The HOUSE on HOARDER Hill

MIKKI LISH & KELLY NGAI

Chicken House

2 PALMER STREET,
FROME, SOMERSET
BA11 1DS

Text © Mikki Lish & Kelly Ngai 2020
Cover illustration © Maxine Lee-Mackie 2020

First published in Great Britain in 2020
Chicken House
2 Palmer Street
Frome, Somerset BA11 1DS
United Kingdom
www.chickenhousebooks.com

Cover and interior design by Steve Wells
Cover and interior illustration by Maxine Lee

Typeset by Dorchester Typesetting Group Ltd
Printed and bound in Great Britain by CPI Group (UK) Ltd, Croydon CR0 4YY

The paper used in this Chicken House book is made from
wood grown in sustainable forests.

1 3 5 7 9 10 8 6 4 2

British Library Cataloguing in Publication data available.

PB 978-1-912626-21-2
eISBN 978-1-913322-03-8

For Rufus and Xavier – K. N.

For Adrian, Aleks, Thorley, Josie,
Annika and Ryan – M. L.

'And above all, watch with glittering eyes
the whole world around you because the
greatest secrets are always hidden in the
most unlikely places. Those who don't
believe in magic will never find it.'

ROALD DAHL

PROLOGUE

The stone raven dreamt of flying. She dreamt of rising on currents of warm air and chasing other smaller birds, of swooping into the woods, hungry for a catch. But this pleasant dream was interrupted by a voice.

'Help them,' it said, 'help them find their way.' It was the voice of the Missing One. The Missing One was never seen, but the raven had heard the voice before. It belonged to the Great House somehow.

Help who? And how? the raven thought back. *What can I do, stuck here on the roof? I can only dream of flying, after all.*

And then she felt it. Freedom, the glorious freedom to move. It began with a tingle at the top of her small head, and spread as though poured like water over her carved body. White stone turned to feather, muscle, a beating heart and darting eyes. The raven shook her wings out in delight, then launched into the air, no longer dreaming but truly in flight. She arced high above the Great House in joyful loops, ignoring the envious calls of the stone gargoyles and dragon grotesques still fixed to the roofline.

'Please. Find them, and lead them here,' said the voice of the Missing One.

'Who?' asked the raven, surveying the land beneath her.

The Missing One showed the raven a vision of a flock of humans in a red car – a girl, a boy, a woman and a man.

'Family,' whispered the Missing One.

The raven set off to find them.

CHAPTER 1

THEY'RE JUST TRICKS

A ball of gloom was growing in Hedy van Beer's chest as she stared out of the car window at the snow-covered fields. With every mile, she was closer to what was sure to be the most boring two weeks ever.

It was so unfair of her parents – both archaeologists – to go on a dig in Spain without them. Well, perhaps it was sensible to leave Spencer behind; he was only eight. But Hedy was eleven, a Guide, and had already learnt a few Spanish phrases from a language app.

'Will you come back early if there's an emergency?' she asked.

'What kind of emergency?' asked Dad. He was in the middle of choosing another song for the stereo while Mum was driving.

'Say, if Spencer's finger is cut off?'

Spencer looked up from his book of magic tricks. 'Grandpa John's a magician. He'd be able to stick it back on with magic.'

Hedy shook her head. 'You're so gullible.'

'What does "gullible" mean?'

'It means you believe anything. Anyway, he's not a magician any more, so don't expect anything interesting.' Hedy leant forwards until her face was between the front seats. 'So *would* you come back early if Spencer's finger got cut off? Since magic isn't real?'

'Depends which finger,' said Dad.

Mum smothered a laugh. 'Of course we would.' She reached back to pat Hedy's cheek. 'But try not to create any emergencies, OK? This trip is very important to Dad and me. It could mean a lot of new work for us. Then I promise: you, me, Spence and Dad on other trips.'

Other trips. As the fields and trees and hills whizzed by, Hedy put her headphones on, cuddled into her mum's stripy scarf and imagined herself in Egypt, gazing up at the Great Pyramids and the Sphinx. But out of the corner of her eye, she noticed Dad glancing at her to see if she was listening to them. When he turned back around, she hit 'pause' on her music, suspecting he might be about to say something interesting.

'They'll be OK with him, won't they?' Dad was asking softly.

'Of course,' Mum said. 'He may be preoccupied and . . . *funny* about his things, but he wouldn't let any harm come to them.'

'Isn't this the time of year your mother . . . ?' Dad trailed off with a sympathetic look.

Mum sighed. 'It'll be good for him to have some company here. He never stays long when he visits us.'

At long last, their little red car stopped in the centre of Marberry's Rest. It was a sleepy, higgledy-piggledy village, dotted with only a few small shops. Although it had the feel of a place that never changed, Hedy's family were confused by the five-way junction at its centre every single time.

'Why can I never remember the street?' Mum muttered.

'Give me a second,' Dad said, as he tried to get the map working on his phone.

Spencer had exhausted his pocket's usual stockpile of lollies and started munching the last of his cheese sandwiches, as though he thought they would be there for a while.

Hedy spotted a large white bird circling overhead. Now it came flapping towards them.

'Is that a white ... raven?' she breathed.

Closer and closer it flew, until, to everyone's shock, it landed on the bonnet of the car.

It was enormous, even bigger than the ones Hedy had seen at the Tower of London. It tilted its head to the side as though sizing them up, then cawed. With a lazy flap, it took off down one of the narrow streets. They all stared; Mum seemed frozen to her seat, too surprised to move. The raven circled back, and landed on the bonnet of the car again. It hopped close to the windscreen and gave Mum a stern look, then propelled itself down the same narrow street once more.

Hedy had a funny, thrilled feeling where her ball of gloom had been. 'It's like it wants us to follow it,' she said.

'I don't know about that,' Mum said, 'but I think it's the right street.' She put the car in gear, and they followed the raven all the way to Grandpa John's house.

Although they hadn't visited in a long while, the house was exactly as Hedy remembered: three floors of pale stone with a dark roof rising steeply into the sky. On the roof were carved stone creatures and a short tower, which Mum said was called a belvedere and was built to show off the view, but which Hedy thought of as a turret from which you could watch the enemy approach. Nestled deep in the shadowy porch was the black front door. The garden, behind a wrought-iron fence, was strewn with leaves and snow. There was none of the hustle and bustle of their own home, or the homes of Hedy's friends, but it wasn't unfriendly, exactly. It was more like Grandpa John's house was taking a long time to think before it started speaking.

The white raven that had led them here – Hedy was sure it *had* been leading them – flew up to the roof and settled up there amongst the other small statues that were more fantastical, like dragons and gryphons.

Hedy gave Spencer a nudge and pointed. At one of the windows on the top floor stood Grandpa John, his white hair sticking up in untidy crests. His face crinkled into a smile and he stepped back from the window, disappearing from sight. And the very next moment, faster than anyone could cover the distance, he was opening the heavy front door. Spencer's mouth popped open and Hedy blinked in surprise.

Grandpa John smoothed his hand down his shirt buttons and then did a nimble turn, all the way around to face them again. To their astonishment, he was now wearing a brightly coloured tie.

'Ladies and gentlemen,' he called in his deep, warm voice, 'welcome.'

The children crowded around Grandpa John to give him a hug. He smelt of peppermints and pipe smoke, as always. Hedy secretly measured how tall she was, pleased to find she was now up to Grandpa's third shirt button.

'Grandpa,' Spencer burst out immediately, 'if I've got a finger that's cut off, can you stick it back on with magic?'

Grandpa John lifted Spencer's hands to his face to study them. 'All of your fingers appear to be attached. Why do you ask?'

'Hedy doesn't believe in magic,' said Spencer.

'Well,' he replied, 'one might say that magic is a very

sensible thing *not* to believe in.'

Hedy was surprised; Grandpa John used to be a very famous magician.

Grandpa John regarded Hedy for a long moment then, as though wanting to say something but not able to find the words.

'She looks like Mum, doesn't she?' Mum said, stepping up to join them. There was an awkward moment when neither she nor Grandpa John were sure which cheek to kiss, or whether to simply hug.

Grandpa John cleared his throat. 'More than ever.'

They were speaking of Hedy and Spencer's grandmother, Rose, which hardly ever happened. She had disappeared when Hedy's mum was still a young child. Looking like Grandma Rose gave Hedy a small glow of satisfaction until she realized that Grandpa John's eyes were shiny with tears. It made him miss her, Hedy thought. But before she could decide what to say next, Dad stacked the last of the bags and came to greet Grandpa John with a handshake. The moment to ask questions disappeared.

The hallway seemed unchanged since their last visit three years ago. One wall was lined with sculpted heads and carved statues. On the opposite wall, over a hall table, hung two large paintings in gold frames. Hedy placed her new-old phone (a hand-me-down from Dad, which he'd given her to use while they were away) on the edge of the table.

Each painting was a portrait of a person with a human body but the head of an animal: one was a skunk and the other a magpie. They were dressed in really old-fashioned clothes and had strange collections of items: jewellery, gloves, fruit, a small knife. Curiously, there were also modern objects in the paintings: a Rubik's cube, a set of keys and a CD of some band called The Smiths.

'Look, my team!' Spencer said, pointing to a West Ham beanie painted in the corner. He snapped a photo with the Polaroid camera he'd taken almost everywhere since his birthday.

'I hope you kids don't mind sharing,' Grandpa John was saying. 'I'm afraid I haven't had time to clear out more than one bedroom.'

That got their attention. Hedy had a sinking feeling that this holiday was about to go from boring to downright annoying. 'But I have my own room at home,' she said hopefully.

'What's wrong with sharing a room with me?' huffed Spencer.

Hedy rolled her eyes. 'You smell like a monkey's bum.'

'That means you go around smelling monkey bums!' Spencer cackled.

'Hey!' Mum waggled a finger. 'No fighting. You're sharing. And if you don't share nicely, you'll go on sharing when we get back home. Now let's get these bags up to your room.'

With a sigh, Hedy picked up the phone – and frowned. It was now at the back of the table, leaning against the painting of the skunk, the earphones almost stuck to the painting. Had Spencer just moved it?

'Come on, Hedy,' called Dad from the stairs. 'Don't forget to bring your pillow.'

Hedy checked her earphones for paint and found nothing, so she grabbed her things and scrambled after the others.

'Why are the doors all different colours?' Spencer asked Grandpa John as he led the way up the stairs.

'This was a bed and breakfast once upon a time,' Grandpa John said. 'Perhaps it helped guests remember which room they were in.'

Their bedroom had a door that was a faded mauve colour. Two beds were already made up inside, and even though it felt very still, there was a fresh smell of lavender in the air.

On the walls hung framed maps of all the continents, and plates painted with famous ancient structures from around the world, like the Pyramids of Giza and the Great Wall of China. At the foot of each bed were large trunks, each one big enough for the children to hide in.

Spencer bolted to the bed closest to the window. 'This one's mine!'

'I'm going to the kitchen to make some tea with Grandpa,' Mum said. 'You guys come down when you've put some of your things away, OK?'

'But don't touch anything on your way down,' said Grandpa. 'There are things here that are locked away for good reason. Do you understand?'

Although they had heard it umpteen times on their way here, there was a note of warning in Grandpa John's voice that stilled the children. They nodded. 'Yes, Grandpa.'

To unpack, Spencer stood inside his trunk and turned his bag upside down so that all his things fell in around him. His bag wasn't quite empty, though, and when he lifted it up for a final shake a sock full of marbles fell on his head. Hedy shook her head at her brother's messy ways. 'Doesn't Grandpa have like six bedrooms here?' she asked. 'Why can't I have my own room?'

'Grandpa's collected a lot of things over the years,' Dad said, studying a battleship in a bottle. 'The other rooms are probably full of stuff.'

Spencer's eyes lit up. 'Does he collect stuff for his magic?'

'They're just tricks, Spence,' said Hedy, 'not real magic.'

'He doesn't do much magician stuff any more, Spencer,' Dad said.

'Not since Grandma disappeared,' added Hedy.

Dad was startled. 'How did you know that?'

'I heard you and Mum talking about it once.' Her grandmother was so rarely brought up that Hedy listened keenly for any mention of her, even if she wasn't supposed to hear.

'What's magic got to do with Grandma?' asked Spencer.

Dad heaved a sigh. 'I don't know, Spence,' he said,

although Hedy thought he knew more than he was saying. 'Come on. You've got a couple of weeks to ask him all these questions. I bet there'll be a few interesting stories for you to hear.'

The kitchen had a feeling of order that was different from the clutter of the rest of the house, as though someone else was in charge here. It was well scrubbed and airy, with windows overlooking the frosty back garden and another door that led to the laundry. Grandpa John was at the oak table with his cup of tea, rolling a couple of small steel balls through his fingers. Up, over and around they moved, as though they were dancing. Spencer hurried to Grandpa's side in awe, eyes fixed on the steel balls. They flashed in the light, chasing each other around Grandpa John's wrists and palms and then, suddenly, they were gone. Mum and Dad clapped. Grandpa John smiled at Spencer over his teacup.

'*You* said he doesn't do magic any more!' Spencer said to Hedy triumphantly.

'That wasn't magic,' said Hedy, 'it was knowing how to do cool stuff with your hands. Wasn't it, Grandpa?'

'Indeed,' said Grandpa John. 'No magic performed in this house. Strictly tricks only.' He seemed to be reminding himself of a rule that mustn't be broken.

Over thick wedges of lemon cake, Mum took Grandpa John through a page of instructions about Spencer's asthma, urged the children to wrap up, and reminded them for the hundred-and-first time not to touch Grandpa John's things.

And then it was time for their parents to go. All of a sudden, the gloom ball sat right on top of Hedy's heart again. They hugged goodbye on the porch, and when Spencer and Mum started sniffing, Hedy found herself getting teary too. Even Dad looked a little red around the eyes. 'Look after Spence,' he whispered into Hedy's hair, 'and we'll see you on Christmas Eve.'

'I will.' Hedy saw their mum whisper something to Spencer that made him glance at Hedy, nod and put on a brave smile.

The little red car coughed to life, and their parents' arms waved out of the windows until they turned the corner and were out of sight.

'What did Mum say to you?' Hedy asked Spencer.

'That I have to look after you,' Spencer said, pulling on the furry aviator cap their dad had given him before leaving. He reached out to take Grandpa John's hand. 'And we *both* have to look after Grandpa.'

CHAPTER 2

A FRAME, THICK WITH DUST

Hedy and Spencer helped Grandpa John wash the cups and plates, not yet knowing what else to do with themselves. Drying the forks, Hedy drifted over to the fridge, which was covered with a mass of magnets. Amongst the little Eiffel Tower from Paris, the miniature Statue of Liberty from New York, and tiny temples and castles, were coloured letters, just like the ones Hedy and Spencer used to play with as little children. The letters spelt out a message: WELCOME TO OUR HOME. Spencer came to see what she was looking at, as he often did. He used some of the other letters to spell out: THANK U.

'Grandpa, what's for dinner?' he asked.

'Spence,' snorted Hedy, 'we've only just had afternoon tea, you greedy guts.'

'I'm not saying I'm hungry *now*.'

Grandpa John joined them at the fridge and yanked open the freezer. 'I'll have to see what Mrs Vilums has made.'

'Who's Mrs Vilums?' asked Spencer.

'She does some housekeeping and cooking for me.' He pulled three containers out, labelled FRIDAY, SATURDAY and MONDAY. 'Which one would you like?' he asked the children. 'You can each choose one.'

'What's in them?' asked Spencer.

Grandpa John looked sheepish. 'I don't really remember.'

'Today's Saturday, so I'll have Monday,' said Spencer. 'It'll be like time travel.'

Hedy picked Saturday, which looked like lasagne to her.

'Excellent,' said Grandpa. 'I'll have Friday. Looks like shepherd's pie.' Setting the tubs on the worktop to thaw, he suddenly seemed lost. 'Well, now, what shall we do?'

'Do you have wifi, Grandpa?' asked Hedy.

'Why *what*?' Grandpa replied, puzzled.

There was no internet here. No video games. No friends. No mobile phone signal. They explored the garden for a short while and found some unusual statues, but headed back inside when sleet began to fall. Grandpa tried to teach them a card game, but neither Hedy nor Spencer could get the hang of the rules.

Spencer slumped further and further on to his arms until he was very nearly head down on the table. The long, dull days began to stretch in front of Hedy, and she worried she hadn't brought enough books with her.

So when the doorbell rang, both children immediately sprang up in the hope of some exciting interruption.

'What is it?' Grandpa John asked, puzzled.

'The doorbell!' they said.

Grandpa John got to his feet, looking a little put out. Grumbling about his hearing, he stalked down the hallway. As he squinted through the peephole of the door, he snorted. 'You old nosey-parker.'

'Who is it, Grandpa?' asked Spencer.

Grandpa John winked at Spencer and turned the four locks of his front door to open it. On the porch stood a man with a grey beard and a wide smile. He was taller than Grandpa John, and had a sizeable round belly, but their eyes and noses were shaped alike. It was their Great-Uncle Peter, Grandpa John's brother. They were supposed to call him Uncle Peter, because he'd once said the 'great' made him feel old.

'What are you doing here?' Grandpa John asked, without a proper greeting.

'I came to see my family, you old grump,' Uncle Peter boomed.

'You missed Mum and Dad,' Spencer piped up. 'They've already left.'

'Did I? I *am* sorry, I was catching up with a dear old friend who loves to talk almost as much as I do. But I'm here now to say hello!' He held his arms wide and swept both of the children into a hug.

'I suppose you'll be wanting tea, then?' Grandpa John sighed.

'Yes please, old boy.'

As they followed Grandpa John back to the kitchen, Uncle Peter whispered, 'I'm surprised your grandfather is letting you stay, considering how he hates people touching his things! I hope this spooky old house doesn't scare you.'

Hedy felt a jolt of loyalty to Grandpa John at that. 'No, we think it's cool.'

'*I'm* a little bit scared,' confided Spencer.

Uncle Peter nodded in understanding. More loudly, he said, 'Any time you want to come and stay, you just tell your grandfather. I'm only about half an hour away, although you'd think I lived in the Arctic with the number of times John and I visit. And your cousins live near me. You haven't seen them since you were babies – a travesty, an absolute travesty. They're about your ages.'

Hedy remembered her mum mentioning these cousins, a girl and a boy.

'I want to learn magic tricks from Grandpa while I'm here,' hinted Spencer.

'Oh, I was a magician too in my day, loads to teach you,' said Uncle Peter. 'More famous than you, wasn't I, John?'

Grandpa John placed the teapot on the table, steam rising from its spout. 'After I retired, perhaps.' Then he thought for a moment. 'No. Not even then.'

Uncle Peter harrumphed and stroked his beard. 'It's

time you met your cousins again. Angelica and Max. I told them you were staying here, and they're bursting to come and meet you.'

Hedy and Spencer looked at each other in hope.

'Please, Grandpa, can they come over?' asked Hedy.

'What? More of you?' Grandpa protested.

'Please?'

Grandpa pointed at Uncle Peter. 'This is your fault. We were all set for a nice quiet time.'

'Pah!' said Uncle Peter. 'Where's the fun in that?'

Uncle Peter stayed for an hour, chatting and joking with the children easily. He had a musical voice that was perfect for the stage, and which he used to impersonate magicians he'd known, including Grandpa John. Both Hedy and Spencer were disappointed when it was time to walk him to the front door.

'I'll bring your cousins over in the next day or so,' Uncle Peter promised, reaching for his hat on the hall table. Hedy was sure Uncle Peter had placed it with the rim down, but now it was turned over, like a bowl waiting to be filled. None of the others seemed to notice. Had she remembered it wrongly? There was something peculiar about this hall table, she decided.

But before she could ask any questions, Uncle Peter hugged the children goodbye, hopped into his car with a wave and zoomed down the hill.

Grandpa John was in a strangely quiet mood during dinner. It drifted over the table like a fog, dampening any chatter by the children. Was he bothered by them being there? The near-silence continued as they cleaned and dried the dishes, and Hedy was relieved when Grandpa suggested it was time they go to bed.

'I wonder how long it would take to learn all of Uncle Peter's tricks,' Spencer said as they padded down the hallway to their bedroom.

'Years, I bet.'

'I wonder how old Grandpa was when he started learning.'

'Why don't you ask him?' Hedy noticed Spencer drawing closer and closer to her. 'What're you doing?'

'It's so much bigger here than home,' said Spencer. 'I wish Grandpa would turn on more lights.'

'Don't be a scaredy cat.'

They passed the doorway to the room next to theirs. The door, a now-faded dark green, was very slightly ajar. 'Let's have a look in here,' Hedy said softly. The door squeaked as she opened it.

'Hedy!'

'It's OK, Spence, he won't hear.'

'Grandpa doesn't want us looking through his stuff!'

Hedy began edging into the room. 'You stand guard.'

But Spencer followed, bumping into her in his eagerness to stay close. 'I hate standing guard.'

The room was crammed from floor to ceiling: towers of boxes looming over a bear rug on the floor; shelves overflowing with books, clocks and strange brass devices Hedy didn't recognize; enormous glass jars holding dried plants and tiny bones; and a large stuffed deer head overlooking it all. Hanging nearby on the wall was a dusty metal contraption that looked like a large bundle of feathers. The feathers were as long as Hedy's forearm, some brass and some like dull steel, and folded down like a Chinese fan. She wondered what they unfurled to.

Drifting closer to a shelf, Hedy couldn't help reaching out one finger towards a small but incredibly lifelike figurine of a Roman charioteer being pulled by two horses. His whip and the horses' manes and tails streamed in an imagined wind. As her finger made contact, she heard whispers of neighing and the thunder of hooves.

Spencer gave her a hard nudge. 'Don't touch!'

Before Hedy could say anything, there was a heavy thump behind them. They spun round.

'What was that?' Spencer asked in a panicked whisper.

On the floor, in the middle of the room, lay a large leather-bound scrapbook.

'It was just that scrapbook falling off the shelf,' Hedy said. But her heart was beating like a drum.

'How did it fall off?' asked Spencer. 'We weren't anywhere near it.'

Hedy didn't answer. She knelt to pick up the book, and out fell a photograph of a woman who resembled their mother. She was dressed in a short outfit with fringing around the hem and a silk top hat.

Dressed like a magician's assistant.

Spencer peered over her shoulder. 'Who's that?'

'Hmmm,' was all Hedy said, although she had a strong feeling she knew who this was.

And then, right beneath their feet, the floor seemed to ripple. A bump in the floorboards, about the size of Hedy's fist, moved in a meandering curve, slowly at first and then faster.

'Argh!' yelped Spencer.

Hedy shushed him – she didn't want to get caught in here – but the ripple in the floor was freaking her out too. They huddled together as it inched closer until, about half a metre away, the bump came to a stop beneath a dark-brown knot in the wood. The bump flattened and disappeared so that the floorboard looked normal. Except . . . the knot in the wood squeezed in tight, and then snapped out again, as though it were a blinking eye.

Just then, they heard Grandpa John coming up the stairs to say goodnight. Hedy crammed the photograph into the pocket of her dressing-gown. She grabbed Spencer by the hand, and they ran.

They were in their beds by the time Grandpa John walked into their room. Hedy's thudding heart slowly calmed as she lay back against her pillow with her mum's striped scarf wrapped around her neck. Had they imagined that strange thing in the wood?

'Grandpa, I'm scared,' blurted out Spencer, eyes like saucers.

'Really? Of what?'

Hedy knew that Spencer was about to get them both into trouble. 'He just misses Mum and Dad,' she threw in hastily, and gave Spencer a look that meant

Don't spill the beans, or we'll both get it.

Spencer shot back a look that said, *Don't butt in when I'm talking,* but also *Fine, I won't say anything.*

Grandpa John didn't catch any of these glared messages as he absent-mindedly pottered around the bedroom. 'I'm sure Mum and Dad miss you too,' he said. 'Do they read to you before bed? I never did for your mother, and maybe I should have. What if I read you a story . . . ?' He plucked an old paperback from the shelf near the windows. 'This book belonged to your grandmother,' he murmured softly. A long, slow sigh escaped his chest, and he seemed to shrink into himself.

'What was Grandma like?' Hedy asked.

Grandpa John put the book back and picked up a pair of metal magician's rings, each about the circumference of a football. He began to deftly play with them, passing them through each other like magic. Neither Hedy nor Spencer could catch how he did it.

'Everybody who met Rose loved her,' Grandpa John said softly. 'She was very quick to joke. Very generous.'

'How did you meet her?' asked Hedy. The metal rings were now balancing steadily, impossibly, on top of one another.

'I pulled her from the audience during a show.'

'Was she ever your assistant?'

Grandpa John didn't reply. He was staring off into a place much further away than the walls of their bedroom.

'Grandpa?'

'Eh? Pardon, my girl?'

'What happened to Grandma?'

The rings began to tremble, clinking and chattering against one another until the top one tumbled down and on to the floor. Grandpa John simply stared at it and said, 'The magic went wrong.'

Spencer slid into the cave he had made of his duvet and pillow, scared but fascinated. Grandpa John bent to pick up the ring and continued softly.

'I had a box for my show. A large one that hid things. I made it. The Kaleidos, I called it. It was brilliant, a showstopper.' He smiled very briefly. 'But one night, the magic box went wrong. She was just . . . gone.'

Grandpa John turned away from them, placing the magician's rings back on his shelf and then looking closely at an old map on the wall. He blew his nose quietly into his handkerchief. Hedy sneaked a look at the photograph in her dressing-gown pocket. The woman who looked like their own mother had to be their missing Grandma Rose.

'Grandpa, can you stay here until I fall asleep?' Spencer said in a half-whisper.

'But Hedy is right here.'

'She's all the way over there, though!'

As Grandpa John tucked Hedy's duvet around her, she noticed his eyes were a little watery. She tentatively hugged him. 'Are you OK, Grandpa?'

Grandpa John gave her a solemn wink, pulled up a chair beside Spencer and turned off the lamp.

Hedy woke as she heard Grandpa John's footsteps leaving their room. She tried flipping the pillow over and covering her head with the duvet, but couldn't get back to sleep. Moonlight slipped into the room through the gap in the curtains, and Hedy finally threw back her covers and opened the trunk at the end of her bed. She pulled out her torch and, checking that the photograph of Grandma Rose was in her pocket, crept out.

She stole into the room next to theirs, closing the faded green door mostly but not all the way, and picked up the scrapbook to flip through it. The first half was filled with newspaper clippings, cut-out advertisements, and flyers for the shows of 'The Amazing John Sang, Magician'. Sometimes a young Peter Sang was the opening act, and sometimes it was other magicians Hedy had never heard of. There was a magician who cut off his own head (*Gross*, thought Hedy), one who seemed to pull a tiger out of a basket and another who turned into an X-ray of himself. There were many photographs of Grandpa John, and some of Rose too. They looked happy.

Hedy found the spot where the photograph in her pocket belonged and replaced it. As she went to return the scrapbook to its shelf, the faintest whisper seemed to drift next to her ear.

Hedy spun around, suddenly remembering the bump in the floorboards. She didn't see anything moving, but her turn knocked a small table, and a large framed photograph wobbled. Hedy leant down to have a closer look with her torch.

The glass of the frame was thick with dust, but Hedy could make out John, Rose and a toddler – her mum, she guessed – wearing party hats and blowing out candles on a birthday cake. As she stared at the photograph, words were spelt out in the dust, as if being drawn by an invisible finger:

FIND ME.

CHAPTER 3

SUTTON'S GENERAL STORE

The muffled *brrrrrng* of a phone downstairs stirred Hedy the next morning. She opened an eye slowly, waking up to sunlight sneaking into the room. Against her back, curled the other way, was Spencer, snoring lightly. Hedy gave a start, properly awake now, remembering in a rush what had happened the night before.

FIND ME.

Hedy shivered and pulled the blanket up right beneath her chin. She had been so frightened to see the words being written in the dust by who-knew-what that she had dropped the frame with a squeak and sprinted back to the bedroom, closing the door with a reckless bang. She had dived into Spencer's bed and lain very still, thoughts awhirl. First there was that thing moving in the floorboards, and now some ghost was in the house, wanting to be found. Hedy didn't even believe in ghosts, but the problem was that this ghost seemed to believe in her.

Just as she was trying to work up the courage to get out of bed without waking Spencer, the sound of Grandpa John's footsteps came down the hallway. 'Hedy! Spencer! Your mum and dad are on the phone.'

Spencer woke in the blink of an eye, and before Hedy could tell him a thing, he tipped out of bed, half-tangled in blankets. 'I want to talk first!'

Hedy scrambled behind him, reluctant to stay in the room on her own. Grandpa John waited for her as Spencer took the stairs two at a time. 'Did you sleep well?' he asked.

Hedy hesitated. Would Grandpa John be cross with her for being in that room? Would he think she was mad, and tell their parents and make them come back early? If they did, they might not get another chance on another dig. She couldn't risk her shot at visiting

Egypt with them one day. So she just nodded at Grandpa and held his hand tightly, looking at the house with new eyes.

'No!' Spencer was saying into the phone. 'Hedy slept in *my* bed, she was so scared!'

Grandpa John looked at Hedy, his bushy grey eyebrows raised.

'Spencer was creeped out in the night, so I kept him company for a bit,' she said, feeling guilty at the lie.

'Nothing . . . bothered you in the night?' Grandpa John asked.

Should I tell him? Hedy wondered for a fleeting moment, then decided against it. 'No, I was fine.'

Grandpa John relaxed. 'Good. How about some soft-boiled eggs for breakfast?'

When Grandpa bustled away, Spencer beckoned Hedy over. Covering the bottom of the large curved telephone receiver with his hand, he whispered, 'Can I tell Mum about that thing rolling in the floor?'

'No, don't,' Hedy whispered back. 'We weren't supposed to be in there, remember? Anyway, I've got something else to tell you.'

'What?'

Hedy took the receiver. 'Later.'

'Hedy,' Mum asked over the phone, 'did you really sleep in Spencer's bed last night? What's wrong?'

Hedy very nearly told her all the strange things that they had seen, but the worry in Mum's voice made her pause. *They've only just got there*, she thought, *I can't make them come back for weird bumps in the night.* 'Nothing. I was keeping Spence company,' she said, and then she began to ask a thousand questions about Spain to reassure Mum that everything was fine.

In the kitchen, Grandpa John was clanking saucepans between the stovetop and the sink while Spencer set the table with cutlery. Hedy felt her fears about last night begin to fade in the warmth of the room with its smell of butter and toast.

'Grandpa,' Spencer said, 'do you know Merlin?'

'Merlin? The magician?' Grandpa held three boiled eggs in his hand and raised them higher than his head. 'How old do you think I am?'

'I don't know. How old is Merlin?'

'Spencer, Merlin was around hundreds of years ago,' Hedy said. Now both children were watching Grandpa as he rolled the eggs around in his hand up near the ceiling.

'Bombs away,' Grandpa murmured. With miraculous precision, he dropped three eggs into three egg cups waiting on the bench. The eggs landed with a satisfying crack, but didn't smash into eggy messes the way they should have, falling from that height.

'How did you do that?' Spencer asked, darting to inspect the perfect eggs. He gently picked off a sliver of shell from one.

'Merlin taught me that one,' Grandpa John replied jokingly.

'Come on, *please* Grandpa, teach me?' Spencer begged.

'Milk please, Hedy,' Grandpa John said with a smile.

Hedy turned to open the fridge and froze. Yesterday the letters had said WELCOME TO OUR HOME. Now they said FIND ME.

'Grandpa,' Hedy asked softly, 'did you make this message?'

Grandpa John placed some plates on the table and came to Hedy's side. 'Spencer, was this you?' he asked, frowning.

Spencer shook his head.

Grandpa John scattered the letters to break up the message and yanked open the fridge door to get the butter. 'It was only me being silly. A poor joke.'

Knowing when someone was fibbing was a skill Hedy had, a combination of listening and watching people's faces and how they moved their bodies. If someone didn't meet her gaze as usual, their hands fidgeted, their shoulders looked a bit stiff and their voice sounded a little tight, the bloodhound in Hedy became alert. And right now, that bloodhound was sitting up very straight with its nose pointed at Grandpa John. He wasn't telling the truth.

After breakfast, Grandpa John gave the children some money and asked them to walk down into the village. 'I'm sure you'd like to get out of the house for a bit,' he said, holding out their jackets. 'And we need some biscuits. Your cousins are coming for morning tea.'

The streets of the village were quiet. Small mounds of snow heaped prettily against fences (inviting Spencer to kick them) and long ropes of Christmas fir decorated with cherry-red ribbon and golden bells were strung between lamp posts. Every house had a Christmas ornament of some sort – a frosted wreath on the front door, or a sign asking for Santa to stop by. Grandpa John's house was the only one not decorated,

Hedy thought, looking back at it on the crest of the hill.

When they were a safe distance away, she tapped Spencer on the shoulder. 'Last night, when you were asleep, something weird happened.'

'What? That thing in the floor again?'

Hedy shook her head. 'I went back to that bedroom, to put the picture away. It's Grandma Rose in the picture, you know.'

Spencer tried to hold back a shiver. 'That room scares me.'

'It's not that bad. Except what happened at the end. I was looking at this photo frame. It had a picture of Mum as a baby, with Grandpa John and Grandma. And then . . .' Hedy stopped to look around. No one was nearby. 'Words just *appeared* in the dust. Like an invisible person was there, writing in the dust with their finger.'

Spencer's mouth dropped open. 'What did it say?'

'FIND ME.'

'That's what it said on the fridge!'

'I know.'

'Find who?'

'I don't know.'

'Find them how?'

'I don't know. That was all it said. After that I ran back to the bedroom.'

Spencer glanced back up the hill towards the house. 'We should tell Grandpa.'

'No, not yet. We weren't supposed to be in that room, remember?'

'You went in there first, not me!'

'Well, you're my accomplice.'

Spencer frowned. 'I don't even know what that means.'

'It means you helped me,' Hedy said. 'I'm sure Grandpa wasn't telling the truth when he said he did the message on the fridge. I don't think we can talk to him about this yet.'

'But why would Grandpa lie about it?'

'I don't know that yet either, Spence. Don't say anything. Promise.'

'Can we tell Mum and Dad?'

Hedy clenched her teeth. So many questions! 'Not unless you really do want to lose one of those fingers!'

Spencer glared at Hedy, then turned his back on her and stomped along the footpath towards the shops. Hedy took a breath, feeling bad for losing her temper.

Why couldn't he trust that she was trying to keep them from getting into trouble? She caught up to him before the end of the street and fell into step.

'Spence, don't worry, I'll look after you. Promise.'

Spencer glanced at her worriedly. 'But what if *I* can't look after *you*?'

Hedy just patted his head, which was encased in Dad's oversized aviator hat. She didn't have an answer.

At the centre of Marberry's Rest was Sutton's General Store. Its front window gleamed in the cold air, dressed with Christmas decorations and a wooden Nativity scene with real straw in the little manger. Hedy and Spencer pushed on the door and a bell jingled to announce their arrival. The shop smelt wonderful inside: ginger snap biscuits, hot chocolate and maybe some kind of freshly baked pie.

Behind the counter sat a rosy-cheeked woman who was knitting. Her body was trussed in a red-and-green apron, from which dangled all kinds of mismatched brooches.

'She looks like a Christmas tree,' whispered Spencer.

The woman put down her knitting and smiled at them. Hedy could tell the smile was genuine, but she could also tell that the woman would start firing questions at them like a cannon any second now.

'Good morning!' said the woman.

'Hello,' both children replied. Hedy started edging towards the large fridge at the back of the shop.

'Can I help you with anything?' asked the woman.

'We're buying some milk and biscuits,' said Spencer.

'You'll find milk in the fridge at the back,' she said just as Hedy reached the fridge door, 'and fresh shortbread is up here with me. Delivered this morning, it was.'

'Thank you,' said Spencer, peering at the pieces of golden shortbread shaped like Christmas trees and stars and snowmen. His stomach gave a pleading rumble. 'Do you sell Polaroid film?'

The woman squeezed one eye closed, as though using it to read a list of goods and locations inside her head. With a victorious, 'Aha!', she ambled from behind the counter, down the central aisle. Three cats followed her, weaving their way through her legs.

At the door, the bell tinkled and another older woman walked in. 'Hello, Melanie!'

'Hello, Lisa dear! Be there in a moment!' the

shopkeeper called back before continuing in a lower voice, 'Polaroid film, eh? No one's asked for that since three winters ago.' At the end of the aisle, the shop-keeper moved a small ladder to the spot she wanted and heaved her large frame up the rungs. 'That was the year Mr Godfrey's toupee was snatched clean off his head by a big bird and turned into a nest in Mrs List's garden.' She pulled two boxes of film from the top shelf and blew a cloud of dust from them. 'Are you . . . passing through with your family?'

'We're staying here with our grandpa for Christ-mas,' Spencer said.

The woman's face creased into happy understand-ing. 'Ah! You must be Mr Sang's grandchildren! Am I right?'

Spencer nodded.

'Well, it is very nice to have you visiting. I'm Mrs Sutton. It's Spencer and Hattie, isn't it?'

'Hedy,' said Spencer. 'H-E-D-Y.'

Mrs Sutton nodded. 'I see, of course. Hedy. Just like the actress – or actress and inventor, I should say. Wonderful, wonderful. Yes, Peter mentioned you would be staying a few months ago.'

'Do you know our Uncle Peter?' asked Spencer,

surprised.

'Oh yes, I know just about everyone in this village. Peter's a lark, isn't he? He used to visit Marberry's Rest quite a bit, before . . .' Her face clouded as she turned some ancient misfortune over in her mind. 'Although not so much these days. But that's by the by. I used to know your mother too, when she was a small girl. I haven't seen her in years. How nice for Mr Sang to have you to stay. Liven the place up, won't you! Now, I'll just go help Lisa over there, and you two look around if you like.'

There wasn't much to look at, as the shop was not very big. Hedy and Spencer drifted between the neatly stocked shelves, and they couldn't help overhearing snippets of hushed conversation between Mrs Sutton and her customer.

'. . . John Sang's grandchildren . . .'

'. . . they never did find her . . .'

'. . . must have run off . . .'

'. . . don't like to think of the alternative . . . why I keep my distance . . .'

'. . . you know, he rarely has visitors . . .'

'. . . heard he was disliked by other magicians . . . rather full of himself . . .'

The children wandered back to the front of the shop, knowing they were the topic of conversation. The two women, their heads huddled close together, coughed and sprang apart abruptly.

'And how do you like it at your grandfather's?' Mrs Sutton asked with a caught-out smile.

Hedy and Spencer glanced at each other, not knowing what to say, what with the ghost and the weird things in the floor and their grandfather's peculiar moods.

'We only got here yesterday,' said Hedy cautiously.

The other customer, Lisa, peered at the children with intense curiosity. 'Doesn't the house spook you? "The mysterious house on Hoarder Hill", it's sometimes called round here.' Her mouth pursed in disapproval.

'Well—' Spencer began before Hedy interrupted.

'Can we have fourteen of the shortbread trees, please?'

Mrs Sutton packed the biscuits into a cardboard tray and slipped in a couple of slices of Christmas cake. 'Don't listen to everything people say around here,' she said. 'And tell your grandfather that Mrs Sutton said to put in his order for the Christmas puddings today. He must buy a tree this year too. Can't have Christmas with children in the house and no tree! No sense in being gloomy *every* year.'

CHAPTER 4

THE BERMUDA TRIANGLE

Hedy and Spencer got back to the house half a minute before Uncle Peter's car pulled up. An extraordinary clamour emerged from the car as its doors were opened and slammed.

'My word, isn't this good timing!' called Uncle Peter. 'Here are your cousins, as promised. Angelica and Max.'

There was no doubting the girl and the boy were siblings; they both had the same large brown eyes, wildly curly black hair and round noses. The eldest, Angelica, bounced towards Hedy and slipped an arm easily through hers, peering into the paper bag that Hedy held. 'Gingerbread from Mrs Sutton's?' she asked.

For a moment, Hedy was taken aback. She and Angelica had been babies when they'd last met, so were practically strangers. But Angelica's wide smile was so friendly that Hedy found herself smiling back. 'Um, yeah. I mean, they're shortbreads actually.'

Max, who looked around six years old, yelled, 'Hello!' and raced around the garden, jumping over tree stumps and puddles. He looked like he'd got dressed out of the costume box: on his head was a black top hat, a light black cape streamed from his shoulders and a tiger tail drooped from his waist.

Angelica led Hedy up the garden path towards the front door. 'On my life, you have *got* to try the gingerbread. They're crazy good,' she said. Hedy couldn't help staring at her cousin. Two twisted horns of hair poked up from her head, dotty red wool stockings emerged from below her purple wool coat and yellow wellington boots crunched along the snowy path. 'I can't believe we haven't seen each other in all these years,' Angelica continued. 'It's basically for ever. Actually, I know why it's been so long.'

'Oh. Um, why?' Hedy was having trouble keeping up with the sudden swerves in Angelica's chatter.

'Your grandpa doesn't like to have us over because he thinks we're *nosy*.' Her grin grew. 'But that's OK. I *am* nosy. Anyway, call me Jelly. I'm so sick of people calling me "Angie". Do you have a nickname?'

'Not really,' Hedy said, disappointed.

'Don't worry,' Jelly assured her. 'I'll think of one.' She reached into the bag of food and pulled out a slice of Christmas cake. Breaking it in the middle, she handed one half to Hedy and began to munch on the other. Hedy smiled and took a bite herself. At the front door, Jelly raised her hand to the doorbell. 'Have you got a key or shall I "bell the ring"?'

But before she could press it, Grandpa John opened the front door. 'I thought I could hear imps approaching,' he half-grumbled, but a small smile played around his lips as he stood aside to let everyone in.

'Hi, Uncle John!' Jelly cried, giving him a brief hug.

Max followed Spencer up the path and Hedy noticed an expression of awe on the little boy's face as he said hello to Grandpa John. A fan of magic, Hedy guessed. She placed the bag of biscuits and milk on the hall table, then started to take off her coat and scarf.

'No!' Jelly snatched the bag off the table.

'Why? What?'

'I've got *so* much to warn you about,' Jelly said, in a strangled whisper. 'But let's wait until everyone goes in.'

'What's in there?' Spencer asked Max, pointing to a glass jar tucked in the crook of Max's elbow.

Jelly groaned with embarrassment as Max proudly held up a small, glistening ball of snot on his finger. Then he stuck the snot inside the rim of his glass jar.

'That's disgusting!' said Spencer, looking both horrified and fascinated.

'Why in the world aren't you using a tissue?' demanded Grandpa John.

'I'm doing an experiment!' Max replied.

'Well, you're not bringing that jar a step further into this house,' Grandpa John said. 'And you wash your hands before you come through to the kitchen. The bathroom is there.' He muttered to himself as he took the biscuits and milk from Jelly and stalked away, followed by Spencer and Uncle Peter.

Jelly pulled Max back by his tiger tail before he could follow them. 'The most important thing,' she said to Hedy, 'is, *never ever* leave anything on this table.' She pointed to the hall table and then made a triangle out of her thumbs and index fingers. 'I call it the Bermuda Triangle. You leave stuff on it, and . . .' She whipped her fingers apart. '*Poof!* Gone!'

'What happens? Where does it go?'

'I don't know. But we've visited here three times, and something's gone missing *every* time. Just . . . *vanished*, in a split second when you're not looking.'

Hedy stared at her cousin.

'You don't believe me,' Jelly guessed.

Yesterday's Hedy would have agreed with her, but today's Hedy was different. Hadn't she thought things had been moved on this table? And hadn't she been contacted by some sort of ghost in the night, seen strange movement in the floor *and* been messaged by fridge magnets? 'I *might* believe you.'

Jelly grinned. 'Let's do an experiment. Hey, Max,' she said to her little brother, 'put your jar on the table.'

Max dutifully placed his glass jar where Jelly pointed, then stood back to look at it.

Hedy watched her younger cousin and his jar carefully. 'Now what happens?' she asked Jelly.

'Now we have to not look at it.' Jelly gave Max a nudge towards the bathroom. 'Go and wash your hands, bogey-boy.'

She took Hedy's hand and said, 'OK, walk and don't turn until I say.' She counted as they walked down the hall. 'One, two, three, four, five, TURN!'

Hedy spun around and her jaw dropped open. 'It's gone!' She ran back to the table and checked all around. There was nothing on the floor, no sign of it anywhere.

'See what I told you? Crazy, right?' Jelly's eyes were alight.

'Where did it go?'

'Who knows?' Jelly said. 'I reckon this house has magic in it.'

Relief flowed over Hedy. 'I never thought magic was real,' she began, 'but there's something I need to show you—'

'Girls,' Grandpa John called, 'unless you want to lose your shortbread to these gannets, you had better get in here quick.'

Jelly looked worried. 'Come on,' she said tugging Hedy's hand, 'tell me while we eat.' Over her shoulder, she called back to the table, 'Enjoy the bogeys!'

They continued towards the kitchen. A moment later, something hard came hurtling out of nowhere and knocked Jelly on the back of the head.

'OW!' The girls spun around to behold the object on the floor. It was the glass jar.

In the kitchen, Spencer was showing off a new top hat, just like the one Max wore.

'Look, Hedy!' Spencer exclaimed. 'This is a present from Max and Uncle Peter, and so's this!' He pointed to a box of tricks on the table, called 'Marvellous Magic'.

'Where's that jar of yours?' Grandpa John asked Max as he poured some tea.

'Out there. On the table,' Max said, pointing to the hall. 'Jelly made me leave it there.'

Grandpa John looked at Jelly suspiciously. Hedy wondered if now was the time to tell Grandpa John about all the strange things that had been happening, and she took a breath to speak. Jelly, however, smiled innocently and said, 'I didn't make him do anything. He dropped it when he ran in here. The jar's still out there on the floor.' She took a bite of her shortbread Christmas tree.

'Spencer,' Grandpa John was saying, 'no hats at the table.'

'Goodness, John,' Uncle Peter scolded, 'you can't blame a boy for wanting to be like his grandfather.'

The grumpy look on Grandpa John's face softened. He leant over to take the hat from Spencer, and said, 'Well, you can put it on as soon as we're done with tea. And when you put it on, you should do so with a magician's style.'

The black top hat rolled the length of John's fingers as though some kind of magnetism was holding it in place. He raised his arm up high, and it dropped on to his head perfectly. The boys clapped, and Grandpa John bowed his head once before placing the hat behind him on the bench with a sigh.

'Need a nap already, old man?' Uncle Peter teased.

Hedy saw the belligerence in her grandfather's eyes as he dunked a biscuit in his tea with more force than was necessary. While the boys pestered Grandpa John to teach them a trick, Jelly winked at Hedy and asked loudly, 'Hedy, can you show me your room?'

Hedy quietly led her cousin to the room with the green door. Jelly gawked at stacks of old magician props until Hedy beckoned her to the small table with the photo frame and pointed to the message written in the heavy dust.

'FIND ME,' Jelly read. She dropped her voice to a

whisper. 'Did Uncle John write it?'

Hedy shook her head. 'I saw the letters being written in dust right then when I was looking at it. By nothing.'

'By nothing?'

'Like an invisible finger was . . .' Hedy pantomimed writing with her own finger.

Jelly took the photo frame and studied it, her nose almost touching the glass. 'Then what?'

'That was it. I got freaked out, so I ran back to bed. But this morning, the letters on the fridge said "FIND ME" too. And I don't think it was Grandpa John who arranged them that way, even though he said it was.'

Jelly shivered and put the frame down.

'That's not the only bizarre thing that's happened,' Hedy went on softly, as she and Jelly plopped down on the bearskin rug. 'When Spencer and I were in here earlier in the night, there was a lump moving in the floor. About this big.' She made a fist. 'Like a little mole tunnelling just under the surface, but once it passes, the floor looks normal and flat again, like it never happened.' Hedy hugged her arms around herself tightly. 'But what if I imagined it? It was dark.

Maybe I was just seeing things. Maybe it's just some trick Grandpa is pulling to be funny.'

Jelly raised an eyebrow. 'I don't think your grandpa knows *how* to be funny.'

'Yes, he does!' Hedy protested.

Jelly just shook her head. 'Anything else?'

'Before Spence and I saw that thing moving in the floor, a book fell off the shelf. By itself. I think.'

Jelly started counting on her fingers animatedly. 'Bermuda Triangle. Message on the fridge. Message on the photo. Thing in the floor. Book jumping from the shelf. That's five.'

'Five what?' The two girls jumped in surprise. In the doorway stood Spencer. 'What are you counting?'

'What are you doing sneaking up like that?' Hedy demanded.

'Grandpa wanted to know if you want ham or cheese or both on your sandwiches. What are you doing in here?' he asked suspiciously. 'What were you counting?'

Jelly shrugged and looked at Hedy as if to say *He's your brother, what do we tell him?* Hedy waved him in impatiently.

'Is that the photo?' Spencer asked, pointing to the

CHAPTER 5

THE ITCH

'What are you doing in here?'

The three children had been so riveted that they hadn't heard Grandpa John come up the stairs. He was standing in the doorway and his face looked thunderous. Spencer dropped the photograph frame with a clatter.

'I told you not to touch things in this house!' Grandpa strode into the room, swiftly picked up the frame from the rug, and placed it back on the small side table after only the briefest glance.

'The door was open ...' Hedy began in a small voice.

'Open doors are no invitation to break the rules that I set,' Grandpa replied heatedly. He took a deep breath. 'Out. All of you.'

Jelly prodded Hedy in the back and pointed to the photograph frame. Should they tell Grandpa what had just happened?

'Grandpa,' Hedy tried again. 'I think Grand—'

But Grandpa John cut her off. He was calm now, but his face was very stern. 'For better or worse, you're my responsibility for the next two weeks. That means understanding that I need to keep you safe. I shouldn't have to explain every last thing for you to do as I say. If you will not abide by my rules, then you may not stay in this house. I will call your parents right now if I need to.'

Hedy and Spencer shared a brief look and shook their heads. They filed out of the room and Grandpa closed the door firmly behind them.

Hedy and Spencer were quiet throughout lunch, stinging from the telling-off. Luckily, Uncle Peter kept up a patter of cheerful stories that eventually lifted the mood. Grandpa John, seeming to want to make peace, did a series of card tricks for Spencer and patted Hedy gently on the shoulder when she led the other children in clearing the table.

Their mood did not escape Uncle Peter, though. When Grandpa John was out of the room, he asked, 'Everything all right?'

They nodded.

'You know, you can come stay at my house with your cousins any time.'

Hedy pondered the offer as they walked Uncle Peter and the cousins to their car. She had a feeling that staying with Uncle Peter would be more fun, but what would that mean for the message in the dust?

Before Jelly got into the car, she took a purple marker from her bag and wrote a telephone number on the back of Hedy's hand. 'You *have* to tell me everything,' she said. 'You're going to help her, right?'

'I don't know how I *can* help her, when Grandpa John is so strict about us not touching his things. I don't want to get in trouble with him again. Or with my parents.' Hedy considered the house, which somehow seemed more watchful than before.

'If Uncle John knew you were helping your grandma, he wouldn't be such a dictator,' Jelly sniffed. Then her eyes widened, as if a thought had just occurred to her. '*Oh em gee* – unless he doesn't want you to find her!'

Hedy's stomach suddenly felt heavy and tight. Could that be true?

Jelly gave Hedy a lung-crushing hug. 'Call me, promise?'

As Uncle Peter's car sped away with Jelly waving a hand and Max waving his bogey jar out of the window, Hedy felt as though the sun had gone behind a cloud. She didn't usually make friends very quickly, being so much more serious than most other kids at school. But she and her bubbly cousin had just connected, even though they were very different. Hedy missed her already.

'Your grandmother would've liked visits like today,' Grandpa John said unexpectedly. 'People and chatter. She got on well with almost everyone.' He looked as though the sun had disappeared behind clouds for him as well.

It was around half past nine that night when Hedy and Spencer crept into the room with the green door. The afternoon and evening had seemed deathly dull without their cousins and with Grandpa shutting himself in his study. During those dragging hours, Hedy had decided they couldn't wait around for something to happen, and she'd convinced Spencer to stay awake after they'd gone to bed so they could sneak in there.

With trembling hands, Hedy picked up the photograph again. 'Grandma,' she said, 'tell us what to do.'

A long moment of nothing. And then, a strange voice came from up above them.

'It is I, your grandmother. Walk to the middle of the room, children.'

Hedy was glad that Spencer had grabbed hold of her hand. They shuffled to the middle of the room, standing on the bearskin rug.

'Move two steps to the left,' said the voice. The children did so. 'And now to the right.' The children shuffled back again. What was happening?

A rumbling laugh erupted below their feet. They spun and looked down. There on the floor was the head of the bearskin rug, chuckling.

'Oh, that feels good! Stamp on that itch!' the bear laughed. It sounded like rocks rolling around in a drum.

'You owe me for that, Doug,' said the first, higher voice, chortling too. The children looked up now. The stag's head on the wall was looking pleased with himself.

Spencer and Hedy scurried off the rug.

'Oh, come now!' said Doug, the bear rug. 'Just a little more stamping where my right shoulder used to be? It's so itchy.'

'*They're talking!*' Spencer whispered.

'I know,' said Hedy, not believing her ears. 'But it's impossible.'

Doug angled his head up to the stag. 'Stan, they said it's impossible.'

'I heard,' Stan replied.

'I guess that means *you-know-what*.'

Doug and Stan suddenly froze, looking like utterly normal, silent house decorations again. Hedy and Spencer stood as still as statues too. Hedy was ready to creep towards the door when Doug and Stan dissolved into snorts of laughter again.

'I . . . cannot . . .' Stan could barely get the words out. 'Oh, Doug, you should see their faces.'

Stan mimicked the petrified faces of the children as closely as a deer could, with eyes wide open and jaw dropped down in shock. Doug slapped a bear paw on the wooden floor in glee.

'Stop laughing at us,' Hedy said, beginning to feel cross. 'Grandpa will hear. Who are you?'

Doug managed to get control of himself. 'Who are we? We were here well before you two, young miss. I think it would be proper for *you* to tell *us* who *you* are first. Come round in front, where Stan and I can both get a look at you.'

With Spencer clutching Hedy's elbow, the children gingerly walked to where Doug could see them, being careful not to step on him.

'I'm Hedy.' Hedy nudged her brother.

'I'm Spencer,' he managed to croak.

Stan whistled, and Doug drummed his claws on the floor. 'Young cubs of Olivia,' murmured the bear – Hedy couldn't help but think of Doug as a bear now, instead of just a rug.

'Do you know her?' Spencer asked, relaxing at the mention of their mother.

'Knew your mum from the time she was born, I did. I'm Doug, one-time bear and now a luxury floor covering.' Then he hiked a claw in Stan's direction. 'That's Stan, last night's venison.'

Stan sniffed, looking offended. 'I am Stanley, Lord of the Queen's Wood—'

'You weren't lord of anything!'

'Well, they weren't to know that! Look at my antlers; fourteen points on them! Lordly they are.' He waggled his head.

Doug sighed. 'Mount a stag on a wall and all the pomp goes to his head ... cos there's nowhere else for it to go!' He thumped a paw on the floor again, chuckling. Hedy got the feeling Doug had been waiting for an audience for his jokes for some time.

'Does Grandpa know you can talk?' she asked.

Stan's head wobbled to and fro, and Doug's laughter petered out.

'He does and he doesn't,' Stan said.

'Oh, he *does*, definitely,' Doug argued.

'Well, he used to.'

'Do you think he's forgotten, you daft deer? Of course he does. That's why we're his.'

Spencer had lost his fear now and settled himself cross-legged in front of Doug. He reached out one finger to stroke the brown fur. 'What do you mean?'

'Your grandfather collects magical items,' Doug replied.

'For his magic shows?'

'I was never used in a magic show. Haven't left this

house since I got here.' The bear head tilted upward. 'How about you, Stan?'

'Sadly no,' sighed Stan. 'I would have been a great stage presence, however. What a missed opportunity.'

'What a blessing for the magic-going public, more like it.' Doug snorted. 'John doesn't talk to us. Not any more.'

'Why not?' Hedy asked.

There was a long pause while the two furry faces weighed up an answer.

'He thinks it's . . . improper,' Stan tried.

'He's closed off to us,' Doug said, more bluntly.

Hedy climbed up on a chair to get a better look at Stan. His fur was mostly pale brown, with white patches on the underside of his neck, along the top of his nose and around very lively eyes. 'Why can you talk?'

'Was it Grandpa doing magic?' Spencer guessed.

Stan thought intently, his grand antlers drifting from side to side, like bare tree branches swaying in the wind. 'Magic was involved, but it wasn't your grandfather, it was before his time. I don't know why we were made to talk, in fact.'

'For the pleasure of our company,' Doug offered.

'I pity the fool who created *you* for company, you shabby grump,' Stan scoffed.

'Grandpa John seems kind of lonely,' said Spencer. 'He should talk to you for company. I would if I were him!'

Doug gave a sorry smile. 'Well, we're not the sort to go against the Master's wishes, generally speaking. So we don't talk to him. If he piped up first, that would be another thing. Speaking of Master's wishes, why are you two cubs in here? Doesn't he have strict rules about not touching things?'

Hedy and Spencer shifted guiltily.

'Mind you,' Doug went on, 'I wouldn't mind a good scratch right in the middle of my back, if you'd oblige. Come on, sit on me, I can take it.'

Settling themselves on to Doug's back, the children scratched the pelt, finding the fur long and coarse. Doug sighed happily, his nose twitching.

Spencer looked at Hedy with hopeful eyes. She could see her brother trusted these two talking, bodi-less creatures, and something about their crotchety humour put her at ease too. Perhaps they could help.

'We think Grandma's ghost is trying to talk to us,' she said.

Stan whistled through his teeth. Doug twisted his head to look at the children in surprise.

'Your grandmother?' said the bear. 'So *that's* what you were whispering about with the other girl earlier. What did she say?'

'She said to find her. She wrote FIND ME in the dust on this photo frame.' Hedy held the frame out for first Doug and then Stan to have a look. 'And on the fridge, in magnets. And when we asked who it was, she circled her face right there in this picture!'

'How do you know it's her,' Stan asked, 'and not some spirit simply pretending to be her?'

Hedy frowned. 'Why would someone pretend?'

'Not everything you meet has good or straightforward intentions,' Stan replied.

'And some things,' Doug added, 'are downright dangerous. That's why your grandfather's collected them. To keep them out of the wrong hands, influencing the wrong people.'

'Dangerous?' repeated Spencer softly. His skin had gone pale, making his freckles stand out sharply.

Hedy mulled that over. That must be why Grandpa John had been so angry when he caught them in the room. 'How can we tell if it's really Grandma Rose or not?' she asked.

The bear and the stag shared a look.

'Stan, I'm sending you a psychic message right now,' said the bear. 'Are you getting it?'

'But Douglas, the Master wouldn't like it. No one's supposed to know about the *unusual* things in this house, even if they are his grandchildren.'

'Says the stag's head that played a joke on them and showed them we can talk!' exclaimed Doug.

Stan gave an embarrassed cough.

'Please help us,' Hedy said. 'If it's not Grandma, we won't do anything else. But if it's her, we've got to figure out how to find her. And we'll do it whether you help us or not.'

Stan's searching stare was difficult to return but Hedy did it, knowing he had to take her seriously. Finally, he blinked and said, 'If we help you, and if it's *not* your grandmother, the snooping ends here. Is that agreed?'

Hedy raised an eyebrow at Spencer, and he nodded. 'Deal,' she said.

Doug blew out hard through his nostrils. 'All right. No more tonight, though. It'll have to be when your grandfather is out or asleep.'

'Why?' asked Spencer.

Doug's claws clacked on the floor. 'Because you're going to have to sneak us out of this room.'

CHAPTER 6

DO YOU KNOW HOW TO PICK LOCKS?

In the morning, the children plodded down the stairs yawning and rubbing their eyes. Spencer's hair looked like he had been through a tornado, and Hedy felt as if her mind was a twisting muddle too.

'How are we going to get Grandpa out of the house?' Spencer murmured.

'We'll think of something.'

They found Grandpa in the lounge room, adding a log to the fire crackling in the fireplace. 'Goodness, you two look tired. Didn't you sleep well?'

'My dreams were too exciting,' said Hedy. It was

sort of true. In the light of morning, a talking bear rug and stag head mounted on the wall seemed all too dream-like.

'Me too,' said Spencer, holding his hands out to the fire. His stomach growled. 'Can we have breakfast here? Please?'

Grandpa John peeked out the window at the fresh white snow dusting the ground and neighbouring roofs. 'Well, seeing as it snowed last night, why not?'

Not long after, the children sat cross-legged by the fire, cradling bowls of warm porridge dotted with fat currants and topped with small chunks of melting butter.

'Grandpa,' Hedy began, 'the lady at the shop—'

'Mrs Sutton,' Spencer offered helpfully.

'Yes, Mrs Sutton. She said you need to see her today to order the Christmas pudding. And the tree.'

Grandpa John looked startled. 'Christmas tree?'

The children nodded. Spencer was in on the game now, and added, 'And pudding. It has to be today!'

'I already have a Christmas tree,' Grandpa John said, nodding his head at the fireplace mantle, which held a faded plastic Christmas tree, a tiny five centimetres tall.

'You can barely see that!' Hedy said.

'Well, I don't have any decorations.'

'Could we buy some? Or borrow some from Jelly or Uncle Peter. They won't mind.'

'And then have the trouble of getting rid of it all afterwards? No, no. Pudding, however, might be a nice change.' He stood and walked towards the telephone. 'I'll call now.'

Hedy fought back a groan. A telephone call wouldn't buy them enough time. But the line seemed to be engaged, because Grandpa John hung up the phone after a moment muttering, 'That woman is always on the phone. Gossips away most of the day. Well, we should all get dressed and *walk* to Mrs Sutton's! Get the blood moving.'

'We'd really like to go,' Hedy said slowly, thinking desperately, 'but . . . Mum and Dad might call. We don't want to miss them. Especially Spencer. He's missing them like crazy.'

Spencer pulled a miserable face. 'Yeah, I really want to talk to them,' he said.

'But you can go without us. We don't mind,' Hedy went on.

'I can wait,' Grandpa John said.

'No, you should go now,' urged Spencer.

'We were supposed to tell you yesterday,' Hedy said. 'About the pudding and the tree, I mean. We're already a day late. If we miss out, it'll be a disaster.'

'A *Christmas* disaster,' Spencer chimed in, shaking his head sadly.

Grandpa John smiled wryly at their worried faces. 'I suppose it won't do me harm to show my face in the village. Get my yearly chit-chat with Mrs Sutton and any other nosey-parkers out of the way. It won't take me more than forty-five minutes. Don't be shocked if Mrs Vilums lets herself in before I get home. She has a key.' He peered at them with a hint of suspicion. 'Are you sure you'll be all right?'

Hedy stacked their bowls and took them off to the kitchen sink to show Grandpa John how trustworthy she was. 'Yep. We'll wash up and read our books. I've minded Spencer by myself before.'

'Yeah,' Spencer said with a resigned sigh, 'Hedy bosses me around all the time.'

As soon as Grandpa John was a few streets away from the house, the children darted to the room with the green door.

'Set your timer for thirty minutes!' Hedy called to Spencer.

They burst into the room, and Doug gave them a toothy grin. 'Adventure time!' he said.

'Where are we going?' Hedy asked.

'To negotiate with someone upstairs.'

'Who?' Spencer asked.

Doug hesitated. 'Let's get up there first. But Stan and I both have to be there.'

'What's the best way to get you down, Stan?' Hedy asked. 'You look heavy even without a body.'

'We can end the adventure here if you cannot rise to the challenge,' Stan huffed. 'It's hardly my fault I'm an imposing creature.'

'Easy, Stanley, I'll make sure they don't break more than one antler,' Doug said mildly. 'Hedy and Spencer, did you bring money?'

'Money? Why?' Hedy asked.

'You'll need money if you want answers.'

Hedy nudged her brother. 'Spence, go to my backpack and get my purse.'

'Yes!' he said with a gleeful fist pump.

'Don't go thinking it's yours,' Hedy called as he ran from the room.

After pulling Doug out of the way to leave a clear space in front of the fireplace, she began dragging furniture around. By the time Spencer came back, Hedy had shifted a coffee table and several boxes to create a cardboard staircase reaching up to Stan.

'Are you quite confident in this triumph of engineering?' Stan called out nervously.

'Do you want to come down or not?' Hedy asked. 'I bet it's super boring stuck on this wall all the time.'

'I'm only thinking of your well-being,' Stan countered indignantly.

Spencer took a deep breath on his asthma puffer as Hedy slowly climbed up the boxes.

'You'll need to lift me up and then put one hand under my chin and pull me away from the wall,' Stan said. 'That should dislodge me from the screw.'

Hedy did exactly that, trembling as the weight of the head came into her hands.

'Is he heavy?' Spencer asked, biting his thumbnail.

'It's all those brains,' murmured Doug.

'Shut up, Doug,' replied the stag, his voice tight as Hedy retreated back down the box staircase.

'Sorry, Stan,' Doug said sounding not at all sorry, and then whispered loudly to Spencer, 'It's all the antlers, not brains.'

Hedy made it to the floor safely, and gently dropped Stan down. 'Well done, child,' the stag said, relieved, as she gave him a soft stroke on the nose.

'Now put him on my back,' Doug said, 'right in the middle, and we can drag him up to the next floor.'

As the children placed Stan on Doug's back, the stag proclaimed, 'My steed, I name thee Doug the Rug!'

'Watch me charge!' growled the bear, scrabbling his paws on the hard wood floor, which got them absolutely nowhere. The two animals began to laugh. 'You should've seen me chase humans, back when I had a body,' Doug panted.

'We'll have to drag you,' Hedy said. The children each picked up a front paw and began to pull. As they got to the door Doug suddenly gasped and dropped his head like any other rug. A second later, Hedy and Spencer bumped into someone who was standing in the doorway.

'Hello there,' the someone said.

Hedy and Spencer let go of Doug's paws in surprise, and stumbled back to find a tall woman looking curiously at them with dark eyes.

'Hello,' croaked the children.

The woman was beautiful in a severe way. Her skin was alabaster white, and so fine and unlined that she seemed to glow. She didn't seem old, but she didn't seem exactly young either. Her pale hair was pulled back into a tight, neat bun, and looked as though a typhoon wouldn't budge a single strand. Hedy thought she seemed like someone who would be quite comfortable snitching on them to Grandpa.

'You must be Hedy and Spencer,' she said.

Both children nodded. Spencer found his voice first. 'Are you Grandpa's cook?'

'Yes, I'm Mrs Vilums.' She looked pointedly at Doug and Stan, who were now lying lifelessly on the ground. 'Going somewhere with those?'

'Just to our room,' Hedy said.

'I'm not entirely sure Mr Sang would approve. He doesn't like people touching his things.'

'We'll put them back.' Hedy tried to sound light, responsible and utterly non-mysterious. Mrs Vilums craned her neck to study the tower of boxes Hedy and Spencer had built to reach Stan.

'We'll put them all back *super carefully*,' Hedy tried again.

'Promise,' said Spencer.

Mrs Vilums gazed at them for a moment. 'I hope you will call me if you need help.'

'We will,' they assured her.

She gave them an unreadable look before turning back towards the stairs. The children exhaled in relief.

'No time to waste,' Stan said, once Mrs Vilums was gone. 'Take us up to the next floor!'

They each took two of Doug's paws and then clumsily made their way up the stairs.

'Does Mrs Vilums know that you can talk?' Spencer asked.

'I suspect she does,' Stan said.

'She caught us talking one day,' added Doug.

'Arguing,' Stan interjected.

'About . . . what *was* it about, Stan?'

'Bees.'

'Don't be daft, we wouldn't have been arguing about bees!' argued Doug.

'We were! You were telling me about the time a bee got stuck in your nostril and I maintained no sane creature would venture there . . .'

The top floor of the house was shadowy and

subdued. Hedy knew that warm air was supposed to rise, but it felt colder up here. All four doors were closed, and the only light in the hall struggled between twisted branches outside the one small window. Spencer let Doug's hind paws gently drop to the floor and he sidled close next to Hedy.

'We're going to the one with the yellow door,' said Stan.

Hedy nudged Spencer to pick up Doug on the other side.

'I don't like it up here,' Spencer whispered.

'I know,' Hedy said, 'but we have to find out if it's Grandma, don't we?'

From Doug's back, Stan said, 'Young sir, you have with you the fiercest bear rug in England – and, in me, the Lord of the Queen's Wood. Courage. Let us advance with resolve to unravel this mystery.'

Spencer breathed deeply, took up Doug's front left paw, and kept pace with Hedy as she led them to the door that was once a daffodil yellow. The door was locked.

'Shoot!' Hedy fumed, jiggling the doorknob.

'Got the key?' Stan asked.

'No,' Hedy said.

'Do you know how to pick locks?' Doug asked.

Hedy and Spencer both shook their heads.

'Doug does,' Stan piped up.

'Shush, you blabbermouth!'

'You do! You told me years ago that you could open doors and start a fire if you needed to –*and* unscrew nails. Because of that lowly magician thief who made you.'

Doug huffed ashamedly. 'Now what will these cubs think of me? The fiercest bear in England really just a thief's tool!'

'We don't think that!' Hedy exclaimed. 'We think you're honourable. Really. And we're not stealing anything from Grandpa John. We're trying to help him. Finding our grandmother would make him so happy.'

'Persuasive, aren't you?' Doug muttered. 'Well then. Lift my paw up and hold my claw to the lock. That's it. Now, just let me . . .'

Doug's eyes squeezed tight, and then every single strand of fur and hair between the four of them stood on end. The air seemed to crackle. Doug grunted. Hedy could have sworn that a tiny lightning bolt fizzled from his claw through the metal lock.

They heard the lock turn. Hedy tried the door-knob, which was warm to the touch.

The door swung open.

CHAPTER 7

MAJOR CHORDS, MINOR CHORDS

'Top job, Doug,' Spencer said softly as they eased into the room.

'Are you all right?' Hedy asked. 'Your paw's gone pale.'

It was true. The paw Doug had used to open the lock had gone a pale brownish-grey colour. 'Must be getting old,' Doug whispered. 'Let's get on with it.'

The room was a mess. A grand piano loomed above mounds of books on the floor. Old birdcages were randomly scattered about the room, some hanging from the ceiling. A bust of Lord Wellington on top of the piano seemed to gaze out of the window, at the wood that Grandpa John said was called Foxwood.

At the animals' request, they pulled Doug over a chair, facing the piano, and then propped Stan on top of a table.

Hedy gazed around the room in wonder. 'Now what do we do?'

Doug pointed a claw towards a crystal bowl on the top of the grand piano. 'Put some money in that bowl.'

Hedy drew a coin from her purse and dropped it into the crystal bowl with a musical clink.

'Simon,' Stan said softly, 'are you there?'

Hedy wondered who Simon was. There was no sound except for Spencer shuffling nervously from foot to foot.

'Hedy, how much did you put in?' Doug asked.

'Fifty p.' When both Doug and Stan snorted, she asked, 'More?'

'Try a couple of pounds,' answered Doug.

Hedy followed Doug's instructions and Stan tried again. 'Simon, are you there?'

The lid of the dusty grand piano lifted by itself to reveal the black and white keys. Unseen fingers played three keys so that a soft major chord hung in the air.

Spencer climbed into the wing-backed chair, his worried face appearing above Doug's head, while Hedy stepped away from the piano, looking for the invisible musician.

Stan spoke up. 'Was that a yes or a no?'

Doug threw an exasperated eye at Stan. 'What do you mean, *Was that a yes or a no?* He wouldn't be playing if he wasn't here. Simon, we're trying to steer these young 'uns in the right direction. Will you help us?'

The sound of the chord had melted away. Silence.

'Hedy,' Spencer whispered, 'put some more money in.'

Hedy dropped another two pounds into the crystal bowl. 'I'm going to run out soon if we keep going like this.'

The major chord played again.

'Simon,' Stan said, 'something in the house has contacted the children. It says it's the Master's wife, Rose. Do you know if it is her?'

After a moment, the major chord sounded again. Hedy and Spencer looked at each other hopefully.

'Wait,' said Doug, 'does that mean it *is* her or that he *knows* whether it is or it isn't? I don't know which question he answered.'

'What?' Stan's eyes crinkled in confusion.

A low, forbidding minor chord was played on the grand piano, startling them all.

'You're making things complicated, you moth-eaten pelt,' Stan rebuked Doug.

'Because you're not being clear, *Bambi.*'

'Quiet!' Hedy exclaimed, stamping her foot. Doug and Stan both shut their mouths in surprise. Hedy turned to the piano. 'Simon, were the messages from our grandmother?'

The major chord was played, but hesitantly.

'That's a yes, isn't it?' Hedy asked the others. Doug and Stan nodded. 'OK, we have another question. Is Grandma Rose a ghost trapped here?'

There was a long pause. Then a sequence of chords was played: the minor chord, the major one, another minor chord. After a long moment, the sequence was played again.

'What does that mean?' asked Hedy.

'It's like he's saying yes and no,' Stan said.

'But what does that mean? Is Grandma a ghost trapped somewhere, or isn't she?'

Someone let out a loud, irritated sigh, and then – out of nowhere – an imperious-looking man gradually appeared, wearing a wig of long white curls. A yellow waistcoat strained around his large belly, which hung over royal-blue knickerbockers and white stockings. His white shirt was rumpled and had large ruffled sleeves.

And he was completely see-through.

'It *means*,' said the man primly from his seat at the piano, 'she is not a ghost, but she *is* trapped somewhere.'

'Simon!' exclaimed Doug.

'At your service.' Simon stood and gave a deep courtly bow. His voice, with its faint French accent, sounded as though it came from far away.

Hedy and Spencer stared – at him and at the rest of the room, which they could see clearly through his body.

'Monsieur de Polignac, this is an honour,' Stan said, bowing as far as a large head on a short neck could bow.

'I thought it best to make an appearance. You and your companions are dreadful at interpreting my music and I did not want to be here all day.' Simon flapped a hand in the children's direction. 'Did you not warn them what to expect? They have gone mute.'

'We didn't know we'd have the privilege of seeing you,' Stan said.

'Give them a moment,' Doug added. 'They took to us pretty quickly, all things considered.'

Simon raised an eyebrow and did his best to wipe the haughty expression from his face. He tinkled a few keys of the piano, and Hedy noticed that he had a much kinder look when he touched the instrument. It softened even more when he ran a tender hand over a bundle of sheet music, tied with a navy-blue ribbon, which sat upon the slender stand. On the first page, Hedy could see dashes and dots of inky, hand-drawn notes, and she had a strong feeling that the music was his own composition.

It was Spencer who unfroze first. 'Can I touch you?' he asked.

'You may try,' Simon said doubtfully.

Spencer climbed down from the chair and inched forwards until he was close enough to swipe a finger through Simon's arm as though it was just air. Emboldened, he did it again with a whole hand, then shivered. 'Cold!' he said to Hedy with a grin. 'Try it.'

Simon rolled his eyes skywards and muttered, 'O, the ignominy of death.'

Hedy stepped forwards and eased her hand into Simon's chest, wiggling her fingers, which were still visible from within Simon. Spencer was right: from her fingers to her wrist she felt chilled to the bone. When she drew out her hand, she brought it to her lips and blew warm air on it before tucking it under her other arm. 'Simon, my name's Hedy and that's my brother, Spencer. We're John's grandchildren. Can you speak to our grandmother, Rose?'

Simon shook his head. 'I know the other ghosts in this house. She is not among them.'

'There are more?' Spencer interrupted.

'Oh yes.'

'Where?'

Simon shot a critical glance at Doug and Stan. 'Well, it would be rather unkind of me to disturb *their* rest by telling you where to find them.'

'We didn't wish to disturb you,' Stan insisted. 'Douglas and I thought another ghost might be tricking the children into thinking it was their grandmother.'

'That didn't seem like *your* style,' Doug added, 'and you're the only ghost here who's decent enough to talk to people.'

Simon was mollified. 'Well, I am cert[...] one of the others. I do not believe your g[...] a ghost. I would see her if she was. She is no[...] same place I am.'

'But . . . you're here,' Hedy said, confused. 'And you said she was here.'

Simon held out a transparent arm. 'I am not all here, as you can see. I am mostly somewhere else.'

'Where?' asked Spencer.

The ghost averted his gaze uncomfortably. 'That I may not say. I *can* tell you that your grandmother is not in the "somewhere else" at all. She is not dead.'

'But she asked for our help,' Hedy said, feeling a little sick, 'so it can't be good.'

The alarm on Spencer's watch beeped. 'Grandpa will be home soon,' he said.

Simon played a few rippling arpeggios. Something seemed to occur to him and he tilted his head. 'There may be somebody who knows something more. Well, not somebody. Nobody, actually.' He rocked back and forth as the notes rose into the air. 'But in this house? Finding things or nothings or somebodies or nobodies is next to impossible. Lord knows, even Master wouldn't be able to find everything, short asking the Woodspies.'

'Woodspies?' Hedy repeated, struggling to follow his nonsense.

'Come *on*, Hedy. It's time to go!' Spencer urged.

The children thanked Simon over their shoulders and scuttled from the room, each pulling on one of Doug's hind paws. At the stairs, Stan very nearly fell off Doug's back. 'Careful!' called the stag.

'Sorry,' Hedy said over her shoulder, 'we don't have much time.'

'At least down is easier than up,' said Spencer.

Doug winced as they bumped his head down the steps. 'Maybe for you!'

Back in the room with the green door, Hedy darted to the window. 'I can see Grandpa! He's nearly here.'

The children straightened Doug on the floor in front of the fireplace, and hoisted Stan to the precarious tower of boxes that Hedy had built to get the stag head down. She climbed up and Spencer passed Stan to her by his antlers.

'Stan,' Hedy asked, 'do you know what Simon was talking about? About "somebody" or "nobody" knowing something about Grandma?'

'And what are Woodspies?' Spencer added.

Stan's nose twitched nervously. 'What a can of worms this is turning out to be.'

Hedy's arms trembled as she raised Stan up to the large screw from which he usually hung. For a brief moment she wobbled dangerously, struggling to keep her balance under his weight, the boxes shifting beneath her feet.

Stan closed his eyes and said in a strained whisper, 'Now is possibly not the best time to go into all of this. Get me up safely first.'

With a grunt, Hedy shoved Stan up and on to his hook. Hedy admired her handiwork before stepping back just a little too far and falling off her staircase of boxes.

'Hedy! Are you OK?' Spencer yelped.

Hedy groaned. Her tailbone throbbed painfully.

'Is it your bum?'

'Yeah.'

'Anything else?' Doug asked.

'The bum's quite enough, thank you,' Hedy said, struggling to her feet.

They put the boxes back as best they could, then Spencer skidded to the doorway and poked his head into the hall. 'He's downstairs!' he said.

'You two get out of here and come back when you get a chance,' Doug said. 'We'll tell you what we know.'

Both Hedy and Spencer hesitated in the doorway. In a short and very strange time, a rug and a hunting trophy had become their friends, and now neither of the children wanted to close the door on them.

'Thanks, guys,' Hedy said.

Doug gave a cheery waggle of his ears and Stan smiled as he said, 'That was the grandest fun I've had in years.'

CHAPTER 8

THE PALISADE

Although the cold of touching Simon lingered in Hedy's hand, her lungs fizzed as she and Spencer headed to the kitchen. From the look on Spencer's face, he felt the same way; his eyes were dancing, and he seemed to be clamping his mouth around a smile that was fighting to get out. *The grandest fun in years*, Stan had said. But when Hedy caught sight of the fridge door and the magnetic letters on it, she was reminded that they had a serious mystery to solve.

The pain in her tailbone certainly wiped the smile off her face as she sat down. 'Ouch!'

Grandpa John broke off his study of – of all things – a tin of Spam. 'What's happened?'

'Hedy fell over,' Spencer answered.

Hedy sensed Mrs Vilums pausing in her chopping. Wanting to keep Grandpa John off the scent, Hedy said, 'Yeah, in our room. I tripped over Spencer's mess.'

'I did NOT leave a mess!' Spencer cried, outraged.

Hedy frowned at him, willing him to go along with her. Luckily, before it could turn into a proper argument, the phone rang in the hallway.

'Mum and Dad!' Hedy said hopefully, and sprang to answer it.

It wasn't their parents, however. It was a very polite woman who asked for Mr John Sang. Grandpa John spoke for only half a minute before he hastened back in, rubbing his chin. 'I have to go out,' he said.

'Where to?' asked Spencer.

Grandpa John didn't answer immediately, but was clearly wondering what to do with them. Mrs Vilums put her knife down. 'I think it would be best to take the children out of the house, Mr Sang. You wouldn't want them to run out of things to do.'

Hedy wondered what the woman meant by that.

'Of course, of course,' Grandpa John said. 'Well

then, you two, grab your coats.'

'But where are we going?' Spencer asked, jumping for his aviator hat on the hook by the back door.

'The Palisade.'

'What's the Palisade?' Hedy asked.

But Grandpa John wouldn't explain any further, calling goodbye to Mrs Vilums, whom Hedy was beginning to think may spell trouble for their investigation.

They drove for over an hour, Grandpa John listening to the radio the whole time. Hedy studied his fingers tapping on the steering wheel in time with the symphony that was playing. Occasionally he lifted a hand off the wheel and drew it across his chest as though drawing a bow across a violin.

'Can you play the violin?' she asked.

Grandpa John shook his head. 'I just pretend when I'm listening.'

'That's like me,' Spencer said, 'I play air guitar and air drums and air trumpet. We could start an air band, Grandpa John.'

'Your grandmother loved this piece,' Grandpa John said, smiling as he tapped away.

As Grandpa John had brought up Rose himself, Hedy felt bold enough to ask, 'Did you look for Grandma after she disappeared?'

The tapping slowed and then stopped. 'What do you think?'

Hedy nodded, feeling silly for asking. Of course he would have. 'Did the police look?'

'The police, me, Peter, her sisters, our friends, our neighbours . . .' He sighed.

'And no one found anything?'

'No one found anything. Your mum used to toddle over to that damned magic box that Rose disappeared into and cry. I thought she was too young to know what happened, but maybe she sensed something. We searched that box a thousand times over. There was nothing there.'

'What happened to the box?' Hedy strained to recall its name. 'The Kaleidos?'

'I got rid of it. Couldn't have it with a toddler around. Couldn't have Olivia anywhere near it.'

Grandpa John turned the radio up, but it was some time before his steering wheel percussion began again, and it was much less lively than before.

*

They reached an ordinary-looking town called Stradmoor, which hummed with cars and bikes and people on their phones. Hedy had found the tranquillity of Marberry's Rest strange and watchful when they'd first arrived there, but she must have got used to it. Stradmoor – which would have felt like a smallish town a few days ago – seemed as chaotic and rowdy as home.

Grandpa John seemed to know his way around well. His car wove away from the newer shops and houses, full of families doing their Christmas shopping, to older streets that were quieter and eventually became narrow one-way lanes, worn and stained with years of footsteps and traffic.

Grandpa John slowed the car alongside a tight row of terraced shops. Each grimy building was covered with graffiti and had heavy security bars criss-crossing its door.

'Is this place safe?' Spencer asked.

'I won't let anything happen to you,' Grandpa John said firmly as he parked, which wasn't exactly an answer. 'Out you get.'

In the middle of the terrace was a house painted a pale-lemon colour. The windows were not filthy like those of its neighbours, but they were hard to see through. On the single unremarkable door was old lettering: *The Palisade – By appointment only*.

With a hearty shove of the shoulder, Grandpa John opened it, and Hedy and Spencer followed him into a large showroom of magic props. Top hats, black capes, wands, silk kerchiefs in a rainbow of colours, playing cards and all manner of other things were stacked neatly on shelves or hung from stands. The air smelt like lemons.

'Mr Sang!' said a voice above.

Sliding down the banister of a creaky set of stairs was a young man wearing baggy trousers and the trainers Hedy was hoping she would get for Christmas. He shook Grandpa John's hand warmly, beaming the whitest, most winning smile Hedy had ever seen.

'How are you, Soumitra? University going well?' Grandpa John asked the young man.

Soumitra raked a hand through his scruffy hair. 'You know I'd rather be here. But Mum says I need a backup in case magic takes a dive.' He crooked his head at Hedy and Spencer. 'You guys Mr Sang's apprentices?'

'I am!' Spencer said.

Soumitra gave him a fist bump, a friend already. 'And how about you?' he asked Hedy.

Grandpa John cleared his throat loudly. 'Thank you Soumitra, I think they're a bit young to settle on careers. Ah, Mrs Pal!'

A woman with white-grey hair slowly descended from the level above, her walking stick thumping with each creaking step. Soumitra vaulted two steps at a time to help her down. Despite her limp, her cane and thick-rimmed glasses, her gaze was keen and quick.

'Good morning, Mr Sang,' Mrs Pal said, shaking Grandpa John's hand. Hedy recognized her voice from the phone call earlier on. 'You brought your bodyguards today?' she added, with a kindly glance at Hedy and Spencer.

'My driver and my removalist. Mrs Pal, may I introduce Hedy and Spencer.'

As the children said hello, Mrs Pal slipped her glasses down her nose to get a better look. 'It's an honour to meet you.' To Grandpa John, she added, 'Fine strong grandchildren. And smart, I think.'

'If they would listen to me as well, I'd say I'd won the lottery,' Grandpa John said dryly.

Mrs Pal chuckled. 'One day they will save us old

people and we will be glad for their rebellion. Come,' she went on. 'Let me show you the new arrival.'

'Could you mind these two rascals, please?' Grandpa John asked Soumitra apologetically.

'No problem,' the young man said. 'Loads to show them.'

Grandpa John fixed the children with a look. 'We won't touch anything,' Hedy said quickly.

'Of course you can touch things!' Soumitra exclaimed, but catching Grandpa John's frown he added, 'Under my strict and extremely responsible guidance. Scout's honour.' He held up three fingers in a scout's salute.

Grandpa John snorted but followed Mrs Pal up the stairs. When they had disappeared from view, Soumitra gave Hedy and Spencer a can of pop each, cracked one open himself and said, 'I was kicked out of the Scouts, actually.' Hedy, shocked, was about to ask what he had done, but Soumitra strode away calling out, 'Want to see something cool?'

On the far side of the showroom hung an enormous framed poster of a magician on stage. It was a young Grandpa John. He was mid-speech, a silky cloak flowing down his back, pointing his wand at smoke that floated around a small girl on a pedestal. Hedy could practically hear the applause of the crowd watching the act.

'Looked good, didn't he?' said Soumitra admiringly. 'He was pretty famous.'

Spencer grabbed his Polaroid camera from his backpack to take a picture.

'Now check out this guy,' Soumitra said, pointing to a photo of a middle-aged Chinese man clothed in a round dark cap, a dark padded jacket over a pale skirt, and long ribbons draped over his shoulders. His eyes were serious and two sharp cheekbones cast shadows on his face. 'Know who this is?'

Hedy bent to read the small inscription at the base of the photo. 'Tsang Li Ming.'

'Your great-great-grandfather,' Soumitra said. The children stared at him, disbelieving. 'Scout's honour. Well, magician's honour or whatever.'

'But he's Chinese,' Spencer said, puzzled.

Hedy stepped even closer to the photograph, looking for anything in the face of Tsang Li Ming that would draw an undeniable line from that shaven head to her own messy mop, or from those razor-sharp cheekbones to Spencer's round face that was bathed in freckles. She found nothing. 'Are you sure?'

'That's what my grandmother told me,' Soumitra said. 'Somewhere along the line, the T was dropped to Westernize the name. So now your grandad is Mr Sang.'

'I'm part Chinese,' Spencer whispered, delighted.

'One . . . sixteenth,' Hedy said, working it out in her head. 'Is your grandmother a magician too?' she asked Soumitra curiously.

'She sees things that we can't see. But she was never a magician. And now she sells stuff. Normal illusionist props,' he swept an arm around the showroom, 'and the other stuff.'

'What kind of other stuff?' asked Spencer.

'Oh.' Soumitra coughed. 'Boring things, not worth your while.'

But Hedy's inner bloodhound was sniffing like mad – which meant that the 'boring things' were not boring at all.

'Are Grandpa John and Mrs Pal talking about "other stuff"?' she said, trying to sound offhand as she walked around looking at posters of other magicians. She stopped by a colourful photograph of a tiny man with bright-green hair pulling an enormous trombone out of his sock.

'Yeah,' said Soumitra, straightening a rack of magician's capes. 'They get together every few months. My grandmother keeps an eye out for gear your grandad is interested in buying.'

'Grandpa John has loads of stuff already,' Spencer said. 'His house is full of it and no one's allowed to touch anything. It's a waste.'

'He's just being careful, I guess.'

'What sort of things does Grandpa John like to buy?' Hedy asked.

'Super magic stuff?' Spencer added, shaking a box of fake ice cubes.

Soumitra thought. 'Some guys like to collect old cars that don't work any more. The things just sit in their garages collecting dust, but the old guys still enjoy looking at them and thinking about when they were shiny and new. I think that's your grandpa, but with more unusual kit.'

'Some of Grandpa John's stuff still works though,' said Spencer. Soumitra's eyebrows shot up at that, and Spencer hastily added, 'Don't tell Grandpa John we know, though. Right, Hedy?'

Soumitra glanced at Hedy, who had moved further around the walls to a huge poster for a magician called

Sebastian Sello. The illustration showed him soaring above London Bridge with a magnificent pair of wings upon his back.

'Hand on heart, you guys be careful,' Soumitra said seriously. 'Things can be unpredictable. I mean, cars are dangerous if you don't know how to drive.'

Hedy nodded emphatically. It was time to get Soumitra off the subject of what she and Spencer knew. 'This is the first time I've seen him happy to see someone except for our family. I don't think he has any friends. No one ever visits – except for Uncle Peter, his brother.'

'Really?' Soumitra seemed surprised. 'That's good to hear. I guess people grow out of sibling rivalries.'

Sibling rivalry? Hedy thought back on some of Grandpa John and Uncle Peter's chafing at each other and wondered if they used to be even worse.

'He turned his back on the showier side of the business,' Soumitra went on. 'There were people who weren't that kind to him after your grandmother . . .' He trailed off awkwardly before brightening. 'Want to try on some costumes?'

After they'd spent some time rifling through a basket of damaged stage clothes, a phone buzzed in

Soumitra's pocket. He checked the message. 'Your grandfather's ready. I have to help him get this thing into his car.'

'Was that Mrs Pal texting you?' asked Hedy curiously, glancing at the stairs.

Soumitra nodded. 'Easier for her than yelling from up there.'

'I don't think Grandpa John even knows how to use a phone that isn't stuck to a wall,' Hedy said.

Soumitra led them back across the showroom and up the creaky stairs. 'No photos up here,' he softly warned Spencer before he opened the door.

Mrs Pal and Grandpa were standing around a bulky object, uneven in shape and wrapped in a sheet. Hedy also spotted two parcels by Grandpa John's jacket, wrapped in Christmas paper.

'Will it fit in your car, Mr Sang?' Soumitra asked.

Grandpa John pursed his lips. 'Perhaps if we dismantled the three main parts. They could stack on top of one another.'

Soumitra nodded and moved to untape the sheet, but Grandpa John stopped him with an outstretched hand and cleared his throat with a quick look at Hedy and Spencer. He obviously didn't want them to see what it was.

'Maybe you can have a quick chat with Mrs Pal while Soumitra and I pack the car?' he suggested to the children. 'I won't be long.'

CHAPTER 9

THE GOLDEN HANDS

Hedy and Spencer followed in the old woman's shuffling footsteps, down a poky hall to a large work space. A long wooden butcher's workbench ran the length of the room, inset with inkwells and holding a cantilevered toolbox.

Mrs Pal was making her way slowly to a door beyond the workbench. Hedy studied the sliver she could see of the room beyond. Rods criss-crossed the air, hung with a hodgepodge of jumbled objects. There were spectacles, dominoes that seemed to be made of jewels set in glass, some sort of measuring device made up of big and small dials, and many more things besides. Hedy even thought she could see a tin of Spam.

Below all this was a round piece of pale cloth, spread beneath like a safety net. When a shaft of light fell into the room, it bounced and split in every direction. All of the hanging objects glowed with different colours – violet, amber, magenta and emerald. On the cloth below, a few dark squiggles appeared. It was too far to see what the markings were, but Mrs Pal gave a very satisfied tut.

'What's that?' Spencer asked.

'An experiment. A way of seeing things,' Mrs Pal said, closing the door.

'With Spam?' Hedy joked.

Mrs Pal looked amused. 'You may be surprised by what one can see with Spam.'

'Why? Is Spam powerful?'

'Many things can grow or intensify over time – their core qualities simmer and bind until they are much more than they were.' But the old woman chuckled in a way that made Hedy wonder if she was joking.

A clap interrupted them, drawing their attention to the oddest thing yet: a collection of golden hands affixed to a massive wooden board that was mounted on the wall. There were over twenty of them, each clutching cards, scarves or some other prop. As they approached, the hands began to move. Some waggled their fingers, some closed and opened fists, some circled around at the wrist. There were name plaques under each pair of hands, stage names like The Fantastic Forrest Maymon, Ethel the Incredible, The Remarkable Rastafarian.

'What is this?' exclaimed Spencer.

'*Souvenez-vous la main*,' Mrs Pal replied.

Spencer tried to copy. 'Souvenir voo lemon?'

'It's French for "Remember the hand". These hands are all casts of late magicians. Everyone,' she said to the hands, 'these are John Sang's grandchildren.'

All twenty-two hands stopped moving, shocked. Hedy had never felt the weight of scrutiny so heavily before. The hands seemed in awe of them.

The first set to recover waved at Spencer. He nervously approached the hands of Samuel Garcia, Magician, which held up a couple of old coins. Samuel opened his hands flat, palm up, showing Spencer what he had to do. When Spencer opened his own hands, Samuel pointed a long index finger to pretend it was a pistol. First one and then two jolts, at which one coin, and then another, plopped into Spencer's hands. The silver coins were old and unfamiliar, with a cross of shields on them. Samuel's hands cupped and shook, then pointed at Spencer to do the same. Spencer copied the gesture, the coins clinking against each other inside. At Samuel's gesture, he opened his hands. The coins were gone.

'What?!' Spencer exclaimed.

The hands grasped Spencer's and turned them over back and forth, making a show of looking for the coins that had disappeared. Then Samuel indicated Spencer should make a pistol out of his own hand, and fire two pretend shots. One coin, and then another, dropped seemingly out of Spencer's finger, into Samuel's hands. Hedy gaped.

'How did he do that?' marvelled Spencer.

Samuel's hands waved a long index finger to and fro, as if saying *No*.

'Was it magic or a trick?' asked Hedy.

'A true magician never reveals . . .' Mrs Pal trailed off, distracted by something.

Both children turned around to find the old woman examining them intently. The hairs on the back of Hedy's head stood up.

'You have been contacted by something,' Mrs Pal murmured.

Hedy and Spencer glanced at each other. Was she talking about Doug and Stan? Simon? Mrs Pal closed her eyes behind her thick glasses but kept her wrinkly face towards them.

'You have been contacted by a family spirit,' Mrs Pal went on.

'Grandma Rose,' Hedy whispered, heart leaping. 'How do you know? She hasn't said anything to us for ages.'

'Her touch on you is there, even though she is not, like a fading bruise that you've forgotten.'

'Can Grandpa John tell?'

Mrs Pal shook her head and opened her eyes. 'Your grandfather is so bathed in her memory that for him it would be like seeing one raindrop in a storm.'

'She wants me and Spencer to find her,' Hedy blurted.

Mrs Pal's eyes widened.

'We haven't told Grandpa yet,' Hedy added.

'Your grandfather believes your grandmother is dead.'

'Is that what you believe?'

Frowning, the old woman took her glasses off and cleaned them with a silk magician's scarf from her pocket. 'There were rumours. But they were a long time ago, and from sources I would not trust.'

'Why can she touch us but not him?' Spencer asked.

Mrs Pal thought for a long moment. 'Perhaps because you are blood kin, and he is not.' She paused. 'But I think the real reason is that he is closed off now, to the doing of great magic. And in the process he has closed himself off to Rose as well. He collects and he guards, but he chooses not to look magic straight in the eye.'

She rubbed her head thoughtfully, looking just like Soumitra, Hedy thought. As her sleeves rode up, Hedy could see the edges of tattoos on the woman's wrists. 'So, young ones, where is she?' Mrs Pal asked.

'We don't know,' Hedy said. Hesitantly at first, and then in a rush, Hedy told her about seeing 'FIND ME' written in the dust, and about Doug, Stan and Simon. 'Do you know where she would be?'

'Rose must be somewhere in the house if she can see you, but ...' Mrs Pal trailed off helplessly.

'How can we find her?'

The old woman cast her eyes around her work-room, searching for inspiration.

'I hear Grandpa John,' Spencer said.

They could hear steps down the hall and Soumitra making some joke.

'Mrs Pal, what do we do?' Hedy whispered urgently.

But there was no more time to find out. Grandpa John was there, poking his head around the doorframe, asking, 'Ready to go?'

Mrs Pal stood and gave him a genial smile as though they had spoken of nothing but Spam.

As Hedy passed the golden hands, one pair – Ethel the Incredible – waved to bring her to a stop. Ethel brought her hands together in a heart shape and Hedy grinned, returning the gesture. Out of the corner of her eye, she saw Samuel had made a pistol as though shooting at her pocket. With a chuckle, she did the same back at him, then hurried after the others.

The air on the street felt chillier than before, and both children shivered. Soumitra led Hedy and Spencer through a complicated farewell handshake, and Mrs Pal patted both their heads and invited them to visit again. There was no chance for her to answer Hedy's question.

It wasn't until they were halfway to Marberry's Rest that Hedy thought twice about Ethel and Samuel's send-off. A business card had been slipped into her pocket, the one that Samuel had pretended to shoot at. On one side, the card read *The Palisade*, with a phone number. On the other, in very curly writing, was a strange warning:

Ask Nobody for help.

CHAPTER 10

SOMETHING IN BETWEEN

Grandpa John wouldn't bring his purchase into the house while the children were watching. 'Soumitra helped me dismantle it so it would fit,' he said breezily, locking the car. 'It's not so heavy, now that it's in pieces. I'll bring it in later.'

'What about the parcels?' Spencer hinted. 'The ones in the Christmas wrapping paper?'

Grandpa John smothered a smile. 'Go on, into the house,' he said. 'You're shivering.'

It was true. The cold feeling that had begun when they'd poked Simon had spread from their hands up their arms and into their chests, and the wintry outdoor air seemed to bite through their sleeves. Inside the house, Hedy put on her fingerless gloves so that she could still turn the pages of her book while she was warming the hand she'd touched Simon with. Spencer had lost his own gloves, of course, so he pulled a long football sock on to his hand and up to the elbow instead.

Despite Grandpa John's good mood after visiting the Palisade, he wouldn't let Spencer wear a sock on his hand to the dinner table, nor Hedy her gloves.

'But my hand is so *cold*,' Spencer protested.

'Why? What did you do to it?' Grandpa John asked.

They held their tongues. Of course they couldn't say, *We touched a ghost*.

Soup and warm showers did help, but the children pulled on extra sweaters over their pyjamas when they hopped into bed. Hedy flipped the message on the card over and over in her mind, unable to sleep until finally she whispered, 'Spence, what do you think "ask nobody for help" means? It sounds a bit like what Simon told us.'

'Dunno,' he mumbled into his pillow. 'Doesn't it mean don't ask anybody for help?'

'So we're on our own.' Hedy stared at the ceiling. 'Does that mean we shouldn't be talking with anyone at all about this?'

'Doug and Stan don't have any bodies,' Spencer said, 'so it must be OK to ask *them* for help.'

Hedy rolled her eyes at her brother's eight-year-old logic, but something about Spencer's words '*don't have any bodies*' nagged at her like a pea under the mattress. She pressed the heels of her hands over her eyes. A fragile thread of an idea wafted in the dark, ready for her to grasp if she didn't reach out too quickly and scare it away.

Any bodies, somebody, nobody. What was it? *Somebody, nobody, no body . . .*

Hedy sat up in bed.

'What is it?' Spencer asked.

She swung her duvet back and pulled on her robe, slipping Mrs Pal's card into her pocket. 'Come on.'

'Where to?'

'There's something we need to look at.'

'What are you two rogues up to?' Stan asked as they poked their faces around the door.

'We're looking for a clue,' Spencer grinned.

Hedy scanned the shelf for the leather-bound book that had thrown itself on to the floor on their first night. By the time she'd found it, Spencer had rolled himself up in the bottom half of Doug the Rug and was peering at the paw that he'd used to open Simon's door. The fur had turned even more pale and seemed to have spread.

Doug craned his head back. 'What're you doing there, cub?'

'Trying to keep warm,' Spencer said. 'Me and Hedy have been feeling colder and colder ever since we touched Simon.'

Stan shook his head, looking worried. 'I wonder if it was a good idea, sneaking into that room and involving him.'

'Not the best idea you've had,' Doug agreed.

Stan's brown eyes narrowed. 'What was that, you shabby hide? Ah yes, you're right, it was *both* our ideas.'

'Guys, guys,' Hedy interrupted, 'it's OK, I think Simon gave us a clue, about "nobody". And today, the hands of these old magicians told me to "ask nobody for help".' She sat on the floor near Spencer and Doug, opening the scrapbook over her knees. Then she began turning the pages one by one, scanning the newspaper clippings and flyers pasted inside.

'What are you looking for?' Spencer asked, peering over her knee.

'An advert,' was all Hedy would say, afraid that voicing her theory would jinx it into being untrue.

As she read, the right-hand pages began to lift by themselves. It was like they *wanted* to be turned. She took their cue and began to flip the pages over more quickly, through years of the acclaimed shows of The Amazing John Sang, Magician. But then pages began to flick over more forcefully.

'I'm not doing this!' Hedy cried, raising her hands.

The pages were turning in a frenzy now as if the scrapbook had a mind of its own, and a wind whipped up from nowhere. Hedy knocked the book off her knees and scuttled backwards. Spencer shrank his head back into his roll of bear fur.

Driven by the wind, the window suddenly shoved open and frosty air swirled into the room. An entire page tore away from the scrapbook and blew into the air, flying upwards. It fluttered to and fro, like a bird not wanting to be caught, but as it passed between Stan and the wall, he threw his head back. The tip of his antler fastened the page to the wall.

'Oh, well done, Stanley!' Doug congratulated his friend.

The wind died away as quickly as it had stirred. Stan released his head from its awkward angle, and the page drifted calmly to the floor.

'What *was* that?' Spencer asked. 'Was the book doing that?'

'Was it Grandma Rose?' Hedy wondered.

Stan shook his head, unsure. 'First time I've ever seen anything like that in here.'

The children knelt over the scrapbook page and the breath caught in Hedy's throat. There it was. Whatever had torn this page from the book had known what Hedy was looking for: one slightly repellent article that she'd seen on that first night.

The article was about the magician whose most famous trick was self-decapitation – seemingly cutting off his own head and reattaching it later. He called himself The Amazing Albert Nobody.

'Grandpa John knows him!' Spencer exclaimed. He pointed to a photo showing a group of five magicians in cloaks, gleefully throwing top hats into the air. The caption noted that between The Brothers of the Bifrost (Anders and Morten) and The Amazing

Albert Nobody were The Astounding Sang Brothers. It was Grandpa John and Uncle Peter as young men.

'I don't think that's going to help us much,' Hedy said, feeling like the air had been sucked out of her. She had read ahead and the article was really an obituary – a short biographical piece on someone who was—

'Dead,' Hedy whispered, 'Albert Nobody is dead.'

Between their discovery of who Albert Nobody was, and the cold spreading through them, Hedy and Spencer slept badly. They awoke late the next morning feeling like one of Mrs Vilums's frozen dinners. Hedy joined Spencer in wrapping a woollen blanket over her clothes and they waddled down to breakfast wrapped like parcels.

'What's this?' Grandpa John asked, eyeing their blankets askance.

'I think we've caught a cold,' Hedy said, which was sort of true.

'Is there any more of that soup left?' Spencer asked hopefully.

There wasn't, but Grandpa John made them each a lemon and honey tea, and they ate slice after slice of warm toast until the loaf was gone.

Mrs Vilums arrived while they were finishing the washing-up, calling out a cheery hello as she hung her cloak on a hook by the back door. Hedy sensed her observing them as they awkwardly tried to put away dishes with one hand.

Her eyebrows crinkled in concern, and she held a hand to Hedy's forehead, then both her cheeks. 'You're cold,' she said slowly. Hedy had a feeling Mrs Vilums knew all about the ghost at the piano. 'You need to go outside. Into the sunshine.'

'Mrs Vilums, I don't think going outside in the cold is wise when Hedy's caught one,' Grandpa John protested, pausing in the doorway on the way to his study.

'And I don't think there's much sun today,' Hedy added doubtfully.

'Sunlight for this type of cold,' Mrs Vilums said again, urgently. 'You can wrap up as much as you like, for all the good it will do. Don't worry, Mr Sang, I'll keep an eye on them. Spencer?' She beckoned him with a crooked finger and felt Spencer's cheek with a frown. 'You need sunlight too, young man.'

Flinging open the kitchen door, Mrs Vilums stared at the sky, still as the carvings on Grandpa John's roof.

In the distance, a wide strip of blue sky could be seen. She pointed a white finger out to the garden.

'There are many cold things in this house already,' she said quietly as the children trooped outside. 'You should not be one of them.'

That left Hedy more worried than ever.

'Come on, let's go look at those statues again,' Spencer said, nudging her.

A leafless sycamore tree overshadowed the garden that backed down the slope of the hill. The children wandered along the path that led from the house, slippery with old snow and overrun with plants creeping over its borders. Above the path was a long wooden archway of thorns that would turn into a tunnel of rambling roses in summer.

Two walls ran across the garden. The first was a low brick wall, behind which was a barren vegetable patch. The second wall, lower down, was taller and looked older, shielding a haphazard collection of large stone statues.

There was a large Chinese lion with a lion cub under its paw, a ram whose curving horns rose close to Hedy's height, and a robed woman holding a basin that was overgrown with ivy. And at the end of the garden was a bench with two hooded figures of black stone sitting at either end, with a gap in the middle.

'What are all these things d-d-doing here?' Spencer asked, his teeth chattering.

'It's like a statue graveyard,' Hedy said.

Spencer peered into the stone basin held by the ivy-covered woman. 'Hedy, look at this!'

The basin was lined with twigs and dried grass, and inside it were three large eggs. The shells were a dark pebble-grey, although they didn't look like stone. Hedy picked one up curiously and Spencer followed suit. They felt light.

'I think these are real eggs,' she said.

'But from what type of bird?' Spencer asked.

'Too big for chickens,' said Hedy. 'And chicken eggs aren't this colour.' She shivered so violently that she almost dropped the egg; she placed it back gently in the basin to keep it safe. Her toes and fingers were beginning to feel numb.

'Your lips are blue,' Spencer told her, slipping an egg into his coat pocket. 'Are we turning into ghosts because we touched Simon?'

'That can't be right,' Hedy said, trying not to worry that he was right. 'Ghosts are spirits of dead people, not living people turned into spirits.'

'But what if we're turning into something in between?' asked Spencer anxiously.

'We're not turning into anything,' Hedy said, more firmly than she felt. She rubbed her cheeks. 'Mrs Vilums said to stand in the sunlight and we'll be fine. Look.' She pointed to a patch of clear blue sky.

They trudged, blankets flapping, to the bit of lawn where weak rays of sun fell. It was a minute before they felt anything, but slowly, Hedy felt her toes, fingers, arms and legs thaw and loosen up. Spencer lost the cold mauve colour in his lips, and his teeth stopped chattering.

'It worked,' Spencer murmured. 'I'm never poking a ghost again. What would've happened to us if we hadn't managed to get some sunshine?'

Through the kitchen window, Hedy could see Mrs Vilums moving here and there. 'Mrs V seems to know.'

Spencer followed Hedy's gaze. 'Do you think we should ask her about Nobody?'

CHAPTER 11

A TYPE OF LYRE BIRD

Mrs Vilums was waiting for them as they opened the back door.

'How do you feel?' she asked.

'Better. Thank you.'

Mrs Vilums's keen eyes turned to Spencer. 'And you, young man?'

Spencer slipped his aviator cap from his head. 'Yes, better, thank you.'

'I'd say you're all right then,' Mrs Vilums said, and disappeared into the laundry.

The children crept after her. Water splashed into

the laundry sink, and they found Mrs Vilums washing a couple of cleaning cloths. 'How did you know we needed to go out into the sunshine?' Hedy burst out.

'I just knew,' Mrs Vilums said, turning slightly. 'Doesn't it make sense to get sunshine if you are suffering from cold?'

'Not in England. We could be waiting for years for sunshine here.'

Mrs Vilums chuckled.

'Were you a magician, like Grandpa John?' Spencer whispered loudly, with a guarded look behind him.

'Not I.'

Hedy and Spencer watched Mrs Vilums for a few moments, and then, without speaking, they both moved into the room as though blocking an escape. When Mrs Vilums began to organize a mop and bucket, Hedy asked, 'Do you know how we can contact Albert Nobody?'

Mopping fluid gushed everywhere as Mrs Vilums squeezed the bottle too hard. She swallowed, and her ears turned a shade more pink. 'I beg your pardon?'

'Albert Nobody. Is there anything of his here in the house?'

Mrs Vilums busied herself wiping the sink. Finally,

without looking at them, she said evenly, 'I don't know anything about an Albert Nobody.'

Lar! Lar!

All three of them froze, startled. Then Spencer reached into his coat pocket and gently drew out the stone egg. It wobbled ever so slightly in his palm, and fine streaks of copper pulsed in the dark grey of the shell. The muffled warble came again: *Lar! Lar!*

'What have you found?' They all jumped. Grandpa John had materialized in the doorway without them hearing his footsteps.

'An egg!' said Spencer, holding it out.

Grandpa John seemed shocked. He stared at the egg for a long moment, scratching his chin. 'Did you find it like this?' he asked finally.

'It was grey before, like rock,' Hedy said.

'What is it, Grandpa?' asked Spencer, running a gentle finger over the eggshell. 'What kind of bird, I mean.'

Their grandfather hesitated. 'Well, it's a . . . a type of lyre bird. The eggs were in the basin when I bought that statue and I simply left them in there.' He reached one finger out to the egg, but let his hand drop before he touched it. 'I'd like you to put it back where you found it.'

Just then the doorbell rang, and there was a muffled din of children at the front door.

'Max and Jelly are here!' Spencer exclaimed, racing to the hall.

Hedy skipped after him, but almost tripped as she passed through the laundry doorway and saw, out of the corner of her eye, a lump in the wood of the doorframe, just like the one in the floor on their first night. It quivered for a moment before shrinking out of sight.

At the front of the house they found Uncle Peter and Jelly holding a real Christmas tree. A box overflowing with tinsel and ornaments had been abandoned on the porch, almost certainly by Max, who was now lobbing a snowball at Spencer.

'I nicked all my mum's favourite stuff!' Jelly cried, pointing at the box of decorations.

'I hope you're not planning to bring all this inside,' Grandpa John called testily as he eyed the Christmas cheer making its implacable way towards his front door.

Uncle Peter chuckled. 'It wasn't my idea.'

'My gym school was selling Christmas trees as a

fundraiser,' Jelly said. 'So we got you one as a surprise – the nicest one left.'

'You might have called first,' Grandpa John grumbled.

'Grandad was sure you'd be home,' Max said, 'because you're a hermit, which means you never go anywhere!'

Uncle Peter smothered a laugh. 'Sorry, old boy, but it's true.' He pulled a Santa hat from his pocket and crammed it on Grandpa John's head, a twin to his own. 'Don't look so cranky. You can't have your grand-children here and not have a proper Christmas tree.'

Hedy and Spencer delightedly followed their cousins to the lounge room, where Jelly insisted the tree had to be set up. The two grandfathers busied themselves putting the tree in the stand.

'I've got so much to tell you!' Hedy whispered to Jelly at exactly the same time her cousin said under her breath, 'I have something to show you!'

They laughed and sidled halfway out of the room.

'Have you found her?' Jelly asked.

'No, but we discovered a whole lot of other things,' Hedy said. 'Bermuda Triangle-type stuff.'

'Oh em gee. You are in *so* much trouble for not calling me then!'

The two girls bustled their grandfathers off to the kitchen for morning tea as quickly as they could. By the time they returned to the lounge room, Spencer and Max were sorting the decorations into different piles by colour and type. Jelly pulled Hedy and Spencer aside and muttered, 'Here, watch this.' She pressed a phone into their hands and then went to take Spencer's place organizing decorations.

Hedy and Spencer slipped into the narrow space behind the couch and each took an earbud. Jelly had a video saved on her phone, ready to play. It was a clip extracted from a longer video titled 'Great Magician Mysteries'. The clip showed The Amazing John Sang, Magician, at a venue called The Castile. It didn't seem like their grandfather. Even though the timbre of the voice was similar, this young man's stage patter was assured and constant, the spiel of a performer in his prime. Then joining him on stage was the young Rose, in her late twenties, wearing a sequinned costume. Despite the fuzzy footage it was clear that they looked at each other with love. They held hands for a moment, and then parted, walking around a large box that stood about John's waist in height.

Here it was, the box at the heart of the mystery.

'The Kaleidos,' Hedy whispered.

It was a perfect rectangle made of hundreds of mirrored cubes, each about half the size of a fist. They could be moved around in ways that seemed to defy the laws of physics: cascading like water, folded like dough or scattered like dice on a gaming board. After showing the audience the remarkable ability of the Kaleidos to flow and rearrange, John moved to the opposite side of the stage and, without touching the box, waved his hands to reposition the cubes in their box shape again.

John then invited a random audience member up on stage, a burly middle-aged man who tried and failed to make the cubes shift even a centimetre. John moved the Kaleidos around, then had the man stand on top of the only trap door in the floor of the stage, so that nothing and no one could slip through it. Striding back to the box, John pulled down the whole front side, like opening a hatch door. Rose waved to the audience and curled inside the Kaleidos, and then John closed the box.

Flames leapt out of the cubes, a foot high. The man on stage flinched. The audience gasped. John pushed rows and rows of cubes through the middle of the space where Rose should have been, his hands unharmed by the flames. He stood back and motioned at the box from a couple of metres away, flicking the fiery cubes up and around until the whole box had been turned inside out. It seemed impossible that someone was curled up in its centre. John spun the box around and the flames died down. With a flourish, he opened the front side again. He clearly expected Rose to be there, whole and untouched by fire.

But she was not.

John started, and joked that she must be powdering her nose. He closed the front of the Kaleidos again, asked the audience to count to three, and reopened it.

There was a smattering of applause that quickly died as everyone realized this was not how the trick should go. Rose had not reappeared. There was no sound except for John crying out, 'Rose!'

Over a montage of news footage and photographs of newspaper articles, the voice-over explained various theories following her disappearance. She couldn't have been burnt, as one person claimed – there was no burnt body, nor any ashes. Someone in the magician community had tried to stir up suspicion against John, but the police had investigated him and cleared him of wrongdoing. A community search had been set up, but was fruitless. Now almost everyone supposed she had simply run away, lived a life undetected, and died before being found.

Hedy knew that last theory made sense. But those people hadn't seen all the things that they had seen at Hoarder Hill. They hadn't seen messages written in the dust upon glass.

The clip was over. They watched it through once more before crawling out from behind the couch and handing the phone back to Jelly, who slipped a folded piece of paper from her jeans pocket.

'What's this?' Hedy asked as Spencer opened it up.

Jelly leant in. 'I thought you might like this photo of them.'

It was a printout of a newspaper article with a picture of John, Rose and the Kaleidos all in frame. The paper claimed the photograph had been taken just before Rose vanished, and it caught John and Rose from the side rather than the front. Rose was grinning merrily out at the audience. John was a step behind, still holding his wife's hand and beaming proudly at her. Moments after that picture, Rose and John would drop hands and do their trick with the box. After that they would never see each other again.

Hedy felt a lump in her throat, and she sniffed. 'I do like it,' she told her cousin, 'it's just sad too, you know?'

Jelly gave her a hug and told Spencer, 'Me and Hedy will untangle the tinsel. Why don't you go and help Max?' Then she sat Hedy down on the floor and dumped a pile of tinsel before her. 'So, what did you find?'

Hedy quietly told her everything that they'd discovered in the last couple of days, feeling better as she talked. Jelly's large eyes grew wider and rounder at each new twist: Doug and Stan, Simon, Mrs Pal and the golden hands, the cold, Albert Nobody.

Jelly grabbed Hedy's knee. 'I want to meet Doug and Stan!'

'Grandpa wasn't too happy the last time he caught us up there,' Hedy reminded her.

'Ugh, no, he wasn't, was he? We need the boys to keep him busy for, like, ten minutes.' Jelly took a look at the tree. 'They've finished already!'

They had indeed. Spencer had let Max climb on to his shoulders and Max was carefully placing an angel on the top of the tree as the finishing touch. Hedy couldn't resist making some adjustments so that the red was spread evenly rather than clumped together, and icicles appeared at the bottom as well as in a cluster at the centre. To her surprise, there were five ball ornaments with different magicians' stage shows beautifully painted on them. They were all jammed near the top of the tree, so she rearranged those as well, to spread them out evenly.

'Why are you moving the magicians?' Max complained. 'I wanted them all up the top under the angel.'

Spencer rolled his eyes. 'Hedy's a control freak.' Hedy narrowed her eyes at him, and he backed out of the room in a hurry. 'I'm hungry. Come on, Max!'

Jelly put her arm around Hedy's shoulders. 'The tree does look better when it's decorated by a control freak,' she assured her. 'Hey, can I meet Doug and Stan now?'

Hedy led her cousin up the stairs and they tiptoed to the room with the green door, which Hedy was beginning to think of as Doug and Stan's room. 'Guys?' Hedy said as she peered around the door. She ushered Jelly in and closed the door. 'Doug, Stan, this is my cousin, Jelly.'

'I swear,' Jelly said to Doug and Stan, 'I am a friend and I come in total peace.'

But the bear and the stag were absolutely silent and still. Hedy tried again, this time kneeling down and looking Doug in the eyes. 'She's OK. I mean, I told her about you. And Grandma Rose's message. She won't tell Grandpa John.'

Doug didn't even blink.

'Why won't they talk to me?' Jelly asked.

Hedy shrugged, disappointed. 'I don't know.' Casting about, she said, 'Do you want to see the photo of Nobody?'

She and Spencer had spent a good half an hour putting all the blown-out clippings back into the album, which Hedy now pulled from the shelf. The two girls settled on the footstool and flipped through the pages until they found the newspaper article. Jelly bent low over the photo. 'Hey, look at my grandad with no beard. And he's so thin!' She giggled. 'They looked alike back then.' She pointed. 'Is this Nobody?'

'I guess so,' Hedy said, checking the caption again.

'He's pretty cute.'

'I guess so,' Hedy said again, laughing.

'Who's cute?' Spencer's head popped around the door.

Hedy snapped the album closed in irritation. 'Don't you ever knock?'

Spencer stepped into the room, followed by Max. 'This isn't *your* room. Who's cute?'

'Oh, nobody,' Jelly said in a sing-song voice, giggling at her little joke, but of course it wasn't lost on Spencer.

'You think Nobody's handsome?' Spencer asked, incredulous.

'Which one is Doug and which one is Stan?' Max interrupted, wandering around the room and looking at the animal heads.

Hedy gave her brother a black look. 'I can't believe you told him!'

'Why not?' Spencer shot back. 'You told Jelly!'

'Yeah,' Jelly threw in, 'but they won't talk to me, so there's no way they'll talk to Max.'

Hedy checked the hallway. 'Where are Grandpa John and Uncle Peter?'

'They went to the garage,' Spencer said. 'They're arguing about how to make a good hedgehog home.'

'You should go with them, keep them distracted,' Hedy said.

'But I want to look around here,' Max said, who had clambered up on to a table.

'You can't do parkour in here, Max,' Jelly told him.

'I'm not!' Instead, Max lifted the bundle of metal feathers from the wall. Seeing a lattice of brown leather straps with worn buckles hanging from the inner spine, Hedy suddenly recalled the poster of Sebastian Sello at the Palisade and realized the feathers were wings.

'Have you tried these on?' Max asked, wide-eyed.

'You shouldn't be touching Grandpa John's things,' Hedy said briskly.

Max was astonished. 'Why haven't you tried them?'

Hedy glared at Max, who was beginning to worm his own arms through the straps. 'Fine,' she said, more to stop him than anything else. She turned so that the others could help her put the wings on. They were heavy, immovable. 'There's no way these things could fly.'

'Can I try them, then?' Max begged. 'They don't work, so it doesn't matter.'

'One minute only,' said Hedy.

With the wings on – so heavy they made him wobble – Max stood proudly on top of the table. 'I can fly!' he beamed to the ceiling, and then leapt off the table as though he were a superhero launching into the sky.

Snap! A moment before Max hit the floor, one of the wings snapped out to its full span, tilted him off balance and sent him tumbling on to the bearskin rug.

'See? If you were meant to fly, you would've been born with a beak!' huffed Doug crossly.

All four children gaped at Doug.

Finally, Spencer said, 'Bats don't have beaks, and they can fly.'

Doug looked unimpressed. 'No one wants to be a ruddy bat!'

'Master won't like them knowing about us, Douglas,' Stan said, sounding strained.

'I know,' Doug said, scratching his head. 'Bit late now, though.'

Max rolled off Doug and on to his knees, the half-spread wing folding into its spine as he got to his feet.

'How did you get the wings to do that?' Hedy asked him. 'Did you press something?'

Max shook his head. 'I don't know. I just jumped.' He gaped up at Stan.

'Your one minute's up,' Hedy said, unfastening the buckles and looking for a mechanism that might have made the wing spring open.

As soon as he was free, Max crouched down next to

Spencer on the floor, right in front of Doug's face, the wings forgotten. Jelly stood on the footstool to get a better look at Stan. 'We just wanted to see you, like, talking and stuff,' she said.

'Well, you've seen us,' Stan said, 'so you'd better get a run along now, otherwise the Master might catch you in here again – and I wouldn't want to be on the receiving end of that.'

Jelly rummaged in her pocket. 'Can I take a video of you talking?'

'NO!' Hedy and Spencer cried together.

'Why not?'

'No way, they're ours,' scowled Spencer.

Much as she liked Jelly, Hedy suspected her cousin wouldn't be able to stop herself sharing a video with friends, not to mention parents. 'It's too risky. Uncle Peter or Grandpa John might find out.'

Spencer remembered the egg in his pocket. He pulled it out. 'Guys, look what we found. Grandpa John said it's a lyre bird egg.'

'Lyre bird, did you say?' Doug said, looking at it closely. 'Well I never.'

'May I see it?' Stan called from the wall. Spencer jealously refused to let Jelly hold the egg, and stood to show Stan himself.

'Ah, of course,' Stan said with a nod. 'Handsome things.'

'Have you seen lyre birds before?' Hedy asked. 'I thought they were from Australia.'

'Nothing The Lord of the Queen's Wood hasn't seen,' Stan said pompously.

The egg in Spencer's hand wobbled and they all heard the *Lar! Lar!* from inside it. Doug guffawed so loudly that Hedy jumped on to the bear's muzzle to keep the noise down. The laugh made the whole rug ripple, shaking Hedy about as she asked, 'What's so funny?'

'I'll wager my tail that's a *lyre* bird egg,' Doug said when he had calmed down.

'That's what we said,' Hedy said, a trifle exasperated.

'No, an L I A R bird egg,' Doug tried again. 'And it caught The Lord of the Queen's Wood out in his fib. "Nothing the Lord of the Queen's Wood hasn't seen." Hah!'

'It isn't,' Stan sniffed.

'I heard about them back when I was underfoot in that Italian magician's house. They used to put criminals on trial, and a liar bird let everyone know when they weren't telling the truth.'

Jelly clasped her hands together. 'Can I have one? Please?'

'No way,' Spencer said firmly. 'They belong to Grandpa.'

As if summoned, from down below they heard the muffled call of Grandpa John, which meant it was time for them to get out. Hedy beckoned them all to the door.

'There are a million cool things here,' Max said, looking around the room with new eyes.

'Yeah,' Hedy said, 'but none of them are helping us find who we're looking for.'

Perhaps it was a trick of the light, but a dark knot in the floorboard seemed to wink as she said it.

CHAPTER 12

THE CHANDELIER

Tap. Tap. Tap.

Hedy swam up out of her dream, thinking the tapping would stop at the cusp between dreaming and waking. Only it didn't. Her dream, of the swirling mirrored cubes that they'd seen in the video clip that afternoon, began to slip away.

Tap tap tap!

The tapping was more insistent this time, and it was coming from the foot of her bed. Hedy jerked upright. She made sure her limbs and her duvet were on top of the mattress, nothing hanging over the side that could be grabbed by some monster in the dark, and then warily crawled to the foot of the bed.

Tap tap tap!

The yellow light of the lamp was faint, but she still had to squint as her eyes adjusted.

Spencer heaved a big breath, then his eyes struggled open. 'What?' was all he managed.

Tap tap tap!

Spencer's eyes popped completely open. Hedy motioned her head towards the source of the noise. They both scrambled around so their feet were at their pillows, then peered at the floor. Three bumps were circling in figures of eight between Hedy's and Spencer's beds. Every now and then they bumped against the bed frame, three in quick succession, with a *tap tap tap*. One was smaller than the others but just as active.

'Like the first night,' Spencer whispered.

Words clicked together in Hedy's mind. Creatures in the wood. 'Woodspies.'

One bump stopped in its tracks, which the others didn't notice, so they banged into the first one like a trio of cars crashing into one another. 'It's OK,' Hedy whispered to them, getting the feeling the creatures were skittish. 'What do you want?'

'I have an idea.' Spencer picked up his sock of marbles, pulled some marbles out and then reached down to the floor. 'Hey,' he said, tapping the marbles softly on the wood, 'come here.'

At the sound, the Woodspies paused. Spencer rolled the marbles, and each Woodspy in turn claimed one. The way the bump of each Woodspy moved through the floor made the marble roll away from it. They moved to the left or right of the marble to make it change direction, winding in quick circles around it when they wanted the marble to stop.

The children sank to the floor and inched closer and closer. Spencer grabbed his little camera and took a picture. By the time one of the Woodspies knocked into Spencer's leg, it too had lost its nerves.

'Hiya,' Spencer said. 'You guys like the marbles?'

The Woodspies raced their marbles back to Spencer and nudged him.

Simon's parting words floated through Hedy's mind. *Even Master wouldn't be able to find everything, short of asking the Woodspies.* She leant down on her elbows. 'Do you guys know where Albert Nobody is?'

The Woodspies seemed startled, and jolted away with their marbles for a moment before coiling back to

Hedy's elbow and nudging her as well.

'You do,' Hedy decided. 'That's why you came and woke us up, right?'

The Woodspies huddled, then each rolled their marble to a large dark knot in the floor, which opened just a little – and sucked the marbles down one by one before closing again. Slowly the Woodspies moved towards the door, then stopped.

'Do they want us to follow them?' Spencer asked.

'Maybe.' Hedy grabbed her torch from her trunk. 'Let's not lose them.'

Spencer scrambled to his feet. 'I wonder if Nobody could teach me how he decapitates himself and then sticks his head back on.'

Hedy's torch beam found the three Woodspies in the hallway, weaving towards the stairs. Once there, the creatures headed to the floor above.

'This isn't going to get us very far,' Hedy said, 'all the rooms are locked up there.' Nevertheless, they followed the Woodspies, doing their best not to make the steps creak.

'What do you think Nobody will look like?' Spencer asked.

'I don't know,' Hedy said. 'Why?'

'They're not taking us to a dead body, are they?'

'Why would Grandpa John be keeping a dead body in his house?'

'He has so much weird stuff here. A dead body wouldn't even be the weirdest thing to show up.'

'Yes, it would!'

Swinging her torch, Hedy found the Woodspies clustered around another knot in the wooden floorboards. They moved in a slow circle around it, until – *pop pop pop!* Out burst the marbles that had disappeared downstairs. The Woodspies then raced up the hall with their marbles to a blue door.

One of the Woodspies streamed up the doorframe to the lock, and suddenly the latch was shoved back with a click. The door swung open.

Unlike the rest of Grandpa John's cluttered house, there were only two items in this otherwise bare room. One was a low-hanging chandelier. The other was a wooden chest, about the size of the trunks in their bedroom, painted like a domino, one square blank and the other with five dots.

Hedy and Spencer inched cautiously into the room as the Woodspies chased their marbles around.

'He must be in that chest,' Hedy said.

'Should we open it?'

'Go on, then.'

'No, you do it.'

'Why me?'

'You're the oldest.'

The chest was certainly large enough to fit a body. Hedy tried to ignore the tiny shiver that travelled down her neck. She decided to approach this the same way she did the diving platform at their public pool near home: *Don't overthink it, get the worst over quickly.* Hedy strode towards the chest and lifted the lid, heart drumming.

It was empty, except for one deck of playing cards tucked in the corner.

'Hello?' Hedy tried. 'Albert Nobody?'

Nothing. Reassured, Spencer scurried to Hedy's side. 'Do we have to do something to get Albert Nobody talking?' he asked.

'Maybe the Woodspies know,' Hedy said. And that was when she noticed the three creatures clustered beneath the chandelier. She knelt on the floor next to them and looked up. 'Is Albert Nobody in there?'

They wobbled.

'I think that means *Yes*,' Spencer said.

The chandelier was as large and round as a wagon wheel and made of eight tubes on the outside, with brass ornaments hanging from them. At the centre of the tubes was a compartment made of green and black glass, like the skin of a beautiful, dangerous snake.

As Hedy stood, the Woodspies whizzed beneath one of her feet, tipping her off balance and making her knock her head on the chandelier. 'Ow!' she muttered. She could hear a rattling sound, as though something tiny was rolling about inside one of the chambers.

Spencer fiddled with the brass ornament at its base. 'It's coming off!' he said, and as he unscrewed it a tiny white object fell out on to the floor. It was a child's tooth.

'Ugh.' Hedy pulled a face.

'What's a tooth doing in there?' asked Spencer.

'I don't even want to know.'

'Do you think it belongs to Nobody? Maybe he kept his baby teeth.'

The three Woodspies, far from being disgusted by the mysterious tooth, began pushing it around, like one of their marbles.

'Maybe you should put it back,' Hedy said.

'Why me?'

'Because you took it out!'

'I didn't mean to!'

'Then why did you undo that ornament?'

'I didn't know it was – *no!*' Spencer suddenly dived towards the floor. The Woodspies had nudged the tooth to a knot in the wooden floorboard, and before Spencer had a chance to do anything, they sucked the tooth into the wood and disappeared.

'Give it back,' said a voice behind them. It was not Grandpa John's voice.

The children spun round. There was no one there, but the dark glass of the chandelier was glowing royal blue.

'Give the blasted tooth *back*.'

Blue light, like veins, whipped across the chandelier.

Spencer inched closer to Hedy as she asked, 'Albert Nobody?'

The invisible speaker ignored her question. 'What do you mean by causing such a ruckus? Hammering my home like barbarians at the gates? Were you raised by baboons? Give my tooth back and scarper.'

'We'll need to call the Woodspies back to get your tooth,' Hedy said. 'But we actually wanted to talk to you, Albert.'

'Mr Nobody to you, peasant.'

Hedy bit her tongue. They had to win his help somehow. 'You try,' she whispered to Spencer.

'I really like your tricks, Mr Nobody . . .' Spencer began.

'Of course you would, you provincial cretin,' Nobody said in a patronizing tone. 'I'm sure you've never come across a skerrick of magic in your life.'

Spencer looked crestfallen. 'I believe in magic,' he tried again. 'How do you cut off your own head?'

'Why do you want to know?'

'Can I learn it?'

'Why, of course!' Spencer's face lifted in hope at Nobody's suddenly amiable tone. The invisible magician added, 'Come closer.'

Spencer squinted at Hedy. He wasn't going any closer by himself. She took his hand and together they inched forwards until they were only two paces from the chandelier.

'Take a sharp, a *very* sharp, implement,' Nobody said, 'and cut—'

'Stop it,' Hedy barked. 'Don't listen to him, Spence.'

Spencer took a step back and crossed his arms.

'No, cretins,' Nobody said softly, 'the grand-spawn

of John Sang, Self-Importance Personified, *may not* learn *my* defining act of magic.' Tendrils of blue light fluttered across the chandelier. 'Ooh, find me! Find me!' he suddenly chortled.

Hedy leant in. 'What did you say?'

He mimicked a woman's voice. 'Find. Me. Your loving grandmother, Rose.'

'How do you know about her?'

'Because I'm a being of intelligence, dead though I may be. Even locked in this prison I pay attention to what happens on Hoarder Hill. I listen. Unlike some former magicians living here.'

'Where is she?' Hedy pressed.

'Oh, Lord knows,' Nobody said breezily. 'I know what happened to her only up to a point.'

'What point?'

'The point at which she disappeared, never to be seen again, ruining your grandfather's life – and, I dare say, your mother's life – *for ever*.'

Hedy and Spencer shared a look. They hadn't really thought much about their mother's life before they had been born, nor how the disappearance of Rose had changed things for her.

'Will you tell us what happened?' Hedy asked.

There was silence as the invisible Nobody thought. Finally he said, 'I've decided I rather like you two after all. Clever things, aren't you, to have found me?'

Hedy couldn't help feeling suspicious at this sudden change.

'I won't tell you what happened,' Nobody continued. 'I'll do something even better. I will show you. Although you may not like what you see.'

'We can handle it,' Hedy said firmly.

'Can you, indeed? Well, my assistance is conditional.'

'What do you mean?'

'If you want me to help you, unleash me from this prison.'

'How can you be trapped?' Spencer asked, puzzled. 'Can't ghosts move through walls?'

'Who said I was a ghost?'

'Then what are you?' Spencer probed.

'You wouldn't understand.'

Hedy scowled. It was maddening when grown-ups assumed that. 'How do we get you out?'

'Return my tooth and unscrew the chambers of the chandelier. That's all you have to do. Easy. I'll be out of your hair, and your grandfather's too – if he's still got any.'

'Will you teach me your trick?' Spencer asked, sensing this was his time to bargain.

'Oh, of course.'

'We'll think about it,' Hedy said, eyes narrowed, and then she motioned to Spencer. It was time to go.

'Free me,' Nobody called softly, 'and I could help you do the same for your grandmother.'

Neither of the children said anything as they hurried away from the room, leaving it unlocked. The further they got from the odd, bodiless voice, the better they felt.

CHAPTER 13

LAR! LAR!

The next morning, Hedy and Spencer mulled over Mr Nobody's offer. As they cruised from room to room, they kept an eye out for a white tooth, or a moving bump in the floorboards.

'How can anyone trust somebody who's so mean at first and then switches to being nice when they want something?' Hedy whispered.

Spencer gave her an accusing look. 'You're like that to me.'

'I'm never *that* mean to you.' She felt a pang of remorse at Spencer's flat stare. 'Am I?'

Grandpa John usually spent an hour or two in his study after breakfast. 'Writing letters,' he had told them. Hedy had a feeling that was how he found new objects to buy. As soon as his door closed, they stole a moment with Doug and Stan to tell them about their discovery, and Nobody's proposition.

'Don't like the sound of him,' Stan muttered.

Doug flicked an ear. 'I'm with Stan. Not everything in this house that the Master's collected is *good* like us, you know? Some might think he's willy-nilly and collects every-which-thing that has the slightest whiff of enchantment. And others still might say he collects the stuff that *isn't* good and keeps it under wraps to stop it making mischief in the world.'

'Albert Nobody falls into the "Isn't Good" category, if your encounter is anything to go by,' said Stan. 'Fancy calling you, young Spencer, a cretin.'

Spencer shrugged. 'I thought he was calling me one of those crunchy things you put on soup.'

'It's a bad idea to deal with him,' Doug muttered, shaking his head.

'But he's our best chance of finding out what happened,' Hedy said.

Stan and Doug fell silent. They couldn't argue with

that. Finally, Doug said, 'As long as you promise not to trust him.'

'And give away as little as you can,' Stan added.

'*And* I don't think you should let him loose either,' Doug ploughed on. 'He's in there for a reason.'

Hedy sighed. 'We need the tooth back from the Woodspies before we can do any of that.'

Every bit of wood they studied inside the house – floor, door, windowsills, tables and chairs – was as still as it was meant to be. At a loss, they checked things in the garage too, inspecting handles of spades, rakes and hoes, wooden boards, an old wooden set of bowling pins. None of it seemed out of the ordinary.

When they heard footsteps on the driveway, they bustled to replace the bowling pins in their frame.

Grandpa John peered around the garage door. 'What are you two doing in here?' He didn't sound cross, but there was unease in the crease between his eyebrows.

'We, um.' Hedy scanned the garage for inspiration. 'We're looking at your motorbikes. Just looking.'

Grandpa's eyebrow crease smoothed away. 'Well, that one's a Gillet, 1929,' he told them, 'and that's an

Indian. And that orange one is a Honda.'

'Why do you have so many?' Spencer asked.

'Oh, I used to ride around a bit,' Grandpa John said. 'And your grandmother used to join me on the Indian. Good riding in the countryside.'

'Grandma Rose could ride a motorbike?' Hedy was shocked.

'She could indeed. That was her helmet.' He pointed to an old helmet, red with a white stripe running down the centre.

Spencer wandered over to the orange motorbike. 'Did you ride this one?'

'Sometimes. A few other people rode it too. Peter did, a handful of times. We'd join a group riding around and create a whole lot of noise.' He shook his head, reminiscing, and then out of nowhere said gravely, 'Don't forget, you two are the only siblings you've got.'

'Like you and Uncle Peter,' Spencer said.

Hedy, however, couldn't help blurting out, 'You were part of a biker gang?'

'Goodness, we weren't bikers,' said Grandpa John, 'we had other common interests.'

'A magicians' biker gang?'

'You make it sound rather more interesting than it was,' Grandpa John said, taking hold of his box of screwdrivers. 'Like we rode across Britain in capes, casting spells. Now go on – you've been skulking around indoors all morning when you could be enjoying the great outdoors.'

'Are you coming with us?' Spencer asked.

Grandpa John rattled his screwdrivers. 'I have to get on with something.'

Spencer lowered his voice as far as he could and creased his own brow in imitation of Grandpa John. 'But you've been skulking around indoors all morning.'

Grandpa John chuckled and said, 'Next time, you scallywag.'

The great outdoors was cold and overcast, but it was refreshing to be out of the house. Hedy and Spencer wandered the garden path, picking thorns off the barren archway of climbing roses and poking at stones. With some fumbling, they climbed into the lowest branches of the leafless sycamore tree. Hedy cast her eyes over trunk and branches for Woodspies, but after a while she gave up to simply enjoy being in the tree. Looking back at the house, she could see Mrs

Vilums moving about the kitchen, but Grandpa John must have returned to his study with the screwdrivers.

'You know,' she said, 'I think Grandpa John might like us being here now.'

'I wish we lived closer,' Spencer said. 'I'd be a magician by now.'

Hedy laughed. 'You haven't learnt any tricks so far.'

'That's not my fault – we've been busy,' he protested. 'Let's check on the eggs.'

To their delight they found them changed, even the one that Spencer had kept with him for half a day. Where the shells had been a dark, polished grey they were now the lighter colour of distant storm clouds. More and more coppery strands glinted in the surface like fire.

'I wonder if this means they're getting ready to hatch,' Spencer said.

'We could ask Grandpa,' Hedy mused. 'He doesn't seem as uptight about these as he is about stuff inside.'

That was all Spencer needed to hear. He placed the three eggs in three different coat pockets. 'If they hatch, he might let us keep one as a pet!' And he took off up the slope back towards the house with Hedy on his heels.

They slowed down as they neared the rear of the house and then Hedy yanked Spencer to a stop to stare through the kitchen windows. Mrs Vilums was in the doorway between the kitchen and the hall, her back to them. She seemed to be saying something to the doorframe. A few moments later, bumps appeared in the wood, rising up and then disappearing like whales at sea. Mrs Vilums smiled at them and held her face close to the wood so that one of the Woodspies could touch her skin, as though kissing her cheek.

'Mrs V knows the Woodspies,' Hedy breathed.

The cook watched with amusement as the Woodspies chased each other playfully up one side of the doorframe, across the lintel and down the other side. There, they disappeared into the wood of the doorframe. The children ducked down low before Mrs Vilums could turn around and see them spying on her.

'What do we do?' Spencer whispered.

Hedy chewed her lip. 'Let's ask her for help. We need the tooth. For Grandma.'

'What do we tell her?'

'Follow my lead,' Hedy said.

As they walked through the back door, they smiled innocently at Mrs Vilums, who was slicing apples.

Hedy checked there was no sign of Grandpa John coming down the hall, then took a deep breath. 'Mrs Vilums, do you know the Woodspies?'

Mrs Vilums paused a fraction too long before saying, 'I beg your pardon?'

'We saw them here with you a few minutes ago,' Hedy said, patting the doorframe.

'One of them kissed you!' Spencer added.

Mrs Vilums turned to place a plate of apple skins on the table. 'I don't know what you're talking about.'

Lar! Lar! Lar!

Suddenly flustered, Mrs Vilums knocked the plate and apple skins skittered across the table, as she looked around for the source of the chirping.

Spencer half-lifted an egg from his coat pocket. 'Liar bird egg.'

'They know when someone is lying,' Hedy said in a low voice.

'Why am I suddenly the subject of interrogation?' Mrs Vilums threw up her hands.

'Please, Mrs V, we need the Woodspies' help,' Hedy said. 'They've taken something they shouldn't have. A tooth. It's really important they give it back.' Mrs Vilums seemed unmoved. Hedy decided to press harder. 'Does Grandpa John know about you and the Woodspies?'

The cook waved a dismissive hand. 'He wouldn't care.'

Lar! Lar! Lar!

'You know about the Woodspies,' Hedy said. 'You knew how to cure us of that cold feeling. You're not just someone who cooks and cleans for Grandpa John, are you?'

Mrs Vilums looked like she wanted to bolt through the back door. Spencer pulled a liar bird egg out completely and held it in two hands. Coppery filaments glimmered in the shell, and the whole egg wobbled, agitated.

Staring at the egg, Mrs Vilums said, 'I . . . I was sent here years ago by a rival of your grandfather, to become a part of this household and learn his secrets. The rival wanted me to pass the secrets back to him.'

'Albert Nobody?' asked Spencer.

'No, someone else.' The egg was silent, so Mrs Vilums was telling them the truth. 'He threatened to harm my sisters, but I never told this rival anything of consequence. And in any case, he's dead now.' At Hedy and Spencer's expressions, she added, 'Of natural causes!'

'So why are you still here?' Hedy asked.

Mrs Vilums glanced out the back windows. 'To be close to my sisters.'

There was a sad quiet to the woman's voice that made Hedy hate herself for what she was about to do. 'If you help us get the tooth back from the Woodspies,' she said, 'we won't tell Grandpa John what you just told us.'

Blackmailing someone didn't agree with Hedy; it brought an uncomfortable, prickly flush to her cheeks. She tried to soften the cruelty of her words by adding, 'It could help us find our grandmother.'

Mrs Vilums's eyes flashed with anger and surprise. Hedy glanced at Spencer for backup, but he was staring into his coat pockets.

'Um,' he said, 'this egg is hatching.'

CHAPTER 14

CARD TRICK

Not only was the egg in Spencer's right pocket hatching, but the one he held in his hand was too, and the third one. Within a few minutes, the children lifted three wet chicks from the broken shell and goo and placed them in a makeshift nest of tea towels. Their greyish-pink skin showed through slick feathers and they seemed exhausted.

Hedy and Spencer had never seen freshly hatched birds before. They bent down close over the chicks, admiring them in whispers, studying their small dark eyes and tiny beaks that kept opening and closing.

Even Mrs Vilums was charmed by the chicks, crooning a gentle lullaby to them in a language the children couldn't understand. 'We should tell your grandfather,' she said as she finished her song.

It took a long time before Grandpa John strode into the kitchen, scratching his head and insisting he never expected the things to hatch. For a while, Hedy, Spencer and Grandpa John were consumed with watching the chicks dry into silvery-brown balls of fluffy down, with short crests on their heads the colour of a dying fire. Over mugs of hot chocolate, the children peppered Grandpa John with questions – where had they come from, what should they be fed, what was he going to do with them?

Sometime during all of this, Mrs Vilums slipped out of the back door unnoticed. When Hedy realized, her heart sank, and she wondered if Mrs Vilums was gone for good. But when the children headed to their bedroom for the night, there in the middle of the floor was the tiny white tooth.

Spencer's alarm went off at midnight and the children struggled awake, yawning heavily and feeling dull-eyed. With the tooth in Spencer's robe pocket, they tiptoed down the hall and up the stairs to Nobody's room. Hedy paused at the door.

'Ready?' she asked.

Spencer hesitated. 'I don't want to learn his beheading trick any more,' he murmured.

'I won't let him hurt you,' Hedy said. Her voice sounded tougher than she felt. She took a deep breath before turning the doorknob and entering, Spencer on her heels.

'Ah!' cooed Nobody as they sidled around the wooden chest with the domino design. 'If it isn't the Sang spawn – I mean, the Sang *children* – back so soon.'

'Our last name isn't Sang. It's van Beer,' Spencer muttered to the blue light as it coiled and uncoiled in the glass.

'Of course, silly me,' Nobody said. 'I'm not surprised your mother didn't want you having any hint of the Sang name hanging about such wonderful children, sullying your futures. I presume you have the tooth?'

Spencer held the tooth up. 'Here.'

'Well, aren't you clever? It's time for me to be released, then,' Nobody said, his tone wheedling.

Hedy took half a step forwards, then stopped herself. 'No, you have to show us what happened to our grandmother first.'

'How do I know you won't just run away once I show you?' Nobody said, sounding hurt. 'One of us has to give in first, and *you're* the ones who came to find *me*.'

But with Doug and Stan's warning ringing in her head, Hedy stood her ground. 'Show us what you know first.'

The blue light travelled through the green glass in an annoyed flicker. 'Stubborn as your grandfather, eh?'

'That's right.'

Nobody sighed very loudly. 'Very well. A show you want, a show you'll get. But there will be consequences if you don't keep your word,' he said. 'You need to put the tooth back. I can't do anything with you holding it.'

Neither of them was keen to touch the chandelier again, but they reached up to unscrew a cylindrical chamber. A very small disc about the size of a finger-nail fell out, on to the floor.

'Quick, pick it up, fools,' Nobody hissed. 'That's the wrong chamber. The tooth belongs in the next one around, clockwise. Don't mix them up or I'll end up with teeth growing out of my fingers.'

It was a horrifying thought, but before they could ask what he meant, three familiar bumps appeared in the surface of the floorboards. The Woodspies had been drawn by the fallen disc. Hedy scrambled to pick it up before the Woodspies could steal the thing, and realized that it wasn't just the size of a fingernail, it *was* a fingernail. Not just a clipped end, but a full nail, ripped off a finger. She almost dropped it in disgust. It was very dark in colour, somewhere between red and purple and black. Trying to hold it with as little of her own fingers as possible, she returned the nail into its chamber and Spencer replaced the cap. They opened the next chamber along clockwise, as instructed by Nobody, and Spencer placed the tooth carefully inside and closed it again.

'OK, now your turn,' Hedy said, backing away from the chandelier and pulling Spencer with her. The Woodspies circled their feet; Hedy couldn't tell whether the little creatures were nervous or being protective.

'There's a deck of cards inside that chest,' Nobody ordered. 'Get them out.'

Hedy opened the lid of the domino chest and extracted the cards lying at the bottom. She gently shook the cards out on to her palm.

'Now throw them into the air.'

'Pardon?'

'Throw them into the air.'

With a doubtful glance at Spencer, Hedy tossed the deck of cards into the air. They fell to the floor with a soft slap.

'Pathetic effort,' muttered Nobody. 'Try again, both of you, half a deck each. And really *throw*. I can't do much if they're just lying on the ground.'

The Woodspies bulldozed cards into Hedy and Spencer's hands until they each had roughly half a deck. Deep in the heart of the chandelier, Nobody's blue light had shrunk to a tight sphere.

'One, two, three,' counted Spencer, and they both flung the cards up.

The cards fluttered and spun. But something else was happening. All the black and red diamonds, spades, hearts and clubs, and the numbers too, lifted off the cards, so that unmarked cardboard wafted to the floor. The small black and red markings gathered together, mysteriously suspended in a large cloud, clustering randomly until Nobody said in a deep, showy voice, 'Behold. The Disappearance of Rose Sang.'

The cloud of shapes and numbers swirled around until they formed an image of a long box. They'd seen it in the clip on Jelly's phone.

'Grandpa John's Kaleidos,' Hedy said. The littlest Woodspy wobbled to and fro excitedly, bumping her toes.

Shapes and numbers wavered and everything swirled again. The Kaleidos reappeared, and a cloud of red and black in the shape of a person approached it – a woman in a short, flared skirt. It couldn't be anyone else.

'There's Grandma,' Spencer said, transfixed.

The shape of Grandma Rose ran an affectionate hand along the Kaleidos, then walked away. The shapes and numbers that formed her figure dissolved. It was just the box again. But now, here came someone new. A taller person with broader shoulders and a cape fluttering behind him as he walked. Like Grandma Rose, his face was indistinct. He knelt at one end of the Kaleidos and extracted a cube, made of a stack of diamonds. Then he too walked away and the markings that formed him disbanded.

'Who was that?' Hedy asked, but Nobody said nothing.

The red and black shapes churned and reformed, showing the box again but smaller, as though seen from a further distance. On one side was a patch of black spade shapes, showing where the Kaleidos was missing a cube.

Doll-sized forms of John and Rose walked out of the swirl of shapes, to take a bow in front of the box at an imaginary audience. Rose curtsied and swung herself into the Kaleidos. The small black John moved his glittering creation around, pushing and pulling and tipping pieces over, red shapes dancing like the flames over it all.

John stopped, made the Kaleidos rectangular again, and opened the side. The box was empty. Small red Rose was gone. The figure of John bent over, crying.

As the cloud of shapes and numbers merged again into one large Kaleidos image, they began to float towards Hedy and Spencer. The empty spot where the missing cube should have been grew and grew, and then came at the children in a rush, the spaces between the shapes disappearing until all was black. It was a tunnel of pure shadow that enveloped them, reverberating.

Hedy couldn't see anything, but she held Spencer's hand tightly. When his other hand came searching through the darkness, she grabbed it. No matter how hard she blinked, she couldn't see anything through the terrifying blackness, nor hear anything. The only slivers of comfort she had to anchor her in the darkness were Spencer's hands, and the bump of a Woodspy underfoot.

Finally, light. The blackness parted, like a tent being unzipped. The shapes all mixed together again, red and black, and then dived down on to the mess of cards, taking their places so that, moments later, the cards looked like they always had.

'And there you have it,' Nobody said blithely. The blue light in the chandelier was no longer a ball shape, and now danced across the glass chambers as normal.

Hedy and Spencer were still clutching each other's hands, breathing hard. Shakily, Hedy asked, 'What was that thing at the end?'

'It was the end.'

'What do you mean?'

'It was the deafening, endless night I believe your grandmother endures. Do you want to see it again?'

Hedy did not. Everything in her instinctively

recoiled at the thought of drowning in the blackness once more. But neither did she want to let Nobody know that she was frightened. 'Who was the man who took the cube?'

'Oh, you know *that*,' Nobody said, his voice taking on a sly tone.

'Who was it?'

'Why, your greatest family magician, of course!'

Hedy felt like her heart had dropped into a deep chasm under her feet. Spencer released her hands from his, stunned and pale as a ghost. 'Grandpa John?' he whispered.

Nobody chuckled deeply for a long time.

'It can't have been Grandpa John,' Hedy managed.

'Really? Why?'

'He loved her. He's so sad, he's been . . . been *broken* ever since she disappeared.'

'The sad, broken form of a guilty man, I say,' Nobody said. 'Or is it an act? Haven't you ever wondered why your mother moved so far away from her only surviving parent? Did she know in her heart what he had done, and hate him for it?'

'Mum and Dad moved for work,' Spencer protested.

And Mum doesn't hate Grandpa John, Hedy thought, holding on to what she thought she knew as if it were a life raft. Moments of their mother and grandfather together played in her mind. Perhaps Mum and Grandpa John were a little awkward with each other at times, and weeks seemed to go by between phone calls. Hedy had never heard them fight, but why did they live so far away? Why didn't they visit more?

'Of course that's what she told you,' Nobody sighed. 'Back in those days, your grandfather was the most arrogant performer on the circuit. We all hated him. Even Peter found him infuriating. John claimed he was the best, but I would have put my money on any number of others. I never did understand why the police dropped the line of questioning that involved The Amazing John Sang so quickly. Your grandfather probably did it for the attention.'

Hedy couldn't put the deep grief of Grandpa John together with someone who would make his own wife disappear.

'Anyway, I've done my part, now time for you to do yours. Set me free,' said Nobody.

'What are you going to do when you're out?' Spencer asked.

There was a pause before Mr Nobody spoke. 'Travel the world to lay the sun on my throat. To look thunder in the eye. To bite at the wind in my teeth.'

The children were momentarily stunned. What did it mean to look thunder in the eye?

'I thought you were going to say you'd haunt somebody,' Spencer said.

'Would you like me to?' Nobody teased.

Hedy tried to think. 'What are we supposed to do now? How do we find Grandma Rose?'

'Well, *obviously*, in order to untrap her you need to find that box she's trapped in and make it whole,' Nobody said.

'But Grandpa John said he destroyed the Kaleidos,' Hedy said, 'to keep our mother safe.'

Nobody snorted. 'Ha! You'd better hope not! Fat chance of you finding her if he did. Now set me free.'

'But are we looking for the missing piece?'

After a long moment of thought, Nobody said, 'If I'm set free, I can help you look for it. And the Kaleidos.'

'How?'

'There are places I can go that you can't.'

Hedy was suspicious. 'Do you promise?'

'Magician's honour.'

Hedy nibbled her thumbnail, thinking. After a long moment, she muttered, 'Fine.'

Spencer grabbed her elbow. 'Doug and Stan said not to trust him!' he whispered.

'I think this will be the fastest way.' She and Spencer slowly edged towards the chandelier. 'What do we do?' she asked Nobody.

'You need to take out all my relics and lay them on the floor. The tooth, the nail, all the items in the other chambers. Take them out and arrange them how I tell you to.'

Hedy and Spencer nervously unscrewed each cap and withdrew the mystery items inside. Not all were unpleasant, although it was creepy to hold things that belonged to a dead man they'd never met. After the tooth and the nail, they found a pocket watch, inside which was a very small photograph of a smiling, bald baby and its smiling mother.

'Who're they?' Spencer asked.

But Nobody wouldn't say. Curtly he told Spencer to place it on the floor. After the pocket watch was a gold ring, a pair of tortoiseshell glasses, a necktie of paisley print in blues and reds, and a lock of brown hair tied with a length of fine black ribbon. Finally, Hedy loosened the cap on the last compartment and reached inside. It was like touching a large raisin, but when she pulled it out it was grey in colour, with a blob of darker colour in one spot.

'Now I shall see,' purred Nobody.

Hedy dropped the thing, feeling queasy.

'What is it?' Spencer asked.

'An eyeball,' Hedy said. She desperately wanted to wash her hands – for hours, days, maybe even until the new year came.

When Nobody insisted the eyeball be moved to a spot between the ring and the nail, completing the circle, Hedy nudged it in with the toe of one shoe. Royal-blue light radiated from the centre of the chandelier, illuminating the relics on the floor.

'What's happening?' Hedy asked.

'All these questions,' Nobody grated. 'No wonder your parents left you here. Now get out!'

CHAPTER 15

PORTSALL

'What do we do, Hedy?'

Spencer was too afraid to sleep in his own bed. He took some puffs on his inhaler, lobbed his pillow to the bottom of Hedy's mattress, and crawled under the covers with his feet towards her head. Hedy couldn't sleep either and sat with her back to the wall, fidgeting with the card that had been slipped into her pocket at the Palisade.

'The golden hands said we should ask Nobody for help,' she said. 'I guess that means Nobody was telling the truth . . .'

'. . . which means Grandpa John did it,' Spencer finished.

Hedy scrunched down under the duvet, feeling a chill come over her that had nothing to do with it being a winter's night. She pictured all the times that Grandma Rose had come up in conversation and tried to recall Grandpa John's face. He had never seemed anything more than lost in grief and yearning for her. Was he simply the world's greatest actor?

From her notebook, she pulled out the article that Jelly had printed for them. And there it was. They had overlooked it completely: a dark empty spot in the sheer side of the Kaleidos that should have held a glittering cube. She stared miserably at the faces of young John and Rose beaming at each other. Was John's smile fake?

Maybe if she broke the problem down, this helpless feeling would vanish. Grabbing a red marker, Hedy began writing in the margins of the page. Down one side, she scrawled, *Where is the cube?*, and down the other, *Where is the Kaleidos?* At the bottom, below Grandpa John, she wrote simply, *Why?*

It was a short list. Instead of feeling inspired by it, she felt more bleak than ever.

'So what do we do, Hedy?' Spencer repeated.

'We'll think of something tomorrow.'

The following morning, they woke late. No great ideas had come to them in the night and they stayed in bed for a long time, until finally Hedy's stomach grumbled even more loudly than Spencer's.

'Do you have any food in here?' Spencer asked.

'Nothing. I guess we'd better go down.'

'Do you think Grandpa John's finished breakfast yet?'

'Maybe.' Hedy reluctantly turned back the corner of her duvet and they made their way from their bedroom to the hall, to the stairs, and down. The blackness that had enveloped them during Nobody's card show last night had left its mark: Spencer insisted on turning on all the lights to banish the shadows.

Grandpa John looked up with a smile when they walked into the kitchen. Spencer kept behind Hedy as much as he could, mumbling 'Good morning' into his chest before clamming up. Hedy had to agree to porridge for both of them as Spencer just stared at the top of the wooden table, speechless.

'What's wrong, my boy?' Grandpa John asked, concerned.

After an awkward pause Hedy said, 'He didn't sleep very well.'

Grandpa John nodded in understanding. 'Breakfast will help. And then what about a ramble to Foxwood today?' He turned to the worktop to make a start on their oats.

'Act normal!' Hedy told Spencer under her breath.

'But I'm scared,' he whispered back.

'He's never tried to hurt us.' As she said it, the assurance settled over her enough to make her doubt, just a little, what Nobody had shown them last night.

By the time he got to the bottom of his bowl of porridge, Spencer looked a bit brighter, although he still hadn't said a word. Hedy had been thinking as she ate, mulling over the magnetic letters on the fridge, long since scrambled and the message lost. Wouldn't Grandma Rose have warned them that Grandpa John had done it? Or did she not know? Questions kept battling in her head, first from one side of the theory, then the other.

Once she had finished and cleaned her bowl, Hedy went to sit by the liar bird chicks that were tucked in a large cardboard box in the warmest corner of the kitchen. Grandpa John had already fed them, and they were sleeping contentedly.

'Grandpa,' she began. Her voice, nervous, came out too loud and croaky. She tried again. 'Grandpa, do you know who was behind Grandma Rose disappearing?'

The teaspoon in Grandpa John's hand clattered to the worktop. Hedy shrank into herself, feeling how clumsy the question sounded, asked out of the blue.

'We've spoken about this before.' Grandpa John frowned. 'Why do you ask?'

Hedy shrugged. 'Well, do you?'

'What a curious way to start the day.' He seemed uneasy. Was it because of the liar birds? 'If I had known, I would have done something about it.'

One fluffy liar bird chick rustled and fluffed, barely opening an eye before settling back into sleep with its siblings. Hedy couldn't tell if it was a reaction to Grandpa John's answer or not. A part of her didn't want to know.

The phone rang in the hallway, and Grandpa John hurried away with some relief to answer it.

'What do you think?' Spencer whispered. 'Is he guilty?'

Hedy frowned. 'He didn't really answer the question, did he?'

Spencer turned his spoon over and over in his hand. 'Can we call Mum and Dad? Ask them to come home early?'

'And tell them what?'

'Tell them everything!'

'But we've got Nobody helping us look for Grandma Rose now,' Hedy reminded him.

In the hallway, Grandpa John was murmuring excitedly to the person on the other end of the line. Hedy edged closer to the hallway entrance to eavesdrop. 'No, of course I still want it,' Grandpa John was saying, 'but does it have to be today? I have grandchildren staying with me . . .'

Spencer sneaked to Hedy's side to listen as well.

'No, no, there's no need for that, I'll take it,' Grandpa John continued. 'Let me make some arrangements.' He hung up the phone, paused for a moment and then dialled a number. 'Hello, it's me,' he said shortly. 'Can you look after Hedy and Spencer for a couple of hours? This morning . . .'

Spencer glanced at Hedy questioningly, and she mouthed back *Uncle Peter*. When Grandpa John hung up the phone, they scurried back to their seats at the table and tried to look surprised when he announced they were going for a drive. 'I'll have to drop you off at Peter's for a short visit. Just while I pick something up.'

'We could stay here by ourselves,' Hedy suggested, thinking of what they might achieve in a few precious hours alone.

Grandpa John looked at her askance. 'This isn't the same as me popping down to the village. Go on, now, get dressed.'

Upstairs, the children brushed their teeth and quickly dressed. When Spencer threw back his duvet to look for his socks, he let out a yelp of surprise. 'What's this?' he asked, turning to Hedy and pointing.

It was a small statue head that took Hedy a few seconds to place. 'That's the head from the Roman chariot guy,' she said slowly. 'The figurine in Doug and Stan's room.'

'What's it doing in my bed?' Spencer bent low to study it. 'Oh, I know. The Woodspies must have put it there.'

'I guess so,' Hedy said. 'I didn't know they could get up there, though. The bed isn't wood.'

Spencer smiled for the first time that morning. 'It's like an offering to a king.'

Hedy pocketed the article on which she had written their short list of matters to investigate. Perhaps Uncle Peter would know something.

Shouldering their backpacks, the children headed downstairs, but on their way past Doug and Stan's room they heard a muffled, outraged grunt. They paused. Hearing Grandpa John on the bottom floor, it seemed safe enough to open the door and quickly check on their friends.

'Are you all right, guys?' Spencer whispered.

'Far from it!' Stan exclaimed from the wall. 'Look!'

Sticking out of his poor nose were three darts. The feathers on the ends of the darts bounced around as Stan tried to get rid of them by screwing up his nose.

'Skewered out of nowhere, he was,' Doug rumbled from the floor.

'Are they magic darts?' Spencer asked.

'Never showed a whiff of enchantment before,' Doug said. 'They've been in this room, still as you please, for years now. Something threw them.'

'Something cruel,' added Stan hotly. 'I thought I'd seen the last of sharp objects coming out of nowhere when that blasted hunter got me. It's not even a sport, what with me immobilized on this wall.'

Doug shook his head. 'Whatever it was, it had good aim.'

While the bear and the stag talked, the children hastily built another tower of boxes so that Hedy could reach up and pluck the darts from Stan's nose. 'Thank you,' Stan said gratefully.

'No problem,' Hedy said, not meeting the stag's eye. An uncomfortable notion was growing in the back of her mind, one that she didn't want to give voice to.

'Hedy, Grandpa's calling us,' said Spencer nervously, one ear to the door.

Stan cleared his throat anxiously. 'Take those darts away, won't you? Get rid of them.'

'The Lord of the Queen's Wood's had enough of Stab the Stag,' Doug joked, humour restored now that the darts had been removed from his friend.

Stan threw him a sour look. 'You'd better hope you're not next, you mangy mat.'

Leaving the two animals to trade insults, Hedy closed the door and shooed Spencer to the stairs. Halfway down the hallway Spencer asked, 'Hedy, who would do that to Stan?' Then he suddenly halted and grabbed Hedy's wrist. 'It was Nobody, wasn't it? He threw the darts – and left the head in my bed.'

Uncle Peter lived in Portsall, about forty minutes' drive away. It lay towards the coast, and there was a faint salt tang in the air when Spencer wound down his window. Like their trip to Stradmoor, arriving in Portsall made Hedy feel displaced somehow, as though she had been in space and missed everything that had happened on Earth for a few days. She'd been quiet for most of the drive, her mind chewing over the figurine head and the darts, but mostly over Nobody's card trick, and what it could mean about Grandpa John.

When they arrived at a wide terrace house of brown brick with a white-trimmed bay window, Hedy and Spencer gladly scrambled out of the car. Within moments Uncle Peter was opening the front door. 'Welcome to the fun house!' he bellowed.

He stepped to one side, and out popped Jelly and Max.

'Surprise!' yelled Max as he tried to get Spencer to chase him.

Jelly threw an arm around Hedy. 'We only live a few streets away, and Mum said we could come over, seeing as you were going to be here.'

'It's about time you visited me, John,' Uncle Peter said. 'Like some tea before you head off?'

'No, thank you, I'm expected elsewhere,' Grandpa John said shortly. 'Be good, won't you, kids? Don't touch anything.'

Uncle Peter let out an amused snort. 'Of course they can touch things, as long as they don't break them!'

Grandpa John pursed his lips, then muttered, 'I'll pretend I didn't hear that.' He told Hedy and Spencer he'd be back in around two hours, and then hurried to his car.

'Do you know where Grandpa John is going, Uncle Peter?' Hedy asked. 'He wouldn't tell us.'

'Not a word to me either, I'm afraid.' Uncle Peter tugged his beard. 'He keeps his secrets from one and all.'

Hedy and Spencer followed their cousins into a tidy boot room where they kicked off their shoes and hung their jackets, then into the house. The hallway smelt wonderful, like some sort of baked treat. Between the scent, and the racket of her cousins, some of the worry that nagged at Hedy ebbed away.

To the right of the hall was the front sitting room, where light from the window was partially blocked by the enormous Christmas tree, festooned with ornaments. Although there were many interesting things scattered around, the room was neat and inviting and ordinary – not a bit like Grandpa John's cluttered house. There was a glossy black upright piano, a pair of leather couches, and side tables holding pictures of the cousins with their parents, Toni and Vincent.

'Come and look at these,' Max said, dragging Spencer to three framed posters of a young Uncle Peter (*Witness the Power of Magician Peter Sang!*) which hung on the far wall. Hedy peered into a tall bookcase with glass doors. It was filled with intriguing things: weathered stone plaques carved with symbols, a small sheathed knife made of silver, brightly coloured enamel eggs with gold filigree, and a few different wooden masks, all with fierce expressions. One silver photo frame held a sepia photograph of none other than Tsang Li Ming.

Uncle Peter spotted Hedy studying the picture. 'That's your great-great-grandfather.'

'Did you ever meet him?'

'Only twice. He was retired and living in China by the time I came along. He was a famous magician, you know.'

'I think I heard that,' Hedy said carefully. 'Is he why you and Grandpa John became magicians?'

Uncle Peter thought. 'I'd say he was the reason John became a magician, but the reason I became one was because of John.' He smiled at Hedy's surprised look. 'Brothers can be competitive.'

As he bustled out of the room, Hedy noticed a small red bag that was, oddly, suspended above the fireplace. 'What's that?' she asked Jelly.

'It's a protective charm. It wards away evil,' Jelly said. 'We have a bigger one at home too, but it's packed up right now because of the renovations at home and there's, like, dust *everywhere*. My nana makes them.'

'Where is she?' Hedy asked curiously.

'She lives in America, in New Orleans, where she's from. She and Grandad divorced before I was born.' Jelly gazed wistfully at the charm for a moment before adding cheekily, 'Your grandpa isn't the only one who can make his wife disappear.' At Hedy's scandalized look, she added, 'What, too soon?'

Hedy couldn't help but dissolve into giggles, and Jelly took her by the arm to show her more of the house.

*

Together, the five of them walked to a Chinese restaurant called The Emperor's Court for a lunch of dumplings, 'in honour of your great-great-grand-father,' Uncle Peter said. The restaurant owner made a great fuss of Uncle Peter, chatting and bringing the children pink lemonades and special dumplings that weren't on the menu. Afterwards, Uncle Peter took them to a nearby ice cream shop, where the manager came out from behind the counter to shake his hand and have a long chat. The manager had a large bucket of lollies behind the counter and let all the children take a handful. Spencer, of course, filled his pocket. Uncle Peter basked in the attention like a benevolent king.

As they ambled back home, Spencer fired questions at Uncle Peter about his career as a stage magician. With immense relish, he regaled them with stories about his performance for the royal family, turning a whole carriage into a pumpkin in the blink of an eye, and the time he used magic to foil a suspected Russian spy. Spencer soaked in every detail and forgot to lick his ice cream, so that butterscotch swirl melted down his hand. *This is what holidays should be like*, Hedy mused.

Jelly pulled on Hedy's sleeve to slow her down, and they walked a little way behind the others. 'What's the latest from Uncle John's House of Horrors?'

'It's not a house of horrors!' Hedy whispered indignantly. She paused and then grudgingly admitted, 'But we did find some creepy stuff.' She filled Jelly in on discovering Albert Nobody, and the revelation about Grandpa John.

Jelly was gobsmacked. 'You're not going to go back to your grandpa's, are you?'

'I can't *not* go back,' Hedy said.

'If he's responsible, and he hid it all this time, you *can't* go back! Aren't you afraid? You could stay with us. Oh, except Max is already bunking with me 'cos his room is being fixed up. But you could stay with my grandad. Want me to ask?'

They had reached the house, and Uncle Peter was waiting for them at the front door. Hedy shook her head firmly at her cousin, not knowing yet what she should do. She was fearful, yes, but what would happen to Grandma Rose if Hedy and Spencer weren't there? Would Nobody still look for the Kaleidos and its missing piece?

Hedy and Jelly found the boys upstairs in the room

where Uncle Peter kept his old costumes, posters and props. 'Can you show me how this works?' Spencer was asking Max, holding up a magician's birdcage. It collapsed just as he said it, painfully pinching his fingers, and they had to call Uncle Peter for help.

'Magic is a dangerous calling,' Uncle Peter warned as he released Spencer's fingers.

Spencer tried to shake the sting away. 'That's what Grandpa says. But this is just a trick, isn't it?'

Max had turned his attention to an iridescent dark-green cape that he arranged around his shoulders. 'Hedy, did you try those wings again? Did you manage to make them work?'

'Wings?' Uncle Peter asked.

Hedy coughed and glared at Max. 'Um . . . chicken wings. Mrs V has a secret recipe.' To cover the slip-up, she stood up in front of her cousin and said, 'Hey, Max, can you bow like this?'

She took a deep, arm-waving bow. As she did so, the printed article in her pocket fell out and dropped to the floor. Uncle Peter picked it up, and his eyes widened at the picture and Hedy's questions surrounding it. 'What are you doing with this?' he asked softly.

Hedy had brought the article so she could ask Uncle Peter about it, but now felt unprepared. 'Um ... we were looking at Grandpa John's Kaleidos.'

'Why?'

'Well, because of Grandma Rose. We ... we want to know what happened to her. Do you know?'

'No one knows what happened.' Uncle Peter shook his head at the photo. 'That damned box.'

'Grandpa John said he got rid of it,' Hedy said, 'so that it wouldn't hurt anyone else.'

A stricken look passed over Uncle Peter's face. 'Are you sure?' Hedy and Spencer nodded. 'I thought he kept it somewhere.'

'Do you know where?' Spencer asked eagerly.

'I don't know. I only thought ...' He trailed off.

'Do you know Albert Nobody?' Hedy asked.

Uncle Peter looked startled. 'That pompous, one-trick show-pony? Why?'

'I read he was there on the night,' Hedy said.

'He was. But he died some time ago, and in any case he wasn't terribly kind about your grandfather when everything happened.' He stared at the photograph and Hedy's handwriting for a long time, and then gave Hedy a searching look. 'Understand that these memories of your grandmother are painful for John. I think it's best not to dredge up this history while you're staying there. He was under suspicion for some weeks, you know. It was a difficult time.'

'But what if we could find her?'

Uncle Peter put a gentle hand on her head. 'You can't. Don't lose yourselves down rabbit holes, chasing the impossible. You'll be going home in a matter of days. Are you going to unearth skeletons only to leave him to deal with them all alone? I couldn't think of anything more unkind. You should throw that article away. Concentrate on the here and now.'

Hedy had an urge to tell him about the writing in the dust, Doug and Stan, the Woodspies, everything, just to prove him wrong. But she stopped herself. It was all too likely he would tell Grandpa John, take his side, and then they'd never find Grandma Rose.

'Could they stay here, Grandad?' Jelly slyly suggested. When Hedy frowned at her, she added, 'Just so we can hang out more.'

'Of course, you'd be welcome,' Uncle Peter said to Hedy and Spencer. 'If you want to?'

Hedy could feel Spencer's pleading eyes on her, and she thought back over their perfectly normal and enjoyable visit here, where things were simple and fun. But then a shaft of light caught the cape that Max wore. That dark green reminded her of Nobody's chandelier, his card trick, and the darkness that had rolled over them – that darkness Nobody had said Grandma Rose was trapped in.

'No,' Hedy said, 'we should go back with Grandpa John.'

CHAPTER 16

ELSEWHERE IS HERE

Grandpa John didn't tell them where he had been, but whatever he had bought had put him in a good mood. From the way his hand kept checking his pocket, it was small.

Spencer was silent most of the way back, and Hedy figured it was because he didn't want to talk to Grandpa John. 'Maybe Nobody's already found the Kaleidos,' she whispered as the car finally wound through Marberry's Rest.

Spencer squinted through the window at Hoarder Hill, which looked especially quiet and lonely after their visit with Uncle Peter and their cousins. 'I hope so.' He glanced at her crossly. 'I wish we'd stayed at Uncle Peter's.'

Grandpa John shifted his shoulders in a way that made Hedy wonder if he had heard. Despite everything, it felt wrong to hurt his feelings.

When they walked into the house, Hedy half hoped that they'd find their grandmother miraculously returned, pacing the hall or perhaps sitting at the large kitchen table. But all was still and silent inside. No Rose awaited them, and while Grandpa John was bustling around, they couldn't exactly go hunting for Nobody either.

Neither Hedy nor Spencer felt very talkative that afternoon. They picked at their dinner listlessly, and then Hedy lied that they weren't feeling very well and wanted to head to bed early. The trouble Grandpa John took to tuck them in and prepare for a night of two unwell children was touching. He put a bucket beside each of their beds in case they suddenly needed to throw up, and made sure Spencer had his asthma puffer nearby. After reading some very detailed instructions that Olivia had written out and placed in the medicine kit she had left, he set up children's paracetamol and crackers on a plate on the shelf, in case he needed to administer them during the night.

'Call me if you need me,' he said, hovering worriedly in the doorway.

'Thanks, Grandpa. I think we just need to sleep,' said Hedy. She scrunched herself under her duvet and forced herself to remember that he might have caused his own wife's disappearance.

As the sound of Grandpa John's footsteps receded, both children sat up in bed. Hedy studied the ceiling. 'Mr Nobody?'

'Is he here?' Spencer asked, hugging his pillow.

Hedy waited a moment. 'I don't think so. I was only checking.' She hopped out of bed, and beckoned Spencer. 'Let's see if we can find him.'

'Where?'

'I guess we should start with his room first.'

They sidled down the hallway to the stairs. Fortunately, there was no movement below; Grandpa John must have gone into his study. When they reached the third floor, Hedy dared to switch on her torch, and they darted along to Nobody's room.

'I'll open the door and you shine the torch inside,' Spencer said. 'That's how the police do it on TV.'

'We're not the police, Spence,' Hedy said, 'and this isn't a gun.' But she agreed to do it his way, which would have been all right except that, in his anxiety, Spencer pushed the blue door a bit too hard and it swung back so forcefully it knocked the wall.

'Be careful!' Hedy admonished him.

She shone her torch inside. The floor where they had placed Nobody's creepy relics was clear, and when they softly called Nobody's name, there was no hint of his blue light, or his voice.

'He's not there,' Hedy said, closing the door.

Spencer edged in closer to Hedy's pool of torch-light. 'Do you think he's still in the house?'

A sharp *pssst* caught their attention from down the hall. Hedy swung her torch. The ghostly head of Simon appeared in the darkness, poking through his yellow door.

'You must warn the Master,' he said, his voice thick, as though he had been crying. 'Warn John.'

'Simon, what is it?' Hedy asked. She shuffled closer with Spencer at her side, feeling the air cool as they approached the ghost pianist.

'Albert Nobody has escaped!'

'He, he . . . he's helping us look for our grandmother,' Hedy stammered.

Simon looked horrified. 'You released him?'

'Remember you said we could ask him about Grandma Rose?' Hedy said defensively.

'Ask him, yes. Release him, *non*!'

'Why? What's he doing?' Spencer whispered.

'He stole my middle C!' Neither Hedy nor Spencer knew what that meant. Insubstantial tears welled in Simon's eyes and ran down his face to fall from his chin, but they disappeared before hitting the floor. 'He stole five keys from my piano. How can I play without them? My concerto sounds like Swiss cheese – full of holes! Why, Wellington's bust atop my piano has been beheaded. The head dented my poor piano when it fell. Nothing is safe with Nobody abroad! You must warn the Master, or I will. I will draw his attention up here and tell him it was your doing!'

'No, please don't tell Grandpa John,' Hedy pleaded. 'Nobody promised to help us look for Grandma Rose. That's all we're trying to do.'

'When we see him, Hedy will tell him to stop this mucking around,' Spencer added.

Simon did not look convinced.

'We'll find the piano keys for you and bring them

back, OK?' Hedy said. 'Do you know where they are?'

Dabbing his eyes with one frilly sleeve, Simon shook his head. 'I cannot travel far from my piano stool. It was on that stool that I took my last breath, you see. So I could not follow him. I do not know where he took them.'

'Did he say anything at all?'

'Only teased me about giving them a "beautiful view".' He crossed his arms mulishly. 'If you cannot find and return them, the Master will have to be told what you have done!'

Hedy and Spencer assured the ghost they would do their best, and he faded from view, still looking pained. They tiptoed away and downstairs, alert to any hint of Nobody. Could he be hiding in one of the other locked rooms they'd never been inside, with doors of muted pink or red or azure?

'Do you think he's going to keep his promise?' Spencer asked.

Hedy crossed fingers on both hands. 'I hope so. If he doesn't, I don't know how we're going to find Grandma Rose.' She paused outside Doug and Stan's room. 'Let's check that Stan hasn't been poked with more darts.'

When they opened the green door, it was a different scene of wretchedness that greeted them. Doug was turned over on the floor, rumpled, as though he had been in a fight. He cocked his head as Hedy and Spencer knelt beside him and said glumly, 'Don't honey the stinger, cubs. How bad is it?'

'How bad is what?' Hedy asked.

'I told him it's not that bad!' Stan called out nervously. 'It isn't really.'

'Turn me over,' said Doug.

Together the children flipped Doug on to his front and had to stifle their gasps. There was a stripe of fur missing from his back, as though someone had taken a razor to it. And not only that: his tail was missing.

'Oh, Doug,' Hedy whispered. Spencer, meanwhile, was speechless.

Doug closed his eyes. 'I knew it was bad.'

'Does it hurt?' Hedy asked.

'In the rump.'

'What happened?' Spencer finally managed to say.

'I didn't see,' Doug said, trying to get a look at the spot where his tail should have been. 'Stan, you tell them.'

Stan licked his nose nervously. 'It was a pearl-handled

blade, shining in the dim light,' he began, 'held aloft by an unseen agent.'

'Here we go,' muttered Doug.

'I'm only trying to give your misfortune a sense of magnitude,' pouted Stan.

'Just get on with it, you nutty pincushion,' said Doug.

'So should I merely blurt out that a knife came out of nowhere, shaved you to resemble a skunk and then hacked off your tail?'

Doug threw his paws into the air. 'Yes!'

'Well,' Stan huffed, 'the conclusion is that we still have no conclusion. We don't know what it was. The Master's done something and it's set off this mischief.'

Hedy found it hard to swallow. 'I think we know what it was.'

Haltingly, the children told Doug and Stan what had happened the previous night – Nobody's card trick, releasing him from the chandelier, the head of the Roman charioteer. As they went on, Hedy spoke less and less, allowing Spencer to fill in the gaps. Small waves of strain had been worrying her lately – of not knowing what to think about Grandpa John, of looking after Spencer, of guilt over Stan's nose, Simon's piano keys and Doug's tail. Now those small waves were fusing into one great swell that was threatening to break over her. She tried to squash it back.

'We did say not to trust Nobody,' Stan said, shaking his head.

'And not to let him out,' added Doug.

Their exasperation brought the tidal wave crashing down upon Hedy, and she began to cry. Spencer stared, baffled by this sudden change in his dependable sister. When he put an uncertain arm around Hedy, she wept even harder.

'Why the tears, little one?' Doug asked.

'I . . . I'm sorry, we let him out,' she sobbed.

'Well, what's done is done,' Stan murmured. 'You were trying to do the right thing.'

'But I feel so bad that you got hurt. And Doug, your tail . . .' The surge of guilt and regret washed over her again and again, and the others did the best thing they could do, which was to let her cry.

It took some time, but her jagged breaths slowly steadied, and Hedy realized there was one thing above all that was bothering her. 'I don't want to hate Grandpa John.'

'Me neither,' Spencer said. His arm was still around Hedy, patting her shoulder every now and then. It was an unusual feeling, being comforted by her younger brother for once, but a heartening one.

'No, indeed,' sighed Stan. 'He's a strange one, even for a human, but I don't like to think he was hiding a secret like that.'

'What are you going to do?' Doug asked.

Hedy took a deep breath, unexpectedly feeling less overwhelmed now. 'We have to find Nobody again. Get him to stop all the trouble-making, remind him that he's supposed to be helping us.'

'Well, he sliced my tail off hours ago,' Doug said. 'I hate to say it, but what if he's bored of making mischief here and sailed off to do it elsewhere?'

'The freed beast doth flail and thrash,' Stan proclaimed.

'Wossat?' Doug frowned. 'A verse?'

'No, I just made it up,' Stan said proudly. 'That's why he's behaving so waywardly. He's like a caged tiger that's got out and wants to claw something.' He paused. 'Perhaps I *could* create a verse out of it.' Closing his eyes, he whispered the words to himself again.

'You'd better get out of here,' Doug counselled Hedy and Spencer. 'He's going to get poetical, and you haven't got that sort of time to waste.'

Small tell-tale signs of Nobody began to appear throughout the house, even though he didn't speak to them or show himself. Hedy and Spencer's tooth-brushes were dropped in the toilet. A page was ripped from the book that Hedy had left in the lounge. Around mid-morning, a Woodspy nudged the head of one of Spencer's wrestling figurines around the floor of their bedroom.

'That's it!' Spencer fumed, picking up the head and jamming it back on to the plastic body. 'Just because he's a decapitation expert doesn't mean he gets to behead my toys!' Grabbing Hedy by the hand, he pulled her downstairs to the laundry, where he started to grapple the vacuum cleaner out of its corner.

'What are you doing?' Hedy asked.

'Maybe we can suck up Mr Nobody with this.'

Hedy gave him a doubtful look. 'Where'd you get this idea? From a movie?'

'Well, do you have a better one?'

She didn't, so they made up a story for Grandpa

John about Mum and Dad having promised to pay them some pocket money if they did some cleaning for him.

'You won't break anything, will you?' Grandpa John asked as he rather sceptically watched them vacuum the hall. 'Perhaps I should pay you *not* to vacuum?'

'We're learning responsibility,' Hedy smoothly assured him. 'And the value of hard work.'

'I've got to find something else to keep you kids occupied,' he said, shaking his head.

Grandpa John watched them vacuum the hallway and the lounge room until he was satisfied they weren't going to accidentally destroy things, and then he eventually drifted off to his study.

'OK,' Spencer said, 'let's try it.'

Together, he and Hedy swung the head of the vacuum up into the air and they slowly wheeled it around the room.

'How will we know if we do suck him in?' Hedy asked.

'Maybe his tooth and his eyeball and other bits will show up in there,' Spencer said, pointing to the clear plastic barrel of the vacuum where dust whizzed around.

They did all the rooms of the ground floor with no sign of Nobody, and then headed upstairs. Arms aching from holding up the hose, they sucked at their bedroom, the hallway, and even did a quick sweep through Doug and Stan's room. But it wasn't until they trundled the vacuum to the bathroom that it worked, although not as Spencer had imagined.

'You two look ridiculous,' said a voice.

Hedy and Spencer dropped the vacuum hose with a clatter. The light on the left side of the bathroom mirror was flickering blue. Hedy swiftly shoved the vacuum out into the hall so that Grandpa John would think they were still working, and then closed the bathroom door.

'Why are you mucking around with our stuff? *And* Grandpa John's things?' Hedy demanded, glaring at the blue light.

'*The freed beast doth flail and thrash*,' Nobody said, mimicking Stan's voice.

Spencer recoiled. 'You were spying on us last night?'

There was a snigger. 'I was investigating!'

'Oh, really? Well, don't try to tell us you were "investigating" when you cut off Doug's tail!' Hedy said.

'Oh, poor tail-less teddy!'

'You owe us.' Hedy's eyes narrowed. 'Have you just been going around hurting things, or have you actually found something?'

'Well, *actually*, I did find something very intriguing – and illuminating – at the top of the house.' Nobody sounded very self-satisfied.

'Do you mean the top floor?' asked Spencer.

'Think higher. *La bella vista*. The belvedere.'

'The thing we call the turret,' Hedy said to Spencer. To the light, she asked, 'What's up there?'

'I'm not going to spoil the surprise,' Nobody purred. 'But you'll find it indeed has a beautiful view.'

Hedy twitched. *Beautiful view*. That was what Simon had said. Were his piano keys up there too?

'So, just say my name when you get up there,' Nobody said casually. 'Oh, and I wouldn't bother lugging the vacuum cleaner up there if I were you.'

Hedy speculated that the way up to the belvedere from inside was probably through the attic, but the door to the attic was firmly locked.

'Doug, you could open it, couldn't you?' Spencer asked the bear hopefully, after they had recounted their exchange with Nobody.

Doug looked uneasily at the forepaw he had used to open the door to Simon's room. The patch of fur that had turned pale brown was now white, and was even bigger than before. 'I'm worried this paw is older than the rest of me after that bit of magical breaking and entering.'

'Remember how limp he was the last time?' Stan fretted to the children. 'He was like a big fur sock that'd been worn too many times. Let's not sap him completely. Bad enough he's a skunk without a tail, I don't want him turning into a comatose polar bear.'

Hedy drifted to the wings on the wall of Doug and Stan's room and ran a finger down the silvery brass feathers. Max had made them work – sort of.

With Spencer's help, Hedy got the wings on and bobbed up and down on her toes. But a sudden vision of herself plummeting from the roof, dragged by the weight of the metal wings, made them wrench downwards, many times heavier than a moment ago. Her knees buckled and she fell to the floor. That decided the matter; this was no time to start experimenting with flying.

Which left only one option: climb.

CHAPTER 17

WHAT HAPPENS TO THOSE WHO SEEK

After lunch, Hedy and Spencer told Grandpa John they were going to explore the garden, and he was preoccupied enough with whatever device he was working on (curiously, it was staining his hands blue) that he cheerily left them to it.

They sneaked a rusty-looking ladder from the garage – which was tricky to do without scratching Grandpa John's car – and crept to the side of the house that was furthest from Grandpa John's study. There, they pushed the ladder out to its full length and leant it against the brickwork.

'It doesn't go anywhere near the third floor,' Spencer pointed out, 'and some of the steps are missing.'

Hedy thought hard. She looked up at the roof and then peered around the corner. On this side, the gutter of the first floor was within reach of the ladder. From the gutter, she could see a way up using a drainpipe and a windowsill, to the bit where the two gables met. Once she shimmied up that, it would be easy to pick her way through the stone grotesques on the roofline to the belvedere and climb over its railing. She pictured what she was about to do, trying to ignore the clenching of her stomach.

'You stand guard,' Hedy told Spencer.

'Again?'

'Do *you* want to go up there? Just tell Grandpa John I'm getting a tennis ball if he comes out.'

Hedy's legs felt shaky as she started climbing up the ladder. She did her best not to dwell on the wobble in some of the rungs, nor look down. When she reached the gutter, she had to stifle a yelp of surprise at a large beetle that crawled out from under some moist leaves. The wind was up, and it tossed Hedy's hair but luckily it also blew most of the snow from the roof, so that it wasn't so slippery to climb. Her hands were very cold, though.

She reached for the gable and then pulled herself up on to the roof. *Light as a feather*, she told herself as she stepped across the tiles that appeared to be in the best shape. She made it to the drainpipe near the windowsill, and told herself that if she fell from it, it was only a very short fall. Taking a firm grip on the drainpipe, she pushed up from the windowsill, found her footing on a decorative brick, pushed up from that, and then edged up between the gables until, miraculously, she was threading her way through the stone grotesques, using them as handholds. The belvedere was within a few steps.

Hedy allowed herself a moment to enjoy the view. The few winding streets of Marberry's Rest, the surrounding patchwork of fields dusted with snow and the stands of leafless trees looked like a large toy play set from up here.

Peeping over the railing of the belvedere, Hedy saw not only the five piano keys that Nobody had taken from Simon's piano, but a brown furry stub of a bear's tail. She grinned and clambered into the belvedere, wondering if Mrs Vilums would be able to help her sew Doug's tail back on. Once the keys and the tail were secure in the inner pocket of her jacket, Hedy checked the single windowless door that led from the belvedere into what had to be the attic of the house, but it was locked.

'You made it. Well done,' said a now-familiar voice behind her.

Hedy turned, and for one heartbeat saw the wisp of a man's face hanging in the air. It faded from view the next instant. 'H-hello,' she said. She told herself the shiver was the frosty wind up here. 'I'm taking the piano keys and the bear's tail back into the house.'

'If you insist,' Nobody said agreeably.

'What did you find up here about Grandma Rose?'

Nobody laughed. 'I found out what happens to those who seek.'

'What does that mean?'

'Your grandfather has a remarkable security system. Crude, but remarkable. Try not to break the roof as you fall off it.'

'What have you found?' she cried.

There was no more taunting from Nobody. The cold wind whistled around the belvedere emptily. But then, out of the corner of her eye, Hedy saw one of the grotesques on the other side of the belvedere – a stone imp – move. It flexed its muscly little shoulders and stood straight, letting loose a guttural croak. Beyond the imp, a scrabbling noise came clicking over the roof and a small pack of grotesques slunk over the tiles.

'Finders!' said the imp in a harsh stony voice.

'What?' Hedy said faintly.

'Enemies!' sneered a gryphon.

'I'm – I'm not an enemy!' she stammered. 'I'm the Master's granddaughter.'

But the grotesques kept coming closer. Hedy crawled over the railing of the belvedere, her breath coming fast, and shuffled as quickly as she could back towards the way she had ascended. In her fear, she slipped, and let out a small scream. The stone dragon she caught hold of to stop her fall shifted under her hand, awakening as well. With a moan, Hedy dropped to her hands and knees and crawled.

'Protect her!' grated the stone dragon closest to her. For a second, Hedy thought it was coming to her aid. Instead it tried to nip her foot. She kicked out as hard as she could, startling the dragon, which retreated towards the safety of the group. But kicking that way made her lose her grip on some lichen, and she skidded down the tiles a little way before a gable broke her slide. The stone creatures were still coming. *This is it*, she thought, *I'm going to have to scream for Grandpa.*

Just as she drew breath, something fluttered from above and landed before her. It was a raven. A raven that rippled from stone to white feather and back. The same huge raven that had led their car to Grandpa John's house on that first day, Hedy was sure of it. She steeled herself for the raven to peck her, but it shot into the air and swooped on the grotesques in menacing circles. It was helping her! The little stone monsters nipped and snarled at the bird, but it darted up and down expertly, claws outstretched. Stone chips went flying and the creatures, now wary, backed away.

Hedy clambered down, resting her feet for a moment on the windowsill below. Her nose was pressed to the dirty glass of the locked window. Through it she could see mannequins wearing magician's outfits, and, in the shadows of one corner, a faint gleam of something metal. This was the attic.

The raven swooped back to Hedy, fixing her with a severe eye. The grotesques were beginning to slink back towards her.

'*Caw*,' squawked the raven urgently.

There was a faint noise inside the attic. Hedy peered in. Was there movement in the shadows?

And then in the grime of the window, just like in the dust of the photo frame, appeared three words: YOU ARE NEAR.

Grandma, Hedy thought. She was near Grandma!

The raven gently swooped at Hedy then, urging her away. She carefully slid and scurried down to the first-floor roof until she reached the top of the ladder that Spencer was still holding steady. 'I'm coming down!' she shouted.

Spencer's jaw dropped as he saw a gargoyle and a gryphon evade the raven and leap down the slate tiles in pursuit of Hedy. 'Watch out!'

She flung herself downwards as fast as she could. Looking up, she saw the small heads of the grotesques, but they did not give chase. They obviously had been given one job by Grandpa John: to keep people from the top of the house.

'What happened? Hedy, are you OK? Those things were chasing you!'

Panting, Hedy dragged Spencer away from the side of the house, feeling like her heart was trying to beat its way out of her chest. They could see the grotesques returning to their spots along the top of the roof and freezing into position. No one would suspect them of being anything but stone carvings now.

'*Caw*.' The raven glided down to the fence and studied them with its intelligent eyes.

'Is that the raven from the first day?' Spencer whispered. 'The one that led us to Grandpa's house?'

'I think so,' Hedy murmured, 'and I think it's a friend. It helped me up on the roof.'

The raven scratched its back with its beak, then with a final '*caw*' it flew off back up to the roof.

They returned the ladder to the garage. Spencer had seen some of the chase lower down on the roof, and now he pestered Hedy with questions about what had happened higher up, until he noticed her hands trembling. He offered her a lolly from the stash in his pocket, saved from Portsall; the sweetness helped to ease the tightness in her stomach. But a lingering dread made Hedy want to put some distance between herself and the house. They scampered to the bottom of the garden, where at least they knew the statues would stay nice and motionless, unlike the grotesques. At last, sitting on the knee of one of the three stone figures on the stone bench, Hedy felt calm enough to fill Spencer in.

'If Grandma Rose said you were near, then does that mean we have to go back up there?' Spencer asked with an anxious squint at the roof of the house.

'I couldn't do the roof again,' Hedy said heavily. 'Nobody must have known they'd attack me. We need to find a way into the attic from the inside.'

CHAPTER 18

NEEDLE AND THREAD

Although a bitter wind was blowing, they stayed in the statue graveyard, working their way through Spencer's lollies and thinking of how to break into the attic, until an hour or so later they heard Grandpa John calling them. They met him halfway up the garden.

'Are you trying to catch frostbite out here?' he asked. 'Come inside. I've got something for you two to do that doesn't involve freezing your noses off.'

In the lounge room Grandpa John had set up a square table with wooden rims, small wooden drawers and green felt across the top. On the table was a large box filled with puzzle pieces.

'Is that a puzzle table?' Spencer asked.

'It's a mah-jong table. It's a family hand-me-down,' Grandpa John said, his gaze wandering over the green felt for a moment. 'Mah-jong's a Chinese game, but don't ask me to teach you, I couldn't remember the rules for the life of me. I thought it would be perfect for you to do this on, though. Two thousand pieces.' He lifted up the top cover box and showed them the image they had to put together: a Christmas scene with Santa in a laden sleigh, fir trees and tons of snow that would be difficult to tell apart.

'Two thousand is a lot of pieces,' Hedy muttered. 'Mum and Dad'll be back . . . tomorrow night!' She could hardly believe it: tomorrow would be Christmas Eve already. With everything that had been going on, she'd completely lost track of the days.

'Well, I'd say you'd better crack on, then.' He smiled. 'You don't want an unfinished puzzle nagging at your brain once you've gone home.'

Unable to argue, Hedy and Spencer sank into two chairs at the sides of the table and reluctantly began sorting pieces into piles. By the time Grandpa John left them to it, however, they were beginning to lose themselves in the activity.

They had pieced together two edges of the puzzle when Grandpa John surfaced and headed to the kitchen, where he began loudly rummaging through the cupboards. 'What's he doing with that funnel and the jug?' Spencer wondered as Grandpa John walked back towards his study.

A moment later, however, there was a loud smash as Grandpa John dropped what he had been carrying and very clearly swore, which they had never heard him do before.

Hedy leapt to her feet and, with Spencer close behind, dashed towards the noise. 'Grandpa John?'

But he hadn't fallen. He was standing in the doorway of his study, broken pieces of the stoneware jug in a puddle at his feet, and the funnel dangling from his hand. At the sound of Hedy and Spencer's footsteps, he turned with a troubled look on his face. 'Did you come in here while I was in the kitchen?' he snapped.

Both children shrank back and shook their heads. 'We were doing the puzzle,' Hedy said. 'Promise.'

Grandpa John sagged and ran a hand through his hair so that it stood in jagged tufts. 'Of course. I'm sorry,' he said, looking it. 'I didn't mean to speak to you like that.'

'What happened?' Spencer asked.

'Something broke while I was in the kitchen . . . I suppose I must have knocked it when I turned around.' But Hedy could tell Grandpa John himself didn't believe that that was what had happened. He backed out of the doorway and pulled the door closed, but not before the children had managed to glimpse inside the study and see a messy, half-built *something* on his desk. It looked like a double helix of undulating scaly tails, surrounded by metal rings and hinges, and half a Spam tin.

Grandpa John asked them to continue the puzzle while he took care of his study, so they half-heartedly flicked pieces of puzzle to and fro without saying what they were both thinking – that Nobody was still at large.

By bedtime, Spencer's wrestling figurine had been beheaded again, and this time the head was nowhere to be found. When he wound a scarf around his neck and insisted Hedy do the same to protect themselves from decapitation, she didn't have the heart to tell him a scarf would be nothing against whatever might cut a head off. Having been tricked into almost falling off a three-storey roof, though, she decided she'd take any defence she could get.

'I need to take a drive today,' Grandpa John said the next morning when they came downstairs.

'To Mrs Pal's?' Hedy asked hopefully. 'Can we come?'

'No, it's someone else. A bit further away than the Palisade and . . . well, I'll need you to stay in the car when we get there.'

Spencer frowned. 'Why?'

Grandpa John fell silent while he doled out some food to the hungry liar bird chicks, whose bright crests bobbed up and down with excitement. Eventually he sighed. 'I'd rather you didn't come into this place, that's all. Don't ask me why. It's simply not a place for children.'

Hedy's mind turned quickly to the bear's tail and piano keys under her pillow, which she hadn't been brave enough to take back during the night. With Grandpa John gone they could use the time to hand Simon his missing keys, somehow reattach Doug's tail and, with any luck, find a way into the attic. 'Is Mrs Vilums coming today?'

'She should be here any minute,' Grandpa John said. 'She said she was bringing some last-minute things for Christmas.'

'Can't we stay here with her?' At Grandpa John's hesitation, Hedy said gravely, 'Kids aren't allowed to be left alone in cars.'

'You can't even leave a dog in the car!' Spencer piped up.

'So if we go with you, you'll have to let us go inside too.' Although Hedy was trying to convince Grandpa John to let them stay, a little part of her yearned to see this top-secret place where children were not allowed.

Grandpa John said they could stay if Mrs Vilums agreed. It was an anxious wait until her arrival after nine o'clock. She greeted Grandpa John as normal, but was distinctly cool in tone to the children. 'They want to stay here with me?' Mrs Vilums asked with a raised eyebrow as she thumped some sweet potatoes down on the worktop. 'Not planning any mischief on my watch, I hope.'

'They know better than that, Mrs V,' Grandpa John said, with a stern glance at Hedy and Spencer. Less than ten minutes later he was driving away, having smuggled something from his study to the car that may have been the double helix artefact from his study.

It was horribly awkward the way Mrs Vilums ignored them today as they hovered around her. Hedy felt her planned plea for help shrivel up as the woman walked around them, silently and very precisely, to polish the dining table, making them feel like intruders.

'Excuse me, Mrs Vilums?' Hedy eventually said. She wanted to ask about the attic, but instead she asked, 'Do you know if Grandpa John has a needle and thread?'

'I believe there's some in the laundry.'

The children sidled out and, after poking about in the cupboards over the laundry baskets, found an old sewing kit with a large needle and some thread.

'Let's go and fix Doug,' Hedy whispered.

They slipped upstairs and retrieved the tail from Hedy's bed before sneaking into Doug and Stan's room.

'You got it back!' the bear exclaimed as Hedy held the tail aloft.

'You should've seen Hedy on the roof,' Spencer said. 'She was so cool dodging all those little monsters up there.'

Hedy was startled by Spencer's open admiration. She shrugged modestly and opened the sewing kit on Doug's back.

'Goodness,' Stan said, his antlers waggling side to side. 'You must regale us with the tale of this heroic recovery! And how are you going to reattach Doug to his tail?'

'Gah!' Doug had just spied the needle that Hedy pulled out. 'You're not going to use that great stinking lance on me, are you?'

On the wall, Stan dissolved into a fit of laughter. 'Now you'll know how I felt, Douglas. What colour thread will you choose? What about a royal purple?'

After suggesting Stan royally sew his lips shut, Doug chose sensible brown thread and gave Hedy the go-ahead to stitch his tail back on. He winced at every pass of the needle through his hide, which was so thick that Hedy's fingers grew sore from the effort of pushing it through. She was glad to let Spencer have a turn while she told Doug and Stan what had happened on the roof.

'We need to somehow get into the attic,' she was saying, when the door to the room swung open.

'What's all this?' Mrs Vilums stood there with her

hands on her hips.

Spencer hurriedly tried to hide the needle under Doug, but it was too late. Mrs Vilums's sharp eyes had spotted it, and there was no disguising the sewing kit on Doug's back. 'I hope you weren't saying you'd try to get into the attic while your grandfather is out.' She stepped into the room. 'What exactly do I need to tell him?'

Hedy's throat had gone dry. 'You don't need to tell him anything, Mrs V.'

'Isn't that what we do here?' the cook asked tightly. 'Blackmail?'

Hedy hung her head. It was a few long moments before she managed to croak, 'I'm sorry about the other day.' She met Mrs Vilums's eyes, which was even harder than talking. 'We won't tell Grandpa John about what you told us. Thank you for getting the Woodspies to give back the tooth.'

Mrs Vilums's expression softened. 'What of your grandmother?'

'Well.' Hedy hesitated. 'That's why we need to get into the attic. I think Grandma Rose is somewhere up there. Do you have a key to get in?' As Mrs Vilums's face darkened again, Hedy hastened to add, 'We promise we won't tell Grandpa John about your past. It's just . . . we need help. Time's running out.'

Mrs Vilums sighed. 'I don't have keys to the locked rooms in this house.'

'But you've been here for ages,' Spencer said. 'I thought he trusted you.'

'Your grandfather seems to have a rule of not trusting anyone.'

At that moment, Doug interrupted them with a shocked grunt. His tail had disappeared into a knot in the wooden floor. 'What's happening?' he cried.

'The Woodspies. They're pulling the needle down!' Spencer exclaimed.

Mrs Vilums strode to the knot in the floor and lowered herself to her knees. With a business-like rap on the wood, she said, 'You're taking too much. Give it back, please.'

Up bobbed three round Woodspies near Mrs Vilums's legs, and they knocked her affectionately. 'Yes, all right,' she muttered, patting each one in turn, 'now return it, please.'

The pull on Doug's tail slackened so that Hedy and Spencer could ease the tail, the thread and the needle out of the hole in the floor. 'Shall I finish this off?' Mrs

Vilums asked the children. They nodded. She expertly made a few more stitches and tied off the thread.

'Thank you, Mrs Vilums,' Doug murmured, giving his tail a cautious wag.

Mrs Vilums cautiously patted his brown fur, then rose to her feet. 'If you two can promise not to try breaking into any other rooms, I'm going to get on with the stew.'

'We have one more thing to do up here,' Hedy said, thinking of the piano keys, 'then we can come down and help you, if you like?'

'I'd like that,' the woman smiled.

'She's not like other grown-ups,' Spencer whispered, staring at her retreating back.

'No,' Hedy agreed, 'but at least she's on our side this morning.' She began to pack up the sewing kit, which was jogging up and down as the Woodspies played under Doug.

Spencer took the needle from her and plucked a spool of thread from the small case, placing it and the needle on top of the dark knot in the wooden floor. 'Can you guys get us into the attic?' he asked.

The Woodspies sucked the needle and spool of thread below the floorboards, and then disappeared themselves.

It took Spencer a while to realize the Woodspies had taken the gifts and run. 'Well, thanks for nothing!' He glowered at the unmoving floor.

'It was worth a try,' Hedy said. 'Let's take the piano keys back to Simon.'

When they knocked on the yellow door, Simon stuck his head through and was overjoyed to see his five missing piano keys in Hedy's hand. '*Mes chouchous!*' he clucked. 'My darlings!'

'I don't know how we're going to get them inside,' Hedy said, for the door remained locked. As they bent on their hands and knees, trying fruitlessly to slide the keys beneath the door, *pop, pop, pop!* – the Woodspies reappeared. The two bigger ones grabbed a piano key before Hedy and Spencer could stop them, but this time they didn't disappear with their prize. As though they understood what Hedy had said, they dragged the piano key low enough to slip it inside the room. Moments later, Simon poked his head through the door to report that they had placed the key back on his piano.

'It is broken, but at least it is back home!' he beamed.

The smallest Woodspy, however, had been struggling

to capture Hedy and Spencer's attention. As the last piano key was returned by the others, it took a run at Spencer's knees and bumped him hard.

'Ow! Hey!' Spencer exclaimed.

The Woodspy knocked Hedy next. She gave it a reprimanding tap with her finger, but now that it was being noticed, the Woodspy whizzed down the hall, and then stopped, waiting.

'What's he trying to tell us?' Hedy wondered.

The Woodspy flowed on, to the door of the attic and up the doorframe. Then they heard the latch pop.

CHAPTER 19

THE ATTIC ROOM

'See? The needle and thread convinced them to help us!' Spencer said smugly. He kept half a step behind Hedy as they tiptoed to the attic door, which was exactly the same colour as the walls, as though doing its best to blend in. 'You open it.'

'Thanks a lot,' Hedy muttered.

The door didn't creak, thank goodness; Hedy didn't think she would be able to smother the butterflies in her stomach if it had. Beyond it was another staircase leading up, with feeble light stretching down from the top.

'I can stand guard here, if you want?' Spencer breathed.

'You hate standing guard,' Hedy reminded him.

They climbed the stairs, holding their breath, and twenty steps later found themselves in the attic. The floor was cluttered with rows and islands of stuff. It was like a maze. Large wooden tea chests were inked with place names such as Siam, Delhi, Nepal, and the mannequins in magician stage costume gave the children an uneasy feeling that they were being watched. Hedy could just make out Grandma Rose's writing on the window, still visible in the dust.

Spencer clutched her elbow and pointed at the suit of armour standing in the dark corner. 'I wish I could try that on!' he breathed.

'You're way too short.' Hedy bent down to the Woodspies butting against their heels and tapped the littlest one. 'Where to?'

The Woodspy streaked away between the clutter to the furthest wall. There, it impatiently rolled back and forth around a rack of suits, and the children moved it to one side. They found another door of plain dark wood, and at its centre was a single golden hand.

'It's like at Mrs Pal's!' Spencer said. 'Like Samuel!'

He took a step forwards and said, '*Souvenir voo lemon.*
Remember the hand.'

Although the golden hand looked just like the ones
at the Palisade, this one didn't give even the tiniest
twitch, let alone play any tricks. The door itself
appeared immovable.

'I wonder whose hand this is,' Spencer said to Hedy.
'Which dead magician, I mean.'

'Or is it Grandpa John's hand?' Hedy bent closer to
study it. The size of the hand and the shape of the
fingers seemed like his.

Spencer reached out to grasp the metal hand before
Hedy could tell him not to, in case it set off alarms or
something. But nothing happened. The golden hand
didn't turn, move, wave or beckon them. It stayed
outstretched and as lifeless as could be.

'Can you open this door?' Hedy asked the Woodspies. They quavered in the wood, which she guessed was
Woodspy for *No.* 'Give it a try,' Hedy said encouragingly.

She heard a light clinking noise, and whipped her
gaze around. All was still. *Paranoid*, she thought to
herself.

The middle-sized Woodspy flowed towards the
door but, unlike the other doors of the house, it

couldn't get through. It tried again and picked up speed, but it was like a bowling ball being rolled against a concrete wall – the Woodspy made a *clonk* sound and was repelled backwards. The others tried, even the small one, but each time they hit the wood of the door or frame they were driven back and away.

Hedy tried the golden hand too, hoping she might find the trick of opening the door, but she didn't have any better luck.

'What's in there?' Hedy asked the Woodspies. The three of them gathered and then seemed to have an idea. They flowed together to the wood beneath the door and disappeared. Seconds later, a narrow gap, a little less than a hand span in width, appeared beneath the door where the Woodspies sucked the floorboards down. The gap quivered, as though keeping the wood pulled down was a strain for the invisible creatures.

'You little geniuses,' Hedy said as she and Spencer scooted forwards on their knees and put their heads down to look through the opening.

They gasped.

On the other side of the door was another, altogether breathtaking room. If a beautiful moonlit wood could be a performance stage and somehow trapped in an attic, this was it. Velvet curtains of rich red hung down, framing what lay beyond: dark tree trunks and woodland undergrowth that looked very real reached up to air that seemed open to the sky, not a closed-in attic at all. Floorboards receded into dirt and grass. Five torches – long sticks with flames burning from their tops like giant matches – stood like sentries surrounding the object at the centre of the room. The moon shone its pale light on it all, but most brightly upon a long, glimmering box in the middle.

'The Kaleidos!' Spencer whispered.

So Grandpa John hadn't got rid of his Kaleidos after all. It was as long as a coffin but much deeper, made entirely of shiny cubes whose surfaces were multi-faceted, like brilliantly cut diamonds. They played the soft moonbeams and reddish flames that lit the magic box in unexpected ways, creating peaks and troughs of reflected light and shadow in constant movement.

'Can you make the hole bigger?' Hedy asked the Woodspies urgently. 'So we can get in?'

The Woodspies zig-zagged to swap positions, but they couldn't widen the gap much more than they had already. When they hauled downwards, disappearing from view, the very floor seemed to fend them off. They came popping back upwards, unable to maintain the gap, and it closed up to a fine sliver again, impossible to see through.

'Damn,' Hedy muttered. It was maddening to be so close to the Kaleidos, and surely to Grandma Rose, but unable to reach her.

That, however, was the least of their problems.

Behind them was the sound of metal on metal, a sliding *shhhhhk* that sounded like a sword being drawn and the creaky *clank* of a metal foot taking a step forwards. The children peered behind them, hoping they were mistaken about what was making the noise. They were not.

The suit of armour that had looked so still in the corner was slowly but surely on the move. Its position was perfect for cutting off escape.

'Stop,' Hedy tried, her voice shaking. 'We're the Master's grandchildren.'

The suit of armour kept clanking towards them. Across the breastplate, a design of snakes was beginning to writhe and blaze as though lit from within.

'What do we do? Where do we go?' Hedy asked the Woodspies in a whisper. But the creatures trembled on the spot, not guiding the children any more. At a particularly loud step, the Woodspies gave a wobble and then disappeared under the floorboards completely.

'Little cowards!' Hedy fumed. As they scrambled to their feet, she calculated the distance to the stairs and the speed with which the suit of armour was moving. The attic suddenly seemed like a labyrinth of boxes and suitcases, but they might just make it. She grabbed Spencer's hand to begin making their way towards the stairs, but before they had gone three steps the suit of armour picked up pace too, and pointed the sword at them.

'This way,' Hedy urged her brother, changing course and pushing him behind a stack of helmets. The clutter not only hampered their getaway, it blocked the suit of armour from taking a direct run at them. In a flash of inspiration, Spencer pushed at a tower of suitcases and they came tumbling down, light but bulky. The suit of armour paused until the suitcases settled, and then started walking again, kicking things out of its way. Hedy followed her brother's lead and began shoving things in the path of their pursuer – mannequins, lampshades, boxes. The armour didn't move all that quickly, but it had an implacable air that was terrifying. If they could lead him further into the attic, they might be able to loop out beyond him and get to the stairs.

That sword looked wickedly sharp and it gave the suit of armour alarming reach. Down it swung. As it *whooshed* past they stumbled to the right. A rolling lampshade tripped Spencer, and Hedy fell to the ground over his sprawled-out legs. She tried to push herself away and let Spencer get to his feet. Over her shoulder, she could see the suit of armour gathering for another swing at them. The snakes on its armour were thrashing frantically. She grabbed an old khaki helmet spinning on the floor, then rolled over with a yell to face the sword heading down towards her.

Hedy punched the helmet upwards. The blade glanced off its rounded top, jarring her arms with its force.

A call came from below. 'Hedy? Spencer?' Mrs Vilums ran up the stairs into the attic.

'Be careful!' Hedy shouted. 'The armour!'

Mrs Vilums hesitated only a moment before striding towards the armour, momentarily surprising it into a few steps of retreat, opening up a very narrow gap of escape. She waved a desperate hand at the children, signalling for them to make a quick getaway behind her.

But the armour caught on to the plan. Raising its sword, it sidestepped to prevent Hedy and Spencer from fleeing.

'No!' cried Mrs Vilums.

Before the children realized what was happening, Mrs Vilums leapt between them and the suit of armour. The sword began its descent. Mrs Vilums drove her hand up and caught the blade coming down. She was silent as its edge sheared into her hand, but there was agony in her eyes as the sword stopped, slicing not into flesh but into rock. There was no blood – Mrs Vilums's hand had turned to black stone.

The suit of armour wrenched its weapon back and Mrs Vilums's stone hand broke away and fell to the ground. Hedy could feel Spencer seizing her arm in disbelief. She clapped a hand over her mouth. But before the armour could attack again, the floor beneath it rolled and dipped, sending it sprawling with a crash. The Woodspies had reappeared.

'They're back!' Spencer shouted.

'For Mrs Vilums,' Hedy guessed.

The Woodspies went berserk in the wooden floor-boards, making it roil like boiling water. The armour could not get to its feet; it could not even get to its knees. The littlest Woodspy flowed beneath the stone hand stranded on the floor, pushed it to a knot in the wood and sucked it down out of sight before rejoining the other two Woodspies, which were still causing havoc.

'Take me to my sisters,' Mrs Vilums gasped.

'What? Where?' Hedy asked. 'We should call an ambulance!'

'No!' Mrs Vilums shook her head violently. 'Garden.'

Hedy and Spencer held her by the elbows and they hurried as fast as they could away from the attic, where the armour was now clashing and smashing upon the floor. Mrs Vilums's arm was turning from flesh to stone with each step.

'What's happening to you?' Hedy asked fearfully.

Spencer stared at the stone elbow in his hand. 'Did the sword do this to you?'

Mrs Vilums shook her head. 'The stone bench at the bottom of the garden,' she panted, grasping for her cloak as they stumbled outside.

The garden had never seemed so long as it did during that dreadful flight. Stone spread through Mrs

Vilums's arms to her torso and began to slow her strides. Hedy and Spencer had to drag her the final few metres to the stone bench, where Mrs Vilums drew the hood of her cloak over her head and stiffly sank down between the two hooded black stone figures at either end of the bench. She nodded her head left and then right. 'My sisters. Maja. And Ewa.'

So when Mrs Vilums had said she wanted to be close to her sisters, she had meant this bench all along; this bench which, Hedy realized, sometimes had two figures and sometimes had three.

'Are you all right now?' Hedy asked with tears in her eyes. 'Is this where you belong? What's happening?'

Mrs Vilums could not move her head any more. 'We were born of stone. I alone was allowed to transform. But I fear I will not wake from this.'

'What can we do for you?' Spencer cried.

Dark, hard streaks now spread over Mrs Vilums's face. 'All unravelling.' Her eyes, wild now, flickered over the children. 'Danger here. Get awa—'

The final traces of Mrs Vilums's pale skin vanished. Her entire form sat locked in black stone, indistinguishable from her sisters except for her missing hand.

CHAPTER 20

EXPLOSION

Hedy and Spencer knelt on the cold ground at Mrs Vilums's feet. Sniffing back tears, they tapped her on the arm, hoping that she would somehow let them know that she was all right. But maybe she wasn't.

Danger here. Get away.

Hedy got to her feet and pulled Spencer up as well, wiping her wet cheeks. 'Come on.'

Spencer stared at the house fearfully as he followed Hedy up the garden. 'Are we . . . are we trying to get into the secret Kaleidos room?'

'The Woodspies couldn't get us in there. Nobody's destroying things. I almost fell off the roof. Stan was hurt; Doug was hurt; and now Mrs Vilums . . . she's hurt too and it's our fault.' Hedy shook her head. 'I can't let you get hurt too.'

'Grandpa John's going to be mad when he finds out we set off that armour.'

'Then he shouldn't have made Grandma Rose disappear. Mrs V's right. We have to get away.'

'I want to call Mum and Dad,' Spencer said.

Hedy put her arm around his shoulder. 'Me too. But they'd be on a plane by now. It's Christmas Eve, remember?'

'What time will they be here?'

'Tonight, I guess. But we have to get away now.'

They paused at the back door, and then crept towards the phone in the hallway. The faint clamour of the suit of armour bashing upon the floor could still be heard.

Hedy quickly found the number she needed, taped to the wall by the phone, and she dialled it. 'Uncle Peter, it's Hedy. Can we come and stay at your house? Now?'

*

'Muddy bells, what happened?' said Jelly, jumping out of Uncle Peter's car an hour later. She was dressed like a rainbow, starting with a red bandana and ending with purple trainers.

'What are you doing here?' Hedy asked, surprised.

'Grandad told us you called for an emergency pickup and I was desperate to get out of going to Max's Christmas concert. That's where he is now, with Mum and Dad. But what happened here?'

Hedy couldn't find the words with Uncle Peter striding through the gate.

'Is everything all right?' he asked. 'Where's John?'

'Let's go now,' Spencer said, untangling himself from Jelly's hug and taking a few steps towards the gate.

'Wait a moment,' Uncle Peter said. 'I can't whisk you away without a word to your grandfather. Now, what happened? Did you have a row?'

Hedy fidgeted with the end of her stripy scarf. 'He's not here.'

'Well, does he know you called me?' Uncle Peter frowned. 'Who did he leave you here with? Mrs Vilums?'

Hedy bit her lip. She had naively hoped that Uncle

Peter would indeed whisk them away, without looking to speak to a grown-up. Instead, he walked through the front door and peered around as though he might find Grandpa John in the house after all. He tilted his head, listening. 'What's that noise?'

'What . . . what noise?' Hedy asked.

'There's a racket upstairs.' Uncle Peter began walking towards the stairs.

'No, Uncle Peter, don't!' Hedy raced in behind him and tried to block his path. 'Don't go up there.'

Uncle Peter stared at her. 'Hedy, I'm even more worried now. What is it?'

Hedy gulped. There was no plausible story to spin, and so the truth came tumbling out. 'It's a suit of armour,' she said at a near-whisper. 'It turned Mrs Vilums to stone. But we didn't mean for her to get hurt. We were looking for Grandma Rose. And we found Grandpa's magic box in a secret hidden room in the attic, but we can't get in. And there's a cube missing from it. And now I think Mrs V is stone for good, but she told us to get away.'

Uncle Peter squinted, trying to keep up. 'The Kaleidos is in the attic?'

Hedy nodded glumly. 'But we can't get in.'

A fleeting look of hope touched Uncle Peter's face. He took off up the steps, two at a time, ignoring Hedy's protests. Spencer and Jelly scurried in, and the three children raced up behind him. Uncle Peter was already halfway down the second-floor hallway when they reached the top of the stairs. The noise of the armour was louder now, and Uncle Peter had slowed. But as he passed the room holding Nobody's chandelier, there was an explosive crash. The blue door cracked and pieces of wood fell away, leaving a gaping window into the room itself. Dust billowed out.

A shard of glass had shot into Uncle Peter's arm, and blood bloomed through his shirt sleeve. He waved for the children to stay back, but they ignored him and rushed to his side.

'Grandad!' Jelly said shrilly. 'Are you all right? What should we do?'

Uncle Peter touched the glass shard and grimaced. 'We'll need to find a bandage before I take this out.'

Through the hole in the door, Hedy could just make out the broken dark-green glass and heavy chain of Nobody's shattered chandelier. The glass abruptly sputtered with blue light – then, moments later, those threads of light twisted off the glass and marshalled in the air. They thrashed over each other in an angry cloud before winking out, leaving a rapidly fading afterglow.

That was the moment, of course, that Grandpa John appeared at the head of the stairs, his arrival below masked by the clamour of the explosion. 'What the devil have you done?'

'You're back already,' Hedy said weakly.

'Too late, it seems.' Grandpa John examined them frostily as he stalked towards them. His jaw muscles were set and his lips were a thin, furious line. 'I knew something had happened,' he went on. 'If only I'd got here sooner and somehow stopped the *wreckage* of my home.'

'Can you have your tantrum downstairs?' Uncle Peter asked, wincing at his bloodied arm. 'I don't want to have to fight whatever it is you have up there.'

Grandpa John tersely waved them towards the main staircase. 'It won't come down from the attic.'

'How do you know?' Hedy asked.

'It belongs to me, doesn't it?'

'But what if your things aren't listening to you any more?'

Grandpa John glowered at Hedy. 'Everyone to the kitchen.'

Spencer got there before anyone else, and sat by the liar birds' box, cradling a chick for comfort. Jelly helped Uncle Peter to a seat, but Hedy couldn't decide whether to stand or sit, and ended up shrinking into the doorway. It was when Grandpa John entered – bandage, bottle and cotton swabs in hand – that he noticed someone missing. 'Where's Mrs Vilums?'

Hedy and Spencer stared at each other. Whatever they said would lead to question after question, and Hedy didn't have it in her to think of a believable explanation. Finally she said, 'In the garden.'

'Why is she out there when half the house is blowing up?'

'She turned to stone.'

Grandpa John froze. 'Not the Medusa Glass?'

'What's that?' Hedy asked, confused.

Grandpa John's eyes darted downwards; he had mentioned something they weren't supposed to know about. 'How did she turn to stone?'

'She's a statue that turns into a woman,' Hedy said, staring at a button on Grandpa John's chest so she wouldn't have to look him in the eye. 'Upstairs when the armour attacked us, she blocked it to save us. And she started turning to stone when the sword struck her. She wanted us to take her to the stone bench in the statue graveyard. That's where she was when she wasn't here as a person.'

Grandpa John rubbed his forehead, struggling to comprehend everything Hedy had just said, then tried a different tack. 'Why are *you* here?' he demanded of Uncle Peter.

'We were scared,' Hedy jumped in. 'We were scared because the armour attacked us and Mrs V said to get away.'

'Of course it attacked, I created it to do so,' Grandpa John said, vexed. 'That's what Sir Roland does, he guards . . . up there.'

Sir Roland? the children mouthed at each other.

Uncle Peter kept his eyes on the floor. 'Guarding your Kaleidos?'

Grandpa inhaled sharply. 'Guarding any number of things that need to be kept safe,' he said softly, 'or kept safely away from people. Hedy, why were you up there? Why does no one in this damned house ever have the courtesy to do as I ask?'

Uncle Peter, his skin looking grey, lifted his wounded arm. 'Can we attend to this before I bleed all over your kitchen floor? Then you can reprimand them all you like.'

Silently, Grandpa John daubed the wound with iodine antiseptic and bandaged it. Uncle Peter refused to go to the doctor. 'I just need to lie down.'

They walked him to the lounge room where he could lie on the couch. Blanketed with his coat, Uncle Peter closed his eyes and thanked them wearily, saying he'd call if he needed them. Before they left the room, a blue filament fleetingly crackled over the tiny bulbs of the Christmas tree lights. Neither Grandpa John nor Jelly saw it, but Spencer jerked and, like Hedy, peered about the room for any sign of Albert Nobody. There was none.

'Maybe it's just wonky lights,' Hedy said hopefully to Spencer. He didn't look convinced, and scuttled from the room ahead of Hedy. She left the door ajar and then, with a remorseful look at poor Uncle Peter, tiptoed after the others.

CHAPTER 21

PLAYING TRICKS

The children awkwardly took seats around the kitchen table while Grandpa John put on the kettle. The air of anger radiating from him could have boiled the water on its own. As his teacup clattered on its saucer Hedy noticed his hands trembling a little. She steeled herself for another explosion, worse than the one in Nobody's room.

'Looks like you've outdone yourselves,' he said at last. 'Why you thought *Don't touch anything* meant sneaking up to the attic and setting off sentries, or detonating God-knows-what to destroy my house, is completely beyond me.' He scowled around the table. 'I should never have agreed to you coming here. So out with it. What's been going on?'

Hedy thought and thought, torn about what to say. An hour ago, she would have said anything to get out of the house. But what if they were never allowed back, never to find Grandma Rose? Who else would save her? There seemed to be only one way to force Grandpa John's hand: the truth.

'You were the one who made Grandma Rose disappear,' she said softly.

Grandpa John's gaze fell upon her, troubled. 'I know that. I know that more profoundly than anyone.'

'But you took a piece of the box out and that's when it stopped working.' Hedy swallowed, her heart hammering. The wrinkles on her grandfather's brow deepened. There was nothing to do now except plough on. 'We were shown what happened.'

'Shown by whom?'

Hedy shot a look at Spencer, who nodded in encouragement. 'By Albert Nobody.'

'Long dead,' Grandpa John said dismissively, but then he suddenly twisted his head, thinking. Comprehension dawned. 'Nobody's –' he said a word that was guttural and incomprehensible, something like *tru-juk-lin-kot*, 'was in the ruined room upstairs. You've been in there. You caused that!'

Spencer finally found his voice. 'We *didn't* cause that!'

'But had you been in there?' Hedy and Spencer's silence was all the answer Grandpa John needed. 'Why? After everything I told you.'

'Grandma Rose told us to find her,' Hedy blurted out. 'She wrote messages to us – she wrote FIND ME in dust, and she wrote it in those fridge magnets too!'

Grandpa John turned in his chair to look at the fridge magnets, which had long been scrambled into gibberish.

'You saw it in the fridge magnets yourself,' she pressed. 'It said FIND ME. And then you scrambled the letters.'

'That was Rose?' he asked, with a catch in his voice.

'Yes.'

'Why would she ask you? Why you and not me?'

'Mrs Pal said it's because you closed yourself off to magic, but—' Hedy said.

'Mrs Pal? You told *her* all this?'

'No, we didn't, she guessed! But if *you* did it,

Grandma Rose wouldn't *want* to ask you for help, would she?'

There was a scraping sound – the fridge magnets were moving again. Four letters only, spelling JOHN.

'It's Grandma Rose!' Spencer cried. 'See? We weren't lying!'

'Look!' Jelly yelped, pointing a finger at a kitchen window. In the frost clouding the corner of the window pane, an invisible finger was writing JOHN. And then on the table in front of them, a small puff of sugar was sprinkled, and through the grains was written, *Help me, John.*

Grandpa John had frozen, stunned. Nothing moved except a tear that fell over his lower lash. Finally he whispered, 'Rosie?'

Me, Rose wrote in the sugar.

A cry escaped from Grandpa John; he tried to muffle it with a hand over his mouth.

Hedy, Spencer and Jelly shared a puzzled look. Grandma Rose had just asked Grandpa John for help. Did that mean he wasn't guilty?

'Seems hard to believe, John.' To their surprise, standing in the doorway with a sceptical look was Uncle Peter. Even the liar birds seemed surprised; they flapped with a great shuffle in their box. Although he was leaning against the doorframe, looking pale, Uncle Peter seemed surprisingly well considering how drained he had been a short time ago.

'What do you mean?' Grandpa John said hoarsely.

'What are the chances of it being her?' said Uncle Peter. Jelly jumped from her seat to give him a hug. He seemed uncomfortable with the embrace, perhaps because of his cut, and briefly put his good arm around her before pointing her back to her seat. 'Like you said, why would she have contacted *them* and not you?' There was something cold about the way he said *them*, and the dismissive wave of his hand in their direction. He was angry with them for causing his injury, Hedy thought guiltily.

Grandpa John walked to the fridge magnets to touch them lightly, a look of wonder on his face. He crossed to the window where his name had been written in the frost and touched the glass with his hand, leaving his own imprint of steam on the inside. 'But it feels like Rose. I can feel her here now.' He desperately wanted it to be true; they could all hear it in his voice.

'You're imagining it,' Uncle Peter said sadly.

'Perhaps you want her back so much that your mind's playing tricks on you.'

'We didn't imagine these messages being written,' Hedy said indignantly. 'We all saw Grandma Rose do it. We didn't imagine those other messages either. It's her!'

Uncle Peter shook his head and pushed himself off the doorframe to stand behind his brother. 'I didn't say you imagined the writing altogether. But what's more likely? Rose suddenly reaching out after being trapped all these years? Or something from one of your locked rooms, something in your collection?'

Grandpa John's head jerked around, glaring.

Uncle Peter scoffed. 'Don't look at me like that, old man. You hoard peculiar things – something in your collection is playing tricks on you.' He pointed his finger at the children. 'Something is tricking the children into turning your house upside down and getting into all the things they're not supposed to. It even tricked them into distrusting *you*. And look what happened upstairs. More of your family could've been lost, because of you.'

A rock formed in Hedy's stomach, plummeting down, down, down. Had the past two weeks been a lie? Had they been played like fools by some nasty spirit, tricked into breaking Grandpa John's rules, into suspecting their own grandfather?

Grandpa John's shoulders fell, and he took a long shuddering breath. Hedy's eyes smarted with tears. Worse than doubting their grandfather, they'd given him hope, only now it was leaking out of him, leaving a smaller, more fragile shell than before.

Uncle Peter placed a hand on Grandpa John's shoulder. Hedy noticed that one of his fingernails had been bruised in the explosion; it was starting to go purple. 'John, I think all this junk of yours is going to be the death of you one day.'

'I keep these things from hurting people,' Grandpa John insisted. 'It's my duty. After what happened to Rose, I shouldered that burden.'

'Maybe, to truly stop these things from hurting people, you need to extinguish them altogether.'

Grandpa John stared at his brother, appalled. 'What?'

'Get rid of this stuff that has a mind of its own,' Uncle Peter said softly. 'Free yourself of the burden. Make the world a less dangerous place by purging it all. Just burn it. Burn these things you own, because right now they're owning you. They're tying you to memories you need release from. You'll be free. Goodness, it could be just like our younger days. Get a couple of motorbikes and ride the land, biting at the wind in our teeth.'

Hedy gave a start. Where had she heard that before?

'I still have the bikes in the garage.' Grandpa John sounded lost.

Uncle Peter nodded. 'Of course you do. You keep everything. Let's build a bonfire and torch the rest of it, the whole dangerous lot.'

CHAPTER 22

BONFIRE NIGHT

The brothers worked non-stop for an hour, carrying armloads of items from the house and dropping them in a pile on a clear patch of dirt in the back garden, while the children sat under the dining-room table and told Jelly everything that had happened since Hedy and Spencer last saw her. Eventually they gathered by the back window, watching the pile of objects grow taller and wider. Small cardboard cartons were stacked like an igloo, hiding unseen artefacts. Ornaments swept from shelves were pitched over the pile. As Uncle Peter walked out with the framed maps that had hung on the walls of Hedy and Spencer's bedroom, he smiled. 'Aren't you misbegotten creatures going to help?'

None of them spoke. Uncle Peter's teasing wasn't as good-natured today.

'We're not supposed to play with fire,' Spencer said finally.

'You weren't supposed to go poking about in all those rooms either.' He scratched his beard as though it irritated him. Something had dirtied his hair, darkening a patch that hung over his brow. 'Come on. Lost your sense of adventure all of a sudden?'

'Do we have to?' Jelly groaned.

Her grandfather suddenly turned on his heel with a chilly look. 'Stop your whining and help.' His tone was quiet and sharp, the usual warm boom of his voice completely absent.

After a breath, Jelly muttered, 'We'll be there in a second.'

As Uncle Peter left the kitchen with a jaunty stride, Hedy saw Jelly rub at tears with a quick dash of her fist. 'Are you OK?' she asked her cousin.

Jelly shrugged, looking stung. 'He's never looked at me like that before. That *mean* look. Never. Mostly it's your grandad who's the grumpy one.'

'Well, he was probably hit on the head by the explosion.'

'I guess so,' Jelly said. 'But does a hit on the head turn you into a troll? You'd think his arm would be bothering him more than anything else.'

Spencer suddenly straightened from the liar bird box. 'Grandpa John's not going to burn the chicks, is he?'

'He couldn't!' Hedy exclaimed.

'But they're kind of magical, so he might.' Spencer wrung his hands. 'We've got to hide them.' He picked up the box of birds, and the creatures inside fluttered and thumped against the cardboard sides. 'One bird's fallen asleep in my pocket. Where can we hide the others?'

Hedy racked her brains. 'They're going through the whole house. What about the garage?'

'What if Grandpa John starts burning things from the garage?' Spencer fretted.

'He wouldn't keep anything magical out there. It'd be too easy for thieves to break into it.'

Spencer grabbed his aviator cap. 'Let's go now before they come downstairs.'

They hurried outside towards the garage. 'Everything's going to be fine,' Spencer crooned to the two chicks in the box.

Liar! Liar! Liar! chimed the birds, betraying Spencer's real thoughts. He clamped his mouth shut.

'Where do we put them?' Jelly asked as she closed the garage door behind them. 'Come on, Spencer, you're the birdmaster.'

He peered around, then pointed to a dark space below a shelf of trowels and coils of rope and chain. 'We could fit it in there, and put the paint bucket in front of it.' He whipped off his aviator cap and tucked the two chicks inside it so they had a warm nest, then slid the box into its hiding place.

'I hope they don't poo in your hat,' Hedy said, trying to joke.

'Good thing it's Dad's,' Spencer said, with only a flicker of his usual cheeky grin. It was hard to laugh with everything that was going on. He peeked into his pocket. 'This little one is *still* sleeping,' he added, satisfied.

Hedy poked her head out through the doors at a particularly loud clatter outside, straining to see what was happening. 'Grandpa John's brought out those big paintings from the hallway. The people with animal heads.'

'But what's wrong with those?' Spencer objected. 'They're cool!'

Jelly scrunched up her nose. 'Actually, they're sort of creepy.'

'Even if they are creepy, it's still nuts,' Hedy said. 'We have to try to stop this.' She ran across the garden, the others at her heels. 'Grandpa John?'

He was stacking the paintings of the skunk and magpie at the edge of the heap. There were tantalizing things on the stack that Hedy had never seen: a skirt made of brilliant peacock feathers, a wide black leather case with a brass clasp, a small wooden foot.

'Grandpa John, don't set all your stuff on fire,' Hedy pleaded. 'I promise we won't touch anything else. We're really sorry about upstairs. We've learnt our lesson, honest.'

Grandpa John looked at her sorrowfully. 'We're beyond that now, Hedy. It's not your apology I'm after. That room upstairs could have exploded while you were in it. Sir Roland could have skewered you with his sword.' He shook his head slowly. 'I won't be responsible for your mother losing either of you, not after she lost her own mother.'

Hedy couldn't think of anything to say. Grandpa John regarded the pyre sadly, then squared his shoulders and turned back to the house to find more belongings to burn, not caring that the children didn't follow him.

'We need a grown-up to talk him out of this,' Hedy said. 'Someone he'd listen to.'

'What about Mrs Pal?' Spencer asked. 'She sold some of this stuff to Grandpa John, didn't she?'

'Good idea, Spence,' Hedy said. 'Her number's on that card. Come on.'

After Hedy had retrieved Mrs Pal's card from her backpack, the children huddled by the phone in the hallway. 'OK, I'll call Mrs Pal and tell her what's happening,' Hedy said. 'When I say go, you get Grandpa John to come down to the phone.'

Dialling on Grandpa John's old rotary phone seemed to take centuries. The three of them clustered around the receiver and waited for the line to ring. After five *brrrrrng-brrrrrngs* the call was picked up.

'This is the Palisade,' said Mrs Pal at the other end.

'Mrs Pal! It's Hedy van—'

'We cannot take your call just now . . .' Mrs Pal's recorded voicemail message went on.

The children all groaned.

'. . . however, please leave a message after the *beeeeep* . . .' Mrs Pal actually imitated the beep noise.

'Leave a message,' Jelly nudged Hedy.

'. . . and we will return your call.' *Beeeeep*.

'Um, um. Mrs Pal, it's Hedy and Spencer,' Hedy stumbled. 'Grandpa John is building a bonfire out of all his magical things, because he's afraid the stuff is dangerous. Please, please, we need you to talk him out of—'

Click.

A finger had come down on the receiver cradle, ending the call. Unnoticed, Uncle Peter had walked up behind them. 'Mrs Pal is just enabling John's obsession,' he said, 'and the worst thing to do is allow that little hawker to buy back these things and resell them. She profits by sending more menace out into the world.'

Behind them the phone rang. It had to be Mrs Pal calling back. But before they could answer, Uncle Peter reached out and lifted the receiver, then immediately dropped it back down, hanging up. 'Let John do what he needs to do.' The phone shrilly rang again, but Uncle Peter hung up on the caller once more. 'You can go and help your grandfather with the bear rug.'

All three of them looked at each other in dread, forgetting the phone. They raced up, taking the stairs two at a time to find Grandpa John had rolled up Doug neatly and was hoisting him off the ground. Doug's eyes were wide with terror.

'No, Grandpa John, please, not that one!' Hedy cried.

Grandpa John grunted as he tossed Doug over his shoulder. 'I can't risk these things hurting people any more.'

'But he wouldn't hurt anyone,' Hedy insisted.

'How do you know?' Grandpa John asked.

Jelly jumped in front of her cousins. 'Uncle John, Uncle John! Let us take this one down for you. We can handle it together. Come on, you two,' she turned and winked very slightly, 'we can get this outside to the fire pile.'

'Yes! We'll take the bear!' Spencer insisted.

Grandpa John released Doug to the three children, and they scooted down the stairs before he could change his mind. They dodged Uncle Peter in the kitchen and hurried Doug to the garage, telling him what was happening in low, urgent whispers. As they hid him under Grandpa John's car, Doug said anxiously, 'Stan. We can't leave Stan behind.'

'We won't,' Spencer promised, already turning to run back to the house with the girls on his heels. But at the base of the staircase, they found Uncle Peter had already carried Stan down, holding the deer head by the great antlers. It was startling that Uncle Peter's wound wasn't giving him any trouble; in fact, a trick of the light was making him stand taller and thinner than before.

'We can help with this one!' Spencer yelled, reaching for the deer.

The girls took hold of Stan's antlers and neck, pleading for Uncle Peter to let go. 'It's too big for you,' he barked.

They tugged this way and that, and then suddenly Stan bashed into the wall, two tips of his antler piercing the plaster.

'Ow!' Stan yelled.

The children froze and Uncle Peter chuckled at their expressions. 'Oh, I already knew he could talk.'

'How?' Hedy demanded, but Uncle Peter didn't answer, instead hoisting Stan out of reach of the children.

'Unhand me!' Stan said in his most imperious tone, but his voice quavered.

'No pets allowed at Hoarder Hill,' Uncle Peter said, shaking his head. He pushed past to take the deer head outside.

'Let me go!' Stan bellowed, to no avail.

The children ran after them. Uncle Peter held Stan aloft, as though he weighed nothing, and tossed the deer on to the pyramid of Grandpa John's belongings. Stan's antlers twisted in the frame of a wooden loom and an open crate, stopping him from tumbling down to be retrieved by the children.

'Don't let me catch you trying to extract him,' Uncle Peter told them, pointing a long finger, 'or I might set fire to this lot while you're up there.'

Hedy stared at the finger. His bruised fingernail had gone completely dark, a colour between red, purple and black. It looked like Nobody's fingernail that had fallen out of the chandelier. The skin on her neck crawled with a dreadful thought. Furtively studying her great-uncle, Hedy realized that his hair had not darkened in places from the dust. Some hairs were actually turning brown. His brow was higher and more square, and his eyes seemed odd – were they too light?

Hedy leant very close to Jelly's ear and whispered

very softly. 'Does he seem different to you?'

Jelly bit her lip. 'He looks weird, and he's all mean.'

'I think he's turning into someone else.' As Hedy voiced the theory, it suddenly felt absolutely right.

'What?' Jelly squeaked. 'You mean he's *possessed*?'

'What are you guys whispering about?' Spencer whispered.

'Hedy thinks Grandad is possessed,' Jelly said, 'and that's why he's being such an ogre.'

Spencer's jaw dropped. 'Ask him a question to test whether it's him or not.'

The girls shared a look, and then Jelly gave Spencer a quick thumbs-up.

They trailed after Uncle Peter who was returning inside. 'Grandad,' Jelly called out, 'what's Nana making us for lunch? I've forgotten.'

Uncle Peter's back stiffened. Over his shoulder, he replied, 'I don't remember. What she usually makes, I suppose.' He wasn't looking the children in the eye.

Jelly's hands shot out and gripped her cousins'. 'Nana lives in New Orleans,' she reminded them softly, 'she has since before I was even born! That's not him!'

'Then who is it?' Spencer asked, horrified.

'Well, think about it. Who could possibly be that *mean*?' Hedy hinted darkly.

Realization swept across Spencer's face. 'Nobody.'

CHAPTER 23

THE COMPOSITION

'How do we get him out?' Spencer shivered as he spoke, as though bugs were crawling over him. 'What if he takes Uncle Peter's head off?!'

Hedy gave Jelly what she hoped was a reassuring look. 'He wouldn't.'

'I don't want to go near him,' Spencer said.

Neither did Hedy, and – after the mention of 'head off' – neither did Jelly. Albert Nobody's cruel manner, what he had revealed about Grandpa John, the headless figurines, what he was doing to Uncle Peter – all of it made wild thoughts of fleeing cross Hedy's mind.

Should they make a run for it?

Upstairs a debate was going on. 'Here, I'll help you,' they could hear Uncle Peter's voice saying.

'No, no, I can manage,' replied Grandpa John.

'Look, you take the music, and I'll take the stool. I'm hardier than you, old man.'

'Nonsense. Oh, fine, then, damn you. Don't break it.' Grandpa John, it seemed, still couldn't help fretting about his belongings.

'Why the devil not?' Uncle Peter scoffed. 'You're about to burn the thing.' Then Uncle Peter – or rather, Uncle Peter's body – came walking down the stairs, holding Simon's piano stool. Behind him was Grandpa John, arms loaded with a tall stack of sheets of music. On the top of the stack was a bundle of paper tied with a navy-blue ribbon: Simon's composition.

'Oh, there are our obliging, cooperative grandchildren,' Uncle Peter called out mockingly. 'Make way.'

All three children drew back from Uncle Peter, gaping at him. His neck seemed to have grown longer, and as he brushed past Hedy something caught on a large button on her coat. Out jerked a gold pocket watch on a chain. It looked exactly like the one she and Spencer had taken out of Nobody's chandelier.

Crash. Uncle Peter's face was gleeful as he – no, as *Nobody*, Hedy reminded herself – tossed the piano stool on to the small hill of Grandpa John's belongings. Grandpa John, struggling with the dense weight of the sheet music, set his stack down on the ground and straightened, rubbing a fist into his back.

'Grandpa John, please let me have the music. Please!' Hedy cried. She pulled the ribbon-tied bundle from the pile, but Grandpa John held out his hand for it to be returned.

'It needs to go, Hedy. We can't start making this exception and that. If I stopped to think of every little thing that I thought *might* be harmless and would *perhaps* be all right to keep, I'd never get this done.' His voice cracked on the last few words. This bonfire would be like cutting off a part of him.

'It's just music,' Hedy pleaded, rolling the papers in her hand.

A firm hand descended and wrenched the roll of music from her, so forcefully that she fell to the ground.

'Peter!' Grandpa John protested.

'Whoops!' exclaimed the person who was not Uncle Peter. Green eyes regarded Hedy, amused. He held out a hand to help her up, but Hedy refused to take it. 'Let's start this now,' he said, stuffing the sheet music along with the other twisted wads of paper into the pyre, like many wicks to set it all alight. 'John, did you get the first pieces of your mad box of woe?'

Grandpa John, who was helping Hedy to her feet, turned pale and shoved a hand in his pocket. Hedy saw that there was something cube-shaped in there.

'John?' Uncle Peter's eyes were ruthless, and trained laser-sharp on Grandpa John's pocket. 'She's never coming back. You have to admit, it's pretty damned morbid keeping a thing like that. It was time to move on years ago.' He ambled over to his brother and held out a hand. 'Give this one to me and I'll help you bring the rest of it down, piece by piece. It might take all night for us to get rid of that box, but we'll do it together. We will *unshackle* you.'

With a trembling hand, Grandpa John withdrew from his pocket a glimmering cube, one of the many that Hedy and Spencer had seen for a short moment in the secret room, a cube of the Kaleidos. 'I could only bring one,' he murmured. 'I don't know if I have the heart to bring more.'

'One is a good start,' Uncle Peter said smoothly. He

plucked the cube from Grandpa John's hand and placed it on the pyre, then pulled a cigarette lighter from his pocket.

'No!' Hedy's voice rang out desperately as Uncle Peter lit a flame centimetres from the roll of Simon's music. 'Grandpa, that's not Uncle Peter. It's Albert Nobody inside him, making him do this!'

Those strange green eyes narrowed, and Uncle Peter's head shook. 'She's lying,' he told a bewildered Grandpa John. Then he tilted his hand and lit the top of the roll of music.

'*Non!*' shouted a voice. Their heads whipped around. Surging from the upturned piano stool was Simon. With a torrent of spat curses, all in French, the ghost curled himself around the composition and the fire withered to a blackened edge at the top of the paper.

Uncle Peter grunted angrily and knelt to light another wad of music, but before he could flick out another flame Spencer ran forwards and, with a yell, kicked Uncle Peter's fist. The lighter went flying. After a shocked moment, Uncle Peter grabbed Spencer by the shoulders to push him hard, metres away. Spencer twisted awkwardly to protect the sleeping chick in his pocket, and crashed near one of the paintings from the hall, knocking the frame with his head.

'Peter! Are you out of your mind?' Grandpa John thundered.

Hedy saw red. She lowered her head and ran at her great-uncle, but his strong forearm stopped her charge, flinging her away so that she flew into Jelly and the pair of them collapsed to the cold ground. The breath was knocked out of her with an *oof*. Trying to find her feet, she helplessly watched as Uncle Peter took a step to retrieve the lighter, but then something astonishing happened.

Simon gave a roar, then flowed that short distance into Uncle Peter, disappearing from sight. Uncle Peter bucked and fell to the ground, convulsing. Grandpa John moved towards his brother, but his attempts to subdue the spasms were in vain, and he took a punishing kick to the ear. Hedy struggled up and pulled Jelly with her, looping around the two old men to help Spencer to his feet. The three children were unable to wrest their eyes from Uncle Peter as he gasped mutely on the ground, eyes bulging, fingers clawing the earth, head beating back.

The dark-coloured patches of hair on his head

lightened back to his usual grey colour, then turned dark again, and then light, unable to settle. Through Uncle Peter's blinks it seemed as though his eyes were changing colour back and forth and an intense blue light seemed to rage under his skin. After a few long moments of agony, he let loose a ravaged howl. On the ground the dark fingernail popped off Uncle Peter's finger with a spark of blue light. He rolled to one side and coughed. There was a flash in his mouth, and he spat out a tooth as the golden watch fell out of his pocket. The darker colour through his hair finally leached away entirely, leaving Uncle Peter's grey curls in their place.

A pale haze gathered and thickened in the air: Albert Nobody. His head appeared clearly enough, like a blue-tinged hologram, though his body was hazy. He was handsome, but there was a contemptuous twist of malice to his mouth and eyes that spoke to his true, ugly nature.

Simon floated out of Uncle Peter and hovered protectively over the lightly singed roll of music that stuck out from the pyre. Uncle Peter sagged on the ground; the wound on his arm began to bleed through the bandage once more. When Jelly hurled herself to the ground to help him up, he could only pat her hand, too drained to stand.

Nobody turned his gaze upon Grandpa John and smirked. 'Look at how old and feeble-minded The Amazing John Sang, Magician, has become,' he jeered.

'Oh, I don't mind being old and feeble,' Grandpa John said steadily. The desolate look about him was gone. He had drawn himself up to his full height and pulled his shoulders back. 'I may not be in my prime any longer, but at least I *had* a prime. Still no body for you, I see. You were a nobody then, and you still are.'

Nobody's mouth tightened. 'How's your wife? Oh of course, silly me – you lost her. No one to stoke your mighty ego for all these years.'

'How did you get out?' Grandpa John asked.

'Your nosy grandchildren, of course.' Nobody chuckled. 'You don't have much of a rein on them, do you, John? You know, I showed them the truth about the night she disappeared.'

'*Truth?* You have them thinking I did it!' Grandpa John seethed.

Nobody gave a satisfied sigh. 'That was very diverting. I'm really very pleased with myself. But the most amusing thing about it? I *did* show them the truth.

They simply got the wrong end of the stick. I showed them that a magician sneaked off with a piece of the box that night before the show. Is it my fault that they presumed the wrong Sang brother guilty?'

Silence befell the group as they tried to make sense of Nobody's words. The wrong Sang brother?

Nobody eyed Uncle Peter. 'You were always so jealous of John, weren't you, Peter? You were lucky if he let your name appear on the poster!'

Uncle Peter had managed to sit up, but his eyes were wide and panicked, as though he was watching a tsunami racing towards him.

'Go on,' Nobody said encouragingly, 'let's make this family confession one to remember. *You* were the one who took that piece of the famed Kaleidos because you wanted it to fail. On stage, in front of everyone. *Splat*, cream pie to the face for John, Peter becomes the most revered Sang! You're responsible for Rose disappearing. And you never . . . said . . . a thing.'

Uncle Peter couldn't manage a word now, but shook his head once. Hedy couldn't tell if it was denial or not wanting it to be true.

'Grandad, he's lying, right?' Jelly pleaded.

'Hedy,' Grandpa John croaked, 'go and get the

birds.' He slipped the Kaleidos cube that Uncle Peter had tried to make him burn into his pocket.

'Here,' Spencer said softly, drawing the blinking liar bird chick from his pocket.

Uncle Peter gazed at the chick, puzzled and fearful.

'Is it true, Peter?' Grandpa John asked. 'Is he telling the truth? Did you make the box fail?'

Uncle Peter looked crestfallen. He shook his head. 'No, John . . . I . . .'

Liar! Liar! Liar!

Everyone stared at the liar bird chick in shocked silence, except Nobody, who giggled in delight.

CHAPTER 24

THE BLINK OF AN EYE

'You lied to me,' Grandpa John breathed.

Face crumpling, Uncle Peter nodded. Tears gathered in his eyes. 'I didn't mean it,' he said. 'I never meant for Rose to disappear. The opposite. I wanted her not to vanish at all. I only wanted to embarrass you.'

Hedy felt hollow in the stomach. It wasn't Grandpa John who had meant the stage show to go wrong. She and Spencer had been tricked by Albert Nobody.

'Why didn't you say anything?' Grandpa John demanded. 'I was suspected of murder at one time, damn you. Why didn't you come forward?'

Uncle Peter made a helpless face. 'I already lived in your shadow. I thought I wanted to get out from under it. But the thought of having the spotlight on me for *that* was far worse. It would have been the end of me. I would've been known for nothing else. Nothing.'

'Why didn't you try to return the piece to the Kaleidos?' Hedy asked.

'I did try, I swear on my life. There were too many people around after the show, police had cordoned off the box. John, I had to wait until you brought the box back here a few days later.'

Grandpa John gave his brother a bitter look. 'I slept on the floor next to it for months.'

Uncle Peter bit his lip ashamedly. 'I thought . . . I thought if I could quietly replace the cube, Rose would reappear. No one need know what I'd done. All would be right again. But the cube disappeared. I know I brought it here safely, in my pocket. I took it out of my pocket and put it down to hang up my jacket. My back was turned from it for three seconds at most, and it vanished. Gone in a blink of an eye.'

A thought whispered in the back of Hedy's mind. 'Where had you put the cube when it disappeared?' she asked.

'I'd put it on the hall table while I hung up my jacket. It was like the table swallowed it up.'

'The Bermuda Triangle!' Jelly exclaimed.

Grandpa John stared at her. 'What do you mean?'

'Things keep disappearing from your hallway table. Haven't you ever noticed?'

Memories flickered over Grandpa John's face as he thought back over decades. 'I'd always put that down to me being careless.'

Could it be the Woodspies? Hedy thought.

'Dear me, John,' Nobody sneered. 'We haven't been as sharp as we thought, all this time, have we?' A fuzzy blue flickering finger appeared as he tapped his own chin thoughtfully. 'I think what I love most about this whole sorry business is that it's really all your fault. Isn't that a poetic conclusion? If you hadn't been such an arrogant, superior, self-important, unjustifiably jumped-up con artist, your brother wouldn't have felt the urge to put you in your place. If you hadn't bought all this . . .' his eyes flickered over the amassed pile of belongings to burn, 'to shut out the rest of *us* from glory—'

'I collect these things to keep them from harming others,' Grandpa John said through gritted teeth. 'I don't want anyone to suffer as Rose has. That was my purpose.'

'But back then you didn't! It didn't start that way! You began hoarding things before Rose vanished. Even then you simply *had* to own these things that could give you an edge on stage, an edge over your brotherhood of magicians.'

'Brotherhood?' Grandpa John scorned. But he didn't deny what Nobody had said.

'Oh, of course, you have no use for brothers, do you?' Nobody jeered. 'You got the head start of a lifetime and then it turned on you. Perhaps your pitiful brother here could have made things right again if something in your house hadn't taken it from him. Don't blame me – I wasn't even dead and trapped in that blasted room upstairs yet. I wonder what it was that you bought, what thing you awoke, that made the missing piece of your Kaleidos disappear?' He sighed happily. 'This is *such* a beautiful life lesson for you. It's almost worth those years of imprisonment to see it.'

Grandpa John had had enough. 'Get you gone, Albert. Now. Away from here.'

'Or what?'

'Or I'll stuff you back into that *trujuklinkot* so hard

- 291 -

that the history books will have a blank space where there used to be your name.'

'And I will drag you back in myself,' Simon called out, his expression determined and fierce. 'If it's the last thing I do.'

'You could barely get me out of decrepit old Peter,' Nobody taunted Simon. 'I put myself in the *trujuk-linkot* once, long ago, but there's no way you have the strength to pull me back in if it's not my will. And anyway, the chandelier is destroyed.'

'I'll fix it,' Grandpa John said, steely-eyed.

Hedy bent to the ground. Swallowing her distaste, she picked up the tooth, nail and pocket watch that had fallen off Uncle Peter. 'These might help.'

Nobody stilled. Hedy had hit a nerve.

'None of you would know how,' he insisted, 'even if you had the other relics.'

There was a crunch of gravel as someone, two some-ones, hurried down the drive towards them. When they came into view, Grandpa John gave a sigh of relief. '*She* would know how,' he said, with a nod at the new arrivals.

'Know what, Mr Sang?' called out Mrs Pal, leaning on her walking stick. Soumitra was at her side.

'What do you know about *trujuklinkotoi*, Mrs Pal?'

'They are difficult,' Mrs Pal said, 'but manageable.'

Grandpa John faced Nobody again. 'Go. Now.'

The blue memory of the cruel, dead magician scowled, and then, with an incomprehensible rumble, streaked away into the sky, up and away. Without warning, the tooth and nail were sucked up into the air in his wake to join him. The pocket watch, heavier, trembled in Hedy's hand as though it too would follow Nobody, but Hedy closed her fingers around it.

'You got our message!' Hedy said to Mrs Pal, dashing to her side and giving the old woman and Soumitra a hug. She expected Spencer to be right behind her, but he was staring at one of the paintings from the hall. He seemed to have missed everything that had gone on, including their friends' arrival. 'Spencer, look who came!'

But he turned to them all, wide-eyed with shock. His outstretched finger pointed at the painting. 'The missing Kaleidos piece! It's in there!'

CHAPTER 25

SUSPICION, HOPE AND LUCK

Grandpa John sat in his study with the paintings propped up against chairs in front of him, barely moving. He had humbly asked everyone to help him bring all his belongings back into the house. 'Let's just get everything into the first spare room upstairs. I'll sort it out later. What a flaming fool I am,' he had added to himself, not quite out of Hedy's hearing.

After he had gingerly carried the painting of the skunk in the frilly dress inside, he had promptly forgotten about everything else, fixated on the small, glittering cube that lay on the skunk's table. He had touched the painted surface, trying to reach into the painting to pull out the key to his happiness. It had been futile, no more than touching oil on canvas.

For a short while, Grandpa John had taken the cube that Nobody had nearly convinced him to burn out of his pocket and held it in the palm of his hand, near the painting. It was as though he were trying to tempt the return of the cube in the painting with its mate out in the real world. But nothing had happened, and not long after that, Grandpa John made one quick trip to the attic where – Hedy presumed – he returned that one cube to the Kaleidos, for safety.

The first things Hedy and Spencer fetched were Doug from the garage and Stan from the unlit pyre. When the bear and stag saw each other, they called out with great relief before starting their usual ribbing of one another.

'I made sure the children didn't forget you, Stan,' Doug said. 'I tried roast venison once and it was very tough.'

'One can't help being a magnificent and muscular animal, Douglas,' Stan replied loftily. 'How was the action wherever you were? Oh yes – nothing happened there, did it? Pity you weren't where all the excitement was like I was. I'm sure the children would have enjoyed sitting on you to watch the show.'

'Go on, then, tell me everything, you great branch-headed milksop. And you needn't try adding in any phony exploits of yours . . .'

Carrying all the artefacts back inside was a quick job, even though Uncle Peter soon had to sit down, wrapped in a blanket and warming his hands around a cup of coffee. As they walked to and fro, Hedy filled in Mrs Pal and Soumitra on all that had happened. The more she spoke, the crazier and more outlandish it all sounded. Soumitra raised a quizzical eyebrow every now and then, but Mrs Pal listened intently, sometimes closing her eyes to catch Hedy's words.

'This house has worlds within it, and you have explored so much in a short time,' the tiny old woman marvelled.

'I wonder if Samuel Garcia knew that Mr Nobody was so nasty,' Hedy said, thinking back to the golden hand that had sneaked the card into her pocket.

Mrs Pal sighed. 'Nobody was like a boil festering away in his prison, letting his resentment grow and twist him. I understand Albert himself was the one who had his spirit preserved in the *trujuklinkot*, the chandelier. He wanted to persist past disease and death, and find greatness beyond. But it seems greatness can't be found when confined like that. Your grandfather has a point when he worries that some of these things are too dangerous and unpredictable to control.'

Hedy gave her a smile. 'We did find out stuff because of him in the end, so maybe it was worth it. But what do we do now? How do we get the cube out of the painting?'

'That's going to be the trick,' Mrs Pal said, quietly troubled.

The light was beginning to fail outside, and it didn't feel a bit like Christmas Eve. By three o'clock, everyone had squeezed into the study to join Grandpa John in scrutinizing the portraits of the skunk and the magpie. On a hunch, Spencer dug out some photos he had taken of the paintings when he and Hedy had first arrived at Hoarder Hill.

'Look,' he said, 'the stuff on the table isn't the same. It must move when no one's looking.'

He was right. Back on their first day, a set of keys had been on a Rubik's cube next to a West Ham beanie and a CD of an album by The Smiths. Today, the keys were on top of a closed music box, the CD and Rubik's cube weren't visible at all and the West Ham beanie had been turned around so its crest couldn't be seen. The miscellaneous collection looked strangely cobbled together over decades, even centuries, but they were part of the image. Everything from the cube to the beanie to the music box was made up of tiny brushstrokes.

Hedy wanted to kick herself. 'On our first day we thought all those things were part of the original painting,' she said. 'I thought the pictures were painted not long ago, and just made to look old, except for little clues of being modern. But those aren't clues of being modern.'

'These thieves steal the items into the paintings.' Grandpa John grunted, disgusted with himself. 'What a blind clod I've been.'

Jelly gave a satisfied sigh. 'So *they're* the Bermuda Triangle.'

'The skunk took it from you,' Grandpa John said to Uncle Peter. 'If only you hadn't had it in the first place.' He didn't look at his brother. All was not yet forgiven.

Uncle Peter looked thoroughly miserable and cold. 'I'm sorry, John,' he said, and lumbered outside. They heard the back door open and close, as though he wanted to punish himself with still more icy air.

'What are we going to do now, Grandpa John?' Hedy asked, when no one else said anything.

He rubbed a hand over his face. 'I have no idea,' he sighed.

In the hush that followed, Spencer's stomach grumbled noisily, reminding them all that they hadn't eaten anything in ages. 'I think we need some food,' Hedy said.

'I make *really* good packet-noodle sandwiches,' Jelly said, clapping her hands.

Spencer brightened immediately. 'Race you to the kitchen!' he yelled, taking off.

The food helped their mood, if not their thinking, even though it was a strange combination that the children served up. When Jelly asked Uncle Peter to come inside to eat, he softly refused, instead looking out into the dusk.

Grandpa John bleakly chewed his crust of bread,

staring at the portrait now leaning against the kitchen worktop. 'We don't even know if anything can come back out once it's gone in.'

'Oh, it can!' Hedy said with a sudden rush of excitement. 'We've seen it – I mean, Jelly felt it – when they threw it at her.'

Jelly's eyes opened wide with recollection. 'Max's jar of bogeys! We tricked them – we didn't know it was the paintings at the time, but we tricked them into grabbing that disgusting jar Max was using to collect his bogeys. And then when we walked away, they chucked it at me and it hit me in the head. I mean, I wasn't knocked out or anything, but one of these things is definitely a good shot.'

A sense of hope rippled through the room. 'What goes into these Theries can come out as well,' Mrs Pal murmured.

'What do you mean, *Theries*?' Hedy asked.

Mrs Pal waved her hand at the portraits. 'These hybrid creatures – with the human bodies and animal heads – are Theries.'

The children all bent closer to the painting, as though knowing what these creatures were called would reveal a new clue about the skunk lady. She stared out of the painting, unblinking and unmoving.

'How do we make her give it back?' Soumitra asked.

'Maybe we turn the cube into a bogey jar so she won't want it any more,' Spencer suggested. Soumitra very seriously gave Spencer a high five.

Jelly snorted. 'Trust you to think of that.'

'What? You said it worked before with Max's jar,' Spencer pointed out.

'But as *if* there's something that would turn—'

Their argument was interrupted by a cough and a groan outside. Out on the back porch, Uncle Peter toppled off the bench on which he had been sitting for so long. Jelly was out of the door first, with Hedy and Spencer close behind, as Grandpa John switched on the porch light.

'Grandad?' Jelly asked.

Uncle Peter's eyelids fluttered for a second and his breath chattered between his teeth. The light of the porch was weak but, even so, it was plain to see that he was very pale, and looked sort of bloodless in the lips.

'Is it your arm?' Grandpa John asked him.

'C . . . c . . . cold,' Uncle Peter stammered.

Grandpa John tried to lift Uncle Peter's head.

'Can you stand? You need to come inside where it's warmer.'

Uncle Peter gave him a despairing look. 'Leave me. D...don't...deserve...'

'Don't be ridiculous. I don't want you freeze to death out here tonight,' Grandpa John grumbled. 'I have enough on my mind.'

It took the combined efforts of Soumitra and Grandpa John to help Uncle Peter hobble inside, where he collapsed into the closest chair.

'Hot coffee's what he needs,' Soumitra said. 'Hell, hot coffee's what *I* need.'

As Soumitra put on the kettle and searched for mugs, Grandpa John, wanting to keep an eye on the painting, sent the children to the linen cupboard for hot water bottles and woollen blankets. When they returned, Mrs Pal was examining Uncle Peter's arm. 'It's not bleeding,' she reported as she changed the dressing, 'but his skin is very cold.'

Soumitra held a mug of coffee out to Uncle Peter, who was drooping so much he couldn't raise his arm to take the mug.

'Here,' Jelly said, grasping the warm drink. She lifted the mug to Uncle Peter's lips and he took a small sip.

They tucked the hot water bottles around his belly and chest and swaddled him with blankets. Gradually, Uncle Peter drained the whole mug, but none of it seemed to help. He looked weaker than ever.

'Why isn't he warming up?' Jelly fretted. 'Do we put him in a warm bath or something?'

'It wasn't *that* cold out there, was it?' Grandpa John murmured to Mrs Pal.

Hedy tried to think back to when she had been that cold, and what had helped her best. When *was* the last time she had been cold? And then the memory of when she'd last been chilled to the bone came flooding back. 'Simon!' she said, grasping Grandpa John's arm. 'It's because of Simon that he's cold.'

'Like we were?' Spencer asked.

Hedy put a hand to Uncle Peter's forehead. It felt like the brow of a marble statue standing out in the frosty garden. 'I'm sure of it.' She quickly recounted to the others what had happened after she and Spencer had touched Simon, and how Mrs Vilums had cured them of the deep chill by making them stand in sunlight.

Spencer thought back. 'But we didn't get that cold that fast.'

'Hedy said you only touched Simon with a finger, or a hand at most,' Mrs Pal said. 'But Mr Sang, you said Simon took over the whole of Peter to oust Nobody. The effect would be stronger, and more immediate. That is why he is fading so fast. I suspect he needs sunlight now.'

'Sunrise isn't for ages,' Jelly said anxiously.

Grandpa John stared at his brother, worry battling with hurt and bitterness on his face. Uncle Peter seemed to feel it. He raised his eyes, took in Grandpa John's expression and whispered, 'Leave me.'

Grandpa John swallowed and brusquely said, 'Soumitra, can you help me get him up the stairs? Hedy and Spencer, bring the painting, please. I don't want it out of my sight.'

The flights of stairs proved too much for Uncle Peter, and at the second landing he dropped to the floor. Soumitra gently heaved him over his shoulder, as if he were a sack of onions.

To their surprise, Grandpa John led them to the attic. At an ominous clank of metal from up the stairs, Grandpa John called, 'Halt! I am thy master and my purpose is pure.'

The clank of Sir Roland fell silent. He was motionless as everyone picked their way behind Grandpa John through the clutter of the attic to the hidden room. Grandpa John reached out to clasp the golden hand in the door. Its burnished metal fingers curled around his, and they shook for a moment, then there was a *snap, clunk, clack* as a hefty mechanism buried deep inside the door unlocked. The golden hand released Grandpa John's, and he pushed the door open to reveal the hushed wood clearing inside.

When Hedy and Spencer had last glimpsed the Kaleidos, it had been lit by moonlight and the torch flames. But now, although outside the house it was night, soft sunlight fell upon the Kaleidos, making it glimmer. Hedy and Spencer stared at the magic box, edging as close as they could without touching it.

Soumitra eased Uncle Peter to the floor, where sunlight could fall upon his body and face. The old man's eyes fluttered, but he was too weak to open them.

'Now what?' Jelly asked, taking her grandfather's limp hand.

Hedy found everyone looking to her for an answer. 'We wait for the sunlight to warm him up.'

Mrs Pal studied the trees around the clearing with

an air of professional curiosity and bent down to touch the earth, finding a small animal bone – a curving rib – half buried. 'Have you ever explored these woods, Mr Sang?' she asked.

'A few times,' Grandpa John said. 'I tied a long rope to the banister of the stairs, tied the other end around my waist, and walked as far as I could go. It was always very quiet here. That's why I chose it as the place for . . .' He trailed off, looking at the Kaleidos.

Mrs Pal eyed the painting of the skunk Therie, an idea seeming to form in her mind. At last, she cleared her throat. 'Mr Sang, your exploration of the wood has given me a thought about the cube.' Everyone fell silent. 'I propose a more direct approach. Rather than trying to convince the Therie to return it, someone' – she looked at Grandpa John – 'enters the painting and takes it back.'

'What are we doing?' Hedy asked as the children and Grandpa John crunched through the dark to the garage. They had left Uncle Peter in the hidden room with Soumitra watching over him. Mrs Pal was guarding the paintings inside.

'We need fishing line . . .' Grandpa John counted on

his fingers, '... cord, rope and chain.'

'Are you building a war machine?' Spencer sounded impressed.

'No. A leash. A line that will tether the bait and tether me.' He yanked open the garage doors and began directing the children to search this or that shelf.

'Who's the bait?' Jelly added with a worried look. 'Are you using Spencer 'cos he's the smallest?'

Spencer had crouched down to dig around in the old bucket, but he now sprang to his feet. 'I don't want to be the bait!'

'No one is the bait!' Grandpa John said, throwing his hands into the air. 'Mrs Pal and I believe, or hope, that the painting is a sort of portal for the Therie. When it wants to – when no one is around, it seems – the Therie opens its portal and takes things from our world into its world. They've been scavenging for trinkets and knick-knacks right under my nose for years. Well, we'll set some tempting item in front of that skunk; that will be the bait. The bait will be tied to some fine fishing line, which we hope will go un-noticed. Mrs Pal suspects that the fishing line will be like wedging a door. It will keep the portal open. The fishing line will connect to me, and the other end of the rope will be anchored to the house. All of the heavy chain is just over-caution, I hope. With any luck, I'll keep a hand on the rope, dart through the portal, snatch the cube and away we go.'

Grandpa John took a deep breath while everyone tried to absorb all that he had said. After hours of frustrating, fruitless watching of the skunk Therie, he was now filled with purpose, moving quickly, the years dropping from him.

But still, Hedy frowned, thinking, *That was a lot of* suspect *and* hope *and* luck.

'Check what I've placed on the hallway table,' Mrs Pal called softly as they returned inside.

A red-and-white decoration, speckled with glitter, had been pulled from the Christmas tree and set on the hallway table. 'There's our bait,' Grandpa John murmured.

Jelly nudged Spencer. 'It looks a bit like you. Ginger on top, pale and freckly on the side ... you *are* the bait!'

Spencer elbowed her.

Grandpa John began unreeling lengths of line and cord and tying them together as fast as he could.

Finally the whole length was linked to the chain that was wrapped around one of the brick pillars of the porch and secured with a large, solid padlock.

Beyond the porch, a very light swirling fall of snow had begun: it was pretty, but couldn't soothe the unease that was starting to rear up in Hedy's mind. She closed the door as far as it would go and pulled her scarf up around her ears for comfort, even though she didn't need it inside.

'I think we're ready,' Grandpa John said to Mrs Pal, slipping the leash through his belt buckle. He held out a hand to stop the children from entering the lounge room, where both the skunk and the magpie portraits had been propped on the floor. 'Keep out of sight now.'

'Out of whose sight?' Spencer asked.

'The Therie's.'

'Why?'

'So she takes the bait. She won't if she knows we're watching her.'

Grandpa John swiftly edged towards the portrait and placed the Christmas decoration on the floor in front of it. Then he retreated to huddle with the others in the doorway, where they hoped the skunk could not see them watching and waiting.

A minute stretched to two, and then five, but the Christmas decoration remained on the floor.

'Is she going to take it?' Spencer whispered.

There was a tense pause. 'The Bermuda Triangle doesn't usually take that long,' Jelly said. 'Hedy, remember when they took Max's jar? We'd only looked away for a few seconds.'

'And when they tried to take my phone, I hadn't turned away very long,' Hedy recalled.

Grandpa John sighed. 'Perhaps she hasn't seen it. Maybe I need to move it closer.'

'Oh, she's seen it.' It was Stan, placed on the seat of the sofa with his antlers tilting up and over the back of it. 'She saw it. She took a look at it. I don't think it's to her taste.'

'Agreed,' Doug rumbled quietly. 'She's not interested. What do you think, Stan? Do they need to try different bait?'

'Yes, good idea,' Stan said. 'Different bait.'

'Your turn,' Jelly teased Spencer.

'Ladies first,' he retorted. Jelly ruffled his hair with a laugh.

'Well, what do we use?' Grandpa John asked. 'I

thought a Christmas decoration was a good idea myself. Sparkly. Pretty to look at.'

'Do we try something that's not sparkly and pretty, then?' Spencer suggested.

Mrs Pal pulled something from her pocket. 'Here, try this.' It was the small, pale rib bone she had picked up from the hidden room upstairs. Hedy and Spencer tugged on the fishing line to reel the Christmas decoration towards them, then cut it from the fishing line with a small blade that Grandpa John had in his pocket.

When the bone was tied on, Hedy whispered, 'Doug, Stan, is it OK to try again now?'

'Looks like it.'

Grandpa John tossed the bone into the room and it landed neatly before the painting. Everyone held their breath.

'She's looking,' Stan whispered.

Moments trickled by.

'She's going for it!' Doug tried to contain his excitement.

A slim hand emerged from the frame. It was glossy and made of many, many brushstrokes, but otherwise looked like a normal woman's hand, with a ruffled

– 311 –

sleeve at the wrist. Lady Skunk's hand quickly plucked the bone from the rug and withdrew into the painting, out of sight. Behind it, the fishing line slowly snaked into the portrait.

CHAPTER 26

ONE FOR SORROW, TWO FOR JOY

Grandpa John let out a few breaths. 'Here I go,' he said as he took a step. Hedy and Spencer scrambled to their feet and hugged him.

'Does this mean your "No magic" rule is broken?' Spencer asked.

'This isn't magic,' Grandpa John said, 'it's repossession.'

'We can help if you need us to,' Hedy added.

'Help? Don't you dare,' he said with stern affection. Then he entwined his forearm in the cord. 'You two stay out here. Stay safe.'

'We'll look after the cubs for you, Master,' Doug called out.

Grandpa John shot Doug a doubtful look. 'Hmm. Grand job you've been doing so far,' he said.

'They're in one piece, aren't they?' Stan said, sounding hurt.

Grandpa John approached the painting and dropped to one knee and then the other, grumbling under his breath about his age. Where the fishing line pierced through the surface of the paint, he poked a finger through.

'What is it like?' Mrs Pal asked quietly.

'Feels squishy,' Grandpa John said. He nodded to them all, then put his head down and crawled into the painting, dragging the cord with him.

The others rushed from the doorway to watch. There stood Grandpa John, completely inside the picture, a fine painted version of himself.

'Why isn't he moving?' Spencer asked.

But Grandpa John and the Therie *were* moving in there somehow. It was like watching a slow, jerky, silent stop-motion picture: first they were in one position, and then a few moments later their positions had changed, without the movements in between being seen. The skunk Therie seemed shocked to find an intruder in her painting. She backed away in fitful lurches from her table of stolen trinkets, the Kaleidos cube among them.

'Get it, Grandpa John!' whispered Hedy.

As she spoke, a tiny flicker of blue light winked along the rope that trailed into the painting. No one paid it any mind because the picture had changed again: Grandpa John was grasping the cube with two hands, a relieved smile upon his face. But in the next moment, the skunk had turned her back on him, her tail up, and Grandpa John had stumbled backwards, his arm over his eyes.

Spencer looked aghast. 'Did that thing just skunk-spray him?'

Grandpa John stretched out his hand along the cord, trying to feel his way back out of the painting. But as he pulled it taut, a large shape of black and white flew at him from above and knocked him down. The cord juddered.

'It's the magpie!' exclaimed Spencer. 'From the other painting!'

Hedy glanced at the magpie's painting by the fireplace. Spencer was right; it was empty. The two paintings were somehow linked. The magpie's splendid coat of black and cream had transformed into wings and the magpie had swooped into that strange place where their grandfather was.

It jabbed at Grandpa John with its large beak. He narrowly ducked it before he tripped, entangled in the cord. In the next moment, he tugged something from his pocket; it was his small blade. He slashed through the cord to free himself, and the magpie soundlessly screeched – Grandpa John had nicked the creature across its thigh.

The magpie suddenly jerked, and for a second blue light crackled over it from top to toe. Then it gazed at Grandpa John with a contemptuous tilt to its head that made it terrifyingly clear to Hedy what had just happened.

'Nobody's gone into that magpie!' she shouted.

'What?' Mrs Pal cried.

'I'm sure of it! Uncle Peter had that look about him when Nobody was controlling him.'

'Mr Sang just cut the creature,' Mrs Pal said, thinking aloud. 'And Peter had an injured arm. I think a wound gives Nobody an opening.'

They watched, horrified, as the magpie engulfed

Grandpa John in its dark wings and tossed him to and fro before hurling him to the ground. The Therie shook each foot into large black bird claws and seized Grandpa John by the belt of his trousers. Stretching out its great wings, it sprang into the air, surging away with Grandpa John who desperately clutched the Kaleidos cube to his chest.

Hedy was vaguely aware that she was yelling as she dropped to her knees and drove her head through the surface of the painting.

It was like a fog clearing, or lifting the pane of a dirty window. The world inside didn't look painted; in fact it looked more than real, with deeply saturated colours: the umber of the earthy ground, the indigo thread of the rug unexpectedly lying under the skunk's table, the intense emerald green of the tumbled potted fern nearby. An unpleasant pungent smell hung in the air, which must have been the skunk spray, but Hedy barely noticed it. All her attention was on Grandpa John's faint cries in the distance. Far away she could see the magpie Therie, with Grandpa John dangling from its claws, flapping beyond a river to a vast tree rearing into the dark sky.

Backing out of the painting, Hedy ignored Spencer

and Jelly's questions. 'Massive tree. Watch them!' she barked. 'I have an idea.' And she raced up the stairs towards Doug and Stan's room, scarf flying, her mind trained on the only thing she could imagine helping right now.

The silver and brass wings were even heavier than she remembered. Her hands shook with nerves and her fingers traitorously refused to disentangle the leather straps. She could feel precious moments ticking by. As she fumbled, Jelly hurried into the room.

'Muddy bells, Spencer *said* this is what you were thinking!' She grabbed Hedy by the shoulders. 'Hedy, no. You couldn't get them to work last time!'

Hedy swallowed uncomfortably. 'Max managed it. So I must be able to somehow. It's the only thing I can think of to get to Grandpa John.'

Jelly chewed her lip unhappily, but then, after a deep breath, huffed, 'Here, let me help you.' She turned Hedy around to wrangle the leather straps across her back and then over the chest. When all was tightly fastened, Hedy rocked back and forth on her feet to gain her balance.

'Ready to channel Max?' Jelly asked her.

'I guess so.'

When they returned to the lounge room, Mrs Pal's face fell. 'Sebastian Sello's wings,' she breathed. 'No, Hedy, I cannot allow it. We must regroup. An adult must go and find him.'

Hedy shook her head. 'What if the skunk sneaks back and throws out the cord and the portal closes for ever? I can't lose Grandpa John too. If I don't go in now, we may never find him again. That place is so big, he might end up anywhere.'

'Then I will go,' Mrs Pal said.

Hedy gave the tiny woman her most stubborn look. 'Mrs Pal, no offence but I'm already taller than you. Just tell me, how do I get the wings to work?'

Mrs Pal buried her face in her hands but finally looked at Hedy, defeated. 'Belief. You must *believe* you can fly.'

'Belief.' Hedy breathed deeply. 'OK.'

At that moment, Spencer sprinted into the room and thrust Grandma Rose's motorcycle helmet into Hedy's hands. 'Just in case,' he panted.

'Did you get this from the garage by yourself?' Hedy asked, surprised. When he nodded, she said softly, 'Thanks, Spence. I know you hate the dark.'

'Yeah. But you're going in *there* by yourself, so . . .'

He gave a little shrug.

For a split second, Hedy couldn't help imagining herself falling out of the dim sky of the painted world and crashing to the earth. With that frightening image, the wings on her back suddenly weighed down, cripplingly heavy. She fully grasped, then, the secret to Sebastian Sello's wings, and obstinately blinked the vision away. 'Do you believe I can do it?'

'Yeah,' Spencer said, 'you can do anything. It's kind of annoying.'

Hedy pulled him into a hug, and then Jelly was crushing both of them, saying, 'I believe in you too, Hedy.'

Spencer lifted his face gravely. 'Be careful of Nobody,' he said. 'He's the worst sort of tricky.'

'Well, then, I'll just have to be trickier,' Hedy said. She patted a small item she had stowed in her pocket all afternoon. 'Keep safe.'

'We'll keep 'em safe, young Hedy, you just look out for yourself,' Doug called out from the couch. 'The Lord of the Queen's Wood over here is just spoiling for a fight.'

Stan cleared his throat as though preparing to recite verse. '*Valiant friends, craven foes . . .*' he began in a deep tone.

Hedy didn't wait around to hear the rest of it. As she knelt to crawl through the frame, Mrs Pal crouched beside her. 'If you fly far, look for the glow of your brother and cousin on this side of the portal. It's called family fire. Look for them to lead you back.'

CHAPTER 27

FAMILY FIRE

Hedy crawled through the painting, awkwardly shuffling with the weight of the wings on her back. She quickly glanced backwards. From this side, the lounge room looked fuzzy, as though she was staring through the surface of a frozen lake, and sound was muffled. But Hedy was most astonished to see what Mrs Pal had just told her: the glowing forms of Spencer and Jelly beyond the painting portal. *Family fire*, she thought, feeling a sliver of reassurance.

The glow shifted as Spencer, Jelly and Mrs Pal poked their faces through the portal to watch her.

Spencer made a gagging face at the smell of skunk spray which seemed even stronger than before, as though it were stewing.

Hedy faced the distant tree, a dark silhouette in the dim light of the painted world. In her mind, she tried to lose the heavy feeling of the wings, pictured her body not falling, but instead rising up as the wings beat upon her back, imagined that the forceful swoop of the magpie's wings was her own, that speed and agility were hers to control and—

The wings snapped to their full span and her feet lifted from the ground. *Whoosh, whoosh, whoosh.* Those brass and silver feathers beat to and fro, propelling her skywards, higher and higher, until she remembered she had to steer.

Spencer whooped. 'You're doing it!'

'Max is going to be so jealous!' Jelly cried.

Flying jerkily, and wrenching forwards as though she were running for her life, Hedy willed the wings to keep going. Not knowing what to do, she pumped her legs, swinging herself off balance. After a few stomach-churning moments, she found that she could steer the wings better by keeping her limbs still and tipping her weight to and fro in smoother, smaller movements.

She lurched towards the vast tree.

As she flew through the air, the skunk Therie showed her face at the entrance to her burrow. The creature reeled back in shock at the sight of Hedy, then hissed at her. Hedy glared in the skunk's direction but otherwise ignored it; there was no time to lose.

No one would describe her flight as graceful, but Hedy did find that it grew easier with each wing stroke. She tried to orient herself, casting another look back in the direction of the portal. The small glow could just be seen.

The tree was immense, growing out of the place where four rivers met. Hedy had no idea what type of tree it was, but its trunk rose an eye-watering height from the surface of the water. No ladder had a hope of reaching its lowermost branches, even if there was ground beneath it.

There was no sign of Grandpa John or the Therie as she approached. She couldn't hover with the wings, so she coursed back and forth a few times, eventually deciding she'd have to look on the other side of the tree. But her heart beat faster: on the far side of the tree, the others wouldn't be able to see her. What would happen to her when she flew out of sight?

'Get it over with,' she muttered to herself. She tipped herself to one side to soar around the tree.

Leaves, branches and more leaves, mostly dark green, while the new growth was a pale golden colour. No magpie in sight, and no other creatures up here either. No birds or squirrels, nor even – if this place was not in England – anything more exotic like chipmunks, possums or monkeys. That was what seemed to be at the heart of its strangeness, she decided; it seemed part wild, but it was too empty of wildlife to feel natural.

When she spotted the faraway tiny glow of Spencer and Jelly at the painting portal again, she knew she had made a full circuit of the enormous tree without finding Grandpa John. She began spiralling around and upwards, scrutinizing the shadowy foliage. By the time her third circuit of the tree was done, Hedy had reached a dizzying height. She chose not to think about how far away the ground was.

What was that? Her ears caught a faint sound. A voice. From where, though?

Up. She had not flown above the tree to check the top of it. Back and forth she flew, up past layers of branches. When the peak of the tree was close, she gathered speed and shot up, to look at the top of the tree from above.

Built into the crown of the tree was a grand nest, the magpie's nest. It was perhaps four metres wide, made of branches as thick as Hedy's arms. Twigs, reeds and grasses were woven between the branches, as well as the odd coloured ribbon, probably stolen over time through the magpie's own portal. Even antlers were interlaced with the branches, their tips jutting out of the nest like thorns. Trinkets, baubles and other random items were heaped within the nest. This was the magpie's hoard.

Amongst it all was Grandpa John. His cheek looked swollen, as though he'd taken a blow, but he was staring defiantly at the magpie Therie that stood over him.

Nobody, Hedy reminded herself, *Nobody has taken over that thing*, for there was an unmistakable disdain in its stance and the way it cocked its head and blinked at Grandpa John. The Therie's wings had disappeared, changed back into its black-and-cream military coat. But worst of all, in its fingers it held the Kaleidos cube.

'I can't give you back those years,' Grandpa John was saying, 'but you're free now. Rose is still trapped. Give me the cube, Albert. We can battle it out later, just let me find Rosie first.'

The Therie's silence was more chilling than Nobody's usual insults. It took a step away from Grandpa John, and another, and another. At first Hedy thought the Therie was letting Grandpa John go, but then it held the cube out past the edge of the nest.

'No, Albert!' Grandpa John cried, struggling to his feet.

The Therie gave a half-shrug and opened its fingers to let the cube fall, all the way down to the currents of dull water below.

Hedy bit back a shout and dived. Behind and above, she heard the Therie's strangled, shocked squawk. Willing herself downwards, she closed in on the cube, and, with an outstretched hand, grabbed it. The cube was hers.

Pulling out of the dive, Hedy beat her wings to streak upwards to the nest, shoving the cube down into her pocket.

Grandpa John's frightened face peered over the edge of the great intertwined branches. 'Hedy, go back now!'

'No!' she yelled back. 'Not without y—'

Hedy's head snapped forwards with a sudden crack. She saw stars for a second, then it happened again, making her cartwheel through the air. She screamed. Nobody was pecking her helmet with the Therie's beak.

She sped upwards, above the nest now, trying to get away. *Crack.* Another flash of stars behind her eyes. Hedy tumbled into the nest with a thud, sending trinkets flying. Grandpa John began picking his way to her side, but Nobody landed in between them, barring his way. With a great shake, his wings transformed back to human arms.

'Go, Hedy!' Grandpa John called.

Nobody's pale hand shot out to yank Grandpa John by the scruff of his sweater towards the edge of the nest. His intent was clear: to send Grandpa John plunging to the dark water far, far below.

'Wait,' Hedy croaked. She reached into her pocket to draw out her only gambit. 'Trade.'

Nobody's feathered head snapped around, and he peered at the pocket watch Hedy held with a hungry gleam in his magpie eyes.

'It's a picture of your wife and child inside, isn't it?'

she asked. 'I'll give it back to you, if you give me back my grandfather.'

Everyone was still. Everything was silent. Then Nobody nodded once, and pulled Grandpa John back in from the edge.

'On three,' Hedy said, feeling her pulse throbbing in her temples. 'One.'

The magpie Therie inched closer, looming tall.

'Two.' Hedy watched his grip on Grandpa John loosen, and extended a trembling hand.

'Three!'

As Nobody let go of Grandpa John, Hedy whipped back her arm and threw the pocket watch as far as she could. It sailed over Nobody, out over the far edge of the nest. Nobody let loose an outraged screech and then launched after the pocket watch, which was now plummeting towards the water.

Hedy hugged Grandpa John tightly for the briefest moment, before yanking her stripy scarf from her neck. She looped it around her waist and through his belt.

'I hope it holds,' Grandpa John said, knotting it tightly.

Hedy closed her eyes and pictured herself in flight,

the silver and brass wings beating on her back. She could feel them wanting to go aloft now.

'It will, if you believe,' she said. 'Ready?'

They gripped each other's forearms tightly, bent their knees and sprang into the air. The scarf pulled sharply at Hedy's waist, but the knot held. Now weighed down by a fully grown man, Hedy could feel the wings working harder. She turned in the air until she could see the glow of Spencer and Jelly, like a tiny lighthouse beckoning her to safety. It was time to get back to Hoarder Hill.

They had covered half the distance when there was a whoosh of air from above. Nobody. All around them was feather and scratching claws and that beak, trying to break their flight. They plunged downwards in a tangle, screams and magpie shrieks filling the air. Hedy wrenched away, trying to regain control of her wings as they fell towards the river below with frightening speed. *Whoosh, whoosh.* She levelled out only just in time to avoid smashing into the riverbed. Grandpa John's feet dragged through the water, sending up a spray. Nobody swept beyond them, but she saw him begin his switchback to assail them again.

Hedy's heart hammered as she tried to pick up

speed. 'Which way?' she asked Grandpa John, climbing upwards. 'Can you see a glow?'

Fifty or so metres up from the surface of the water, Grandpa John pointed. 'That way.'

A gust of air alerted her to Nobody diving again. Hedy barely dodged and a terrifying thought struck her: what if either of them was wounded by the magpie's claws or beak and Nobody tried to change bodies? She let out a small whimper.

'You can do this,' Grandpa John told her firmly.

As Hedy tore towards the portal, small creatures began flapping from it. What on earth were they? Should she change direction?

Wham! Nobody's Therie beak pecked her leg with a painful jab, making her cry out and veer off course. With a clumsy swing, she dropped a few metres to avoid another stab by the magpie's beak. *Go left*, she told herself, *now right, be unpredictable, make him miss.*

The small creatures flying in her direction were more visible now. Cold fear rolled over her. It was the grotesques from Grandpa John's roof. Seven stone creatures jabbering and flapping in a chaotic cloud, and she began to pick out words here and there. Just like that day on the roof, there were growls of 'Finder!'

and 'Protect her!' How had they got in here? She spotted the imp, some garygoyles, a winged ram, every one of them ugly and frightening. Nobody was behind, the grotesques were ahead – there was no way she could outfly them all.

In front, the cloud of grotesques drew into formation, some above and some below. She raised her arms in front of her face, bracing for a collision, but the formation suddenly circled out. As they passed by, a raven – *her* raven – shimmering between stone and white feather, screeched, '*Caw!*'

'Protect her!' snarled the grotesques in answer.

They swarmed Nobody. Claw, fang, horn and beak flew at the Therie in a vicious throng, forcing Nobody to beat them away. It gave Hedy the time she needed to begin her race towards the glow behind the portal, visible again and brighter than ever, beckoning her to safety.

Hedy risked a look behind. The Therie snapped its beak to and fro, flapping its great wings at its smaller assailants. It grasped one gargoyle in its claw and hurled it to the ground, where the gargoyle smashed. That gave the grotesques pause, a moment that Nobody snatched to charge in pursuit of Hedy again.

'We can't fly through the portal, we won't fit,' Hedy called to Grandpa John. 'We'll need to slow down and land.'

Grandpa John nodded. 'Just make sure you go through first.'

Ten metres away from the portal, Hedy dared to slow the beat of her wings. At five metres, she back-winged and set them on the ground. Nobody was closing in.

'Get clear of me, Hedy!' Grandpa John urged, tugging at the knot of the scarf. Hedy struggled to detach herself. She looked longingly at the portal. It was so close!

Nobody screeched, steeling himself to swoop.

But now there was a sudden commotion at the portal. The family fire swirled. In crawled a large brown furry creature, and behind it was a great branching head. Spencer, blanketed with Doug, and Jelly, holding Stan, got to their feet.

'Hedy, get in!' Spencer yelled, controlled fright all over his face.

As Nobody flew in, Doug roared over Spencer's head. The bear's white paw slashed at the air, and Stan, held high over Jelly's head, shook his antlers threateningly and snorted.

Nobody jerked back, stunned. He flapped in alarm when Doug roared again, Spencer and Jelly screaming in concert with the bear this time. The growling of the grotesques came for Nobody again from the rear. With a final infuriated shriek, Nobody flailed upwards, away from the portal, away from Hedy and Grandpa John, and back to the magpie's nest.

The grotesques didn't give chase this time. They settled on the ground like tame, rumbling pets. Facing away from the portal, they surveyed the ground, water and air for danger, with a satisfied aggression that suggested this was exactly what they enjoyed doing.

Grandpa John pulled Hedy into a hug. She allowed herself to sink against him as the wings on her back collapsed down into themselves. 'You smell like skunk,' she said, wrinkling her nose, still breathless.

'I know. Do you like it?' Grandpa John said with a dry smile.

Hedy turned and pulled in Spencer, draped with Doug. 'We'll all have to like it. Come on, Jelly.'

Jelly did her best not to poke them with Stan's antlers as she wrapped her arms around them.

'Now this,' Doug said, 'is what I call a bear hug.'

They all laughed woozily until Stan cleared his throat. 'May I suggest we continue in the house, where the danger is not?'

'I hope you still have the cube after all of that,' murmured Grandpa John to Hedy, a last vestige of anxiety creasing his face.

'I've got it,' Hedy said. She pulled the cube from her pocket and dropped it into Grandpa John's palm.

CHAPTER 28

THE MAGICIAN'S ASSISTANT

'Look who's defrosted,' Soumitra smiled as everyone hurried into the attic room.

Jelly dashed to Uncle Peter's side, feeling his forehead with her hand. He was sitting up now, and his skin was no longer ashen. His eyes immediately fell upon the cube in Grandpa John's hand. 'You got it!'

Grandpa John could only pat Hedy's shoulder gratefully and nod, too exhausted to explain all that had happened.

Uncle Peter's face crumpled with relief. 'I'm sorry, John,' he whispered. 'I'm sorry I wanted to humiliate you. I'm sorry for Rose. For everything.'

Kneeling by his brother, Grandpa John said, 'I was hardly the ideal brother. There were times we should have helped each other and I turned it into a contest.' He sighed. 'Why don't we both do things differently from now on?'

'Can two old men change decades of stupidity?'

Grandpa John chuckled. 'Maybe I've got something hidden away in this house that'll transform us.' He held the cube out to Uncle Peter and said, 'I need both hands for the Kaleidos. Will you look after this for me for a moment?'

Uncle Peter carefully took the cube and held it against his chest.

Grandpa John stood and placed both hands on his Kaleidos, blinking hard. 'It's been so long,' he whispered.

'You know how to do this, John,' Uncle Peter said.

No one dared to say a thing as Grandpa John began to move the cubes. He shifted them over and under one another, folding rows of them this way and that, out of rectangle shape into a rough pyramid, into a sphere, into a shapeless heap, and finally back into the shape of a long box, into which a magician's assistant could fit. Along the short bottom edge of the box of cubes was a hollow space, like a missing tooth, where the lost cube belonged.

Grandpa John was puffed from the effort. He and Uncle Peter both stared at the empty gap, and then Grandpa John said huskily, 'Time to put it back.'

Uncle Peter knelt by the box and, trembling, held out the cube and slipped it into place. It fit perfectly, held there as though magnetized. The Kaleidos was restored.

With two hands, Grandpa John took hold of the front side of the box and wrenched it open. It was filled with darkness inside.

Grandpa John helplessly stared at the space where they had all hoped his wife would be.

There was a sudden rush of sucking air, and doors banged downstairs, throughout the house. The flames of the torches guttered.

'Is that Nobody?' Spencer asked uneasily.

But there was no threatening crackle of blue light, nor any nasty chuckle. Instead, they could hear a soft rustle, and footsteps, and voices calling out. Moments later, a stream of fluttering petals – rose petals – swept up through the doorway. They swirled around everyone, settling on top of the glimmering box. And following in the wake of the petals, as though they had been led up through the house, were Hedy and Spencer's bewildered parents. They stood in the doorway for a moment before both children flung themselves into their arms.

'What on earth—?' Mum began. Then she broke off, staring at the Kaleidos.

The blackness inside the box was fading, like night retreating at sunrise. When it cleared, they could see a woman, lying down on her side. She opened her eyes.

'Rosie!' Grandpa John knelt in front of the box and held out his hands to grasp hers.

Rose Sang, missing for decades, hesitantly inched out of the box. Hedy felt an odd chime of recognition. It was like a picture coming to life – this was the young woman whom she and Spencer had seen in photos, and there were so many of her own features that Hedy could see in her grandmother. She looked the same age as the day she had vanished, and was dressed in the magician's-assistant costume she had been wearing. As she crumpled to her knees on the floor of her secret room, she stared at the old man in front of her, who had tears running down his face.

'John?' Rose said, lifting a weak hand to stroke the tears.

'It's me,' he said, putting his hand over hers.

Rose broke into a sob and fell against Grandpa John's chest. Mum, who had been watching in silent shock, slowly walked forwards and sank to the ground to dazedly look at her mother, whom she only knew as a memory. 'How?' she asked.

Rose sobbed again and held out an arm to her daughter. As the trio cried together, everyone else stood and watched from a respectful distance.

Hedy didn't know how to feel. For the past couple of weeks, her and Spencer's lives had been filled with getting to this moment, had been obsessed with this moment. But the depth of loss that Rose, John and Olivia had felt, now being washed over by a rising tide of joy, was almost unfathomable.

Jelly put her head between Hedy and Spencer's. 'You did it,' she said.

Hedy and Spencer shared an awestruck smile. 'We did,' Hedy said. She let go of a shuddering breath.

As Rose cried and laughed, her messy brown hair began to pale. Before their eyes, with every movement, little by little she began to age, covering the decades she had been gone. Her hair turned an iron grey, and a few very fine lines became evident in her skin. Rose either didn't notice or didn't care; she was too absorbed in taking in the sight of her husband and daughter. Finally, her crying subsided enough for her to lean in to Grandpa John and inhale deeply. 'John, you smell terrible,' she said.

'That was the skunk spray,' Spencer said.

Rose turned to her grandchildren. She staggered to her feet with the help of her husband and daughter, standing like a newborn colt on unused legs. 'Hedy, Spencer,' she smiled, which was invitation enough for them to run to their grandmother and wrap her in their arms.

'Gently,' Mum told them softly.

'No, never mind gently,' Grandma Rose murmured, kissing the tops of Hedy and Spencer's heads.

The children didn't say anything, because there was too much to say. Grandma Rose's hands and face were cool, but her study of them was as warm as the sun.

'So, you finally get to see your grandchildren,' Mum said, blowing her nose.

Grandma Rose pulled her head back slightly to look at them and said, 'I could see you whenever you came to this house. You too, Olivia. For the last little while, Hedy and Spencer were like bodies of light I could see through the blackness, from far away. You lit the house around you when you were here.'

Mum broke into fresh tears, burying her face in her mother's shoulder. 'If I'd known that, we would have come more often.'

'They saved you, Rosie,' Grandpa John murmured. 'These two broke all the rules of the house and saved you.'

'Thank you,' Grandma Rose whispered to them. 'Thank you.'

'Was it bad in there, Grandma?' Hedy asked quietly.

A cloud passed over Rose's face. 'It was dark. And lonely.' She looked fearfully over her shoulder at the open Kaleidos, and Grandpa John hurried to close it.

'This is Will, my husband,' Mum said, putting an arm around Grandma Rose's shoulders and motioning to their father. Looking at Jelly, she added, 'And I'm sure this must be Angelica, Peter's granddaughter.'

Dad wiped his own tears away with his sleeve as he led Jelly towards them. 'I . . . I never thought I'd be able to meet you,' he said.

'Well, come here, then,' Grandma Rose teased, embracing her son-in-law heartily.

He pulled off his jacket to wrap around Rose. 'You seem cold. Wear this.'

'Dad, you just wiped your snot on the sleeve,' Spencer said.

'I won't touch the sleeve,' Grandma Rose said, unfazed. 'Besides, at least it doesn't smell like skunk.' She turned to Jelly. 'How big this family has grown. Angelica, did you say?'

'You can call me Jelly, and I have a younger brother, Max,' Jelly babbled with a hug. 'Oh, my gosh, Auntie Rose, do you even know what Hedy and Spencer have gone through to get you out? Hedy almost fell off the roof – oh, maybe you know that part – and gargoyles attacked her, and then a suit of armour attacked them both – he's just out there – and then my grandad was possessed, and—'

'And Nobody nearly took my *head* off!' Spencer chimed in.

'And did you even know it's Christmas Eve?'

Hedy affectionately put her hands over both of their mouths, laughing, 'Later!'

'That's right. Later,' Mum said, 'but then we want

every little detail.'

Spencer put his hands up and pointed to Doug and Stan on the floor. 'Wait. You have to meet our friends.' The children dragged the rug and the stag head closer.

Stan cleared his throat. 'Madame, I present my companion, Douglas, the fiercest bear rug – nay, the fiercest *bear* – in England.'

'And he's Stanley,' Doug took over, adding in a whisper, 'He'll tell you he's the Lord of the Queen's Wood, and after this adventure he probably thinks he has magical antlers or some such. But don't worry, he's mostly pretty en*deer*ing!' Doug started chortling at his own joke.

'Madame,' Stan muttered, 'I apologize if you find Douglas un*bear*able.'

Grandma Rose laughed and stroked their fur with a marvelling expression. 'If you're friends of the children, then it doesn't matter what else you may be.' She slowly took in the details of the strange woodland room, the trees, the curtains and the earthy ground. Bending to pick up a few rose petals, she held them to her nose and inhaled deeply. Then she caught sight of Mrs Pal. 'Is that you, Rani?'

'Much older, I'm afraid, Rose,' Mrs Pal said. 'But

feeling twenty years younger at seeing you returned.'

Strength seemed to be slowly returning to Grandma Rose's limbs. She crossed the few paces between her and Mrs Pal and gave her a warm embrace. 'Is this young man your grandson?' she asked of Soumitra, who was hovering nearby.

Soumitra wiped a hand on his trousers and held it out to Grandma Rose. 'I'm Soumitra.'

'Thank you, Soumitra, and you, Rani. I could only see bits and pieces, but I know I wouldn't be standing here without your help.'

'Any time,' Soumitra said, then in embarrassment hastened to add, 'but, I mean, I hope never again. Obviously.'

Grandma Rose peered beyond the red velvet stage curtains and through trees of a wood that should not have been there. 'Peter?' she called.

Uncle Peter had crept away from everyone, and was leaning against a thick tree.

'Peter, I hope you're not planning to banish yourself,' Grandma Rose said.

He half-turned, hesitated, and then slowly picked his way between the trees and undergrowth. He had a wretched look on his face as he came to face Grandma

Rose. 'Do you know what happened?' he asked her.

She nodded. 'I heard some of it from the children when I was in there.'

'Well, I'm sorry, Rose.'

'I know.' Grandma Rose placed a tentative hand on his shoulder. If it wasn't forgiveness yet, the seeds of it were there.

The others watched them, all lost for words, until Mum clapped her hands. 'OK, someone in this room smells absolutely awful and needs a shower . . .' She began to shepherd everyone towards the stairs, planning a thousand things at once. Hedy led the way down with Spencer and Jelly, although she slowed herself to stay just in front of her grandparents, carefully negotiating the way down, hand in hand.

'No doctors today, please,' Grandma Rose insisted when Mum tried to suggest it. 'I'd be at hospital all day trying to explain the impossible. Today I just want Christmas with my family.'

Bathed and warm, everyone squeezed around the kitchen table to fall ravenously upon the toasted sandwiches that the children had made with Soumitra.

'John,' Dad asked, picking up his fourth sandwich,

'do we get to hear the whole tale from start to finish now?'

Grandpa John dabbed his mouth with a napkin and looked at Hedy and Spencer. 'If you want the *whole* tale, you'll need Hedy and Spencer to tell it.'

And so the children began to recount what had happened from their first night at Hoarder Hill, slipping into the room they should not have gone into, and the photo album being pushed off the shelf.

'Was that you, Grandma Rose?' Hedy asked.

Grandma Rose nodded, and Spencer shivered happily. 'We were so spooked by that. How come you didn't do stuff like that for Grandpa John?'

'I . . . couldn't *see* John from the darkness the way I could see you,' Grandma Rose said hesitantly. 'You two and Olivia were like lanterns that lit the space around you, but everything else was dark.'

'Family fire,' Mrs Pal said, exchanging a glance with Hedy. 'Blood relations can be visible across the boundaries of worlds, like a beacon. The children and Olivia are your blood kin – but, for all your love of John, he is not.'

Grandma Rose laid a hand over Grandpa John's and continued. 'I could make out a little of what the children said, but it was very muffled, like listening through brick. Touching things here while I was in there was exhausting. I don't know how to describe it. It took an enormous amount of energy even to write in dust or fog; those magnets too. I didn't know where I was either, I just seemed far away. But, somehow, I could speak to the raven. When I saw Hedy take flight, I begged the raven to help somehow. Thank heavens she was able to convince those other stubborn creatures from the roof to join her. I don't know how she could hear me, I'm just glad she did.'

'I tasked the grotesques with protecting you,' Grandpa John said, thinking aloud, 'to keep watch from above. But the raven wasn't one of the carvings on the roof when we moved here. That's the raven you bought in Sweden. You asked me to put it on the roof when we brought it home, so it could have company.'

Mrs Pal tapped her finger on her lips, eyes alight. 'Sweden? Ravens and crows are very powerful in Norse mythology.'

Soft sounds interrupted her: a *shhhhh* and then a *crrrrrt*. By the liar birds' box, now returned to the warm kitchen corner, a dark knot in the floorboard opened up. A stone hand was pushed through the gap:

Mrs Vilums's hand, which the Woodspies had taken from the attic. Everyone murmured in surprise. The Woodspies didn't close up the knot until three single socks were ruefully lobbed up on to the floor as well.

'So *that's* what happens to odd socks,' Grandpa John said with wonder, picking them up along with the stone fingers. He shook his head. 'I wonder how many other things they have secreted down there.'

Hedy and Spencer leapt to his side to touch the stone fingers. 'We can fix Mrs V now, right?' Spencer asked.

Grandpa John glanced at Mrs Pal, who thought for a moment and then said, 'We could bring you some *glue* glue.'

'Magic glue?' Spencer asked.

Soumitra whispered, 'It's glue my grandmother makes a bit *extra*. You know, a bit more super. Not quite magical. But not quite *not*, either.'

'Leave me *some* trade secrets, Soumitra,' Mrs Pal said.

'Can I get some?' Spencer asked Soumitra with bright eyes. 'It'll be super handy if I, like, cut off my finger.'

Their mum cleared her throat warningly. 'Spencer, don't even think about cutting off something, magic glue or no magic glue.'

But Soumitra gave Spencer a wink when he thought Mum wasn't looking.

Later on, everyone trooped to the lounge room to study the Theries' paintings. There were no signs of the skunk or the magpie. Mum and Dad poked their heads through experimentally, but went no further than their chins, and they wouldn't let the children close to the frames.

'It still stinks in there,' Mum reported, screwing up her nose. 'What are we going to do with them, Dad?'

'We'd best board them up to keep them out of mischief,' Grandpa John said. He released Grandma Rose's hand for the first time in an hour. 'Stand back, everyone.'

They all shuffled to the edges of the room, the children hopping up on to the couch with Doug and Stan. Grandpa John put his head through the portal and spoke a few words. Moments later, the grotesques came hopping, crawling and flapping out of the painting, shaking their limbs and wings as though deprived of a fight they had been looking forward to.

'They're less frightening when they're on your side,'

Hedy whispered.

'Only just,' said Spencer.

The raven fluttered on to Grandma Rose's shoulder. As it batted its head against her cheek, Hedy overheard Mrs Pal murmur something like *huginn* and *muninn* to Soumitra.

Grandpa John pulled the whole tether out of the painting and, when he pushed a finger against the painting's surface, it no longer gave way. The portal was closed; it was oil paint upon canvas once more. He ushered the grotesques to the front door, and the snowy night air blew in around the creatures as they obediently filed outside, then began swarming up the posts of the porch or fluttering into the sky, back to their places on the roofline of the house.

Dad and Uncle Peter found old sheets of plywood in the garage and each painting was placed face down on a board, then securely fixed in place with gaffer tape.

'They won't see anything tempting this way,' Grandpa John said. 'But let's take them upstairs where they can be minded.'

In the attic, Grandpa John leant them against a wall and, with a soft word to Sir Roland, gave the suit of armour a new purpose – to watch over the paintings.

When the children yawned heavily, Mrs Pal patted Soumitra on the shoulder and said it was time for them to go, but they were made to promise to return for Christmas lunch the following day.

Mum and Dad set up cushions, sheets and blankets on the floor of the lounge in a makeshift camp for the children, watched over by Doug and Stan. Grandma Rose took a long time to say goodnight to them all. She seemed to find it as soothing as the children did to stroke their hair and lay her cheek against theirs.

At Spencer's request, she left the Christmas tree lights on as the children settled into their blankets and pillows. It was hard to believe it was Christmas Eve.

'We did it,' Hedy said. 'I can't believe we saved Grandma Rose.'

'Did you see the Snowy Paw of Doom?' Doug asked. 'Made that ruddy magpie thing take a turn, didn't it?'

'Most impressive,' Stan agreed generously. 'Nor did that unearthly creature want to contend with the Lord of the Queen's Wood! Never underestimate the ferocity of a pair of prodigious antlers, Douglas!' Stan was then undone by those same prodigious antlers as he waved them with too much swagger and toppled over on to his side.

'I was fierce too, wasn't I, Doug?' Spencer asked.

'If you're not the fiercest cubs we've ever met,' Doug said, 'you are all surely the most courageous. And that's a finer thing altogether.'

The next day, Spencer stirred first – and, with a jubilant cry of, 'Merry Christmas! Presents!' woke the rest of the house. Hedy was thrilled with the trainers and new novels she had been hoping their parents would give her, while Spencer gleefully unwrapped modelling clay and some modelling tools, plus a new video game. They had given Jelly some crazily coloured woollen tights and a beaded necklace, both of which their cousin put on immediately.

The last gifts they unwrapped were from Grandpa John. To Spencer, he gave a very light copper and paper device, about a hand-span in length and shaped like winged sycamore seeds. The device helicoptered through the air just like the seeds and, when Spencer used his hands to move the air around it, it changed the direction in which it spiralled.

Hedy unwrapped a small leather-bound world atlas

with a fine brass telescope attached to the spine on the end of a chain. Inked on the pages inside were the continents and countries of the world – although with the borders and names of a hundred years ago – and the telescope allowed the maps to be magnified in terrifically fine detail. At a certain depth, the wavy lines of the ocean bobbed up and down, and drawn animals could be seen moving in their native habitats. There was an elephant that ambled across the plain of a place marked Bechuanaland (which Dad said was now Botswana), a penguin that shuffled over snow in the Antarctic, and a great many birds and insects to be spotted in the Amazon.

'These are awesome, Grandpa John,' Spencer said. He gazed out at the back garden as though deciding how high a tree he could climb to test his small propeller.

'They're amazing, thank you,' Hedy agreed. 'But I'm sorry we didn't get you anything for Christmas.'

Grandpa John smiled at Grandma Rose, who was talking softly with their mum. 'Of course you did.'

Jelly's parents, Toni and Vincent, arrived with Max mid-morning, and were utterly shocked to find

Grandma Rose returned. They had a million questions of course, but with everyone either restoring the house to some semblance of order or preparing Christmas lunch, the account was very disjointed. It wasn't until the Pals joined them that the whole tale was satisfactorily told again, from start to finish, over turkey, roast potatoes and all the trimmings.

Afterwards, Mrs Pal quietly beckoned Grandpa John, Hedy and Spencer into the hallway. She handed them a squeezy bottle of mustard, chuckling at their befuddled looks. 'This is my *glue* glue,' she explained.

'Will it wake Mrs V and her sisters from the stone?' Hedy asked.

Mrs Pal looked regretful. 'Glue will not.' Her eyes fell on Grandpa John. 'You'll need magic for that.'

An impatient grunt was Grandpa John's answer, which made Mrs Pal chuckle once more and leave to rejoin the others.

'We have to free Mrs Vilums and her sisters, Grandpa,' Hedy said in a low voice.

Spencer nodded. 'Without her, we would've been mincemeat.'

'No magic in this house,' Grandpa John said, rubbing his eyes with a hand. 'Strictly tricks only. That was the rule, wasn't it?'

'You already broke your rule with the gargoyles. And Sir Roland. Think of all the other cool things you could do!' Spencer said, eyes gleaming.

'The problem is I think of all the *harm* I could do,' Grandpa John reminded them. 'I've spent all these years quashing the impulse to do what I'm actually good at because I know my actions have consequences.'

'Are you really going to give up doing magic?' Hedy asked incredulously. She had thought that perhaps the events of the last day were the tip of an exciting new iceberg.

'Maybe I should. Isn't it wiser to quit while we're ahead?'

'You could make this the last one ever, then,' Hedy suggested. 'And if it's the last time you ever do magic, it'll be because you care about someone, not because you're trying to show off.'

Grandpa John looked at them with a mixture of amusement and defeat. 'Will you help me?' he asked unexpectedly. They nodded eagerly. 'All right. Quietly then. And don't get your hopes up. I'm not certain we can pull this off.'

He crooked a finger and they followed him to his

study, where he opened a brown leather box in a bookcase. From the box, he withdrew a long, slim ebony wand, and from a drawer in his desk he retrieved the stone hand.

'Grandpa John, are you an actual wizard?' exclaimed Spencer, gaping at the wand. But Grandpa John rolled his eyes as though it was an absurd notion.

They sneaked through the front door and looped around the side of the house to get to the back garden. The children had to trot to keep up with Grandpa John as he strode through the wooden archway, down the path, all the way to the statue graveyard.

The '*glue* glue' seemed ordinary enough when squeezed out of the mustard bottle. But once they held the chopped-off hand to the stump of Mrs Vilums's wrist, the join between them fizzed. There was a far-off sound of bells, and they watched the seam between the hand and the wrist disappear. It was like it had never been broken.

Grandpa John pulled the wand from under his jumper and turned to face the carved figures of Mrs Vilums, Maja and Ewa. He cleared his throat nervously. 'Both of you take a hold of the wand,' he instructed the children. They did so, and then he placed his hand over the top of theirs. 'Now think of what Mrs Vilums looked like as a person, what she sounded like. Bring her to life in your mind.'

As they raised the wand in the air together, Hedy's mind flitted over different memories of Mrs Vilums: sending them out into the back garden for sunlight, being kissed by the Woodspies, dashing to protect them from Sir Roland. They brought the wand down to point at Mrs Vilums and her sisters.

'Awaken,' Grandpa John whispered, staring hard at the statues. He nodded at Hedy and Spencer to do the same.

'Awaken,' they repeated.

They backed away a few steps and waited for something to happen.

'Do you think Maja and Ewa are as good at cakes as Mrs V?' Spencer whispered into the stillness of the garden.

Hedy stifled a laugh. 'How can you still be hungry?'

A crest of voices and noise suddenly floated from the house, making the three of them turn back, fleetingly worried that some danger had befallen the house. But it wasn't fright or alarm, only laughter.

'That's the most people my house has ever held,'

Grandpa John murmured.

'It's a big house, Grandpa John,' Hedy said. 'There's room for three more, isn't there?'

'Yes, there is,' he agreed.

At that, there was a light cracking sound over the surface of the carved stone statues. Hedy took Spencer and Grandpa John's hands and dared to smile. With a growing sense of hope, they watched dark shards of stone begin falling away to reveal the life that was waiting beneath.

EPILOGUE

The stone raven hesitated.

She was no longer trapped on the roof by her stone form and could take to the wing at will – it was what she loved best. But sitting above the attic window where she had helped the girl fly, she heard a noise that made her pause and look through the glass.

All seemed dim and still in the attic, but there was the noise again. *Peck, peck.* Two large frames rested against a wall. *Peck, peck.* One of the frames quivered, as though it was being tapped. *Peck, peck.* A board covering the front of the frame was marred by a hole that had been chipped through it. If the light had been better, the stone raven might have seen the brown eye of a magpie-like creature, gazing through the opening.

Calls below the great house diverted the stone raven yet again. It was the voice of Rose. She was no longer the Missing One; she was found, and she was with her family. The raven now thought of them as the raven's own flock. She watched them embrace and call out their farewells to one another, and then four of the flock got into their red car to drive away. Even the girl who could fly.

The stone raven leapt and flickered mid-air to feather, muscle and bone. She circled above the car that slowly eased down the hill. When it got to a small terraced house in the village, the red car was flagged down, and the raven had to alight upon a lamppost to observe. The woman who cooked for the Master emerged from the house, smiling widely, followed by two other women who looked very much like her. They passed wrapped parcels through the windows of the car and kissed everyone inside it, laughing and chattering for a while, before allowing the family to leave the village.

The red car sped towards the woods and the raven sped with it. Alongside the trees where many wild things lived, the girl in the car spotted the raven and wound down her window so that her hair flew everywhere and the wind blew her cheeks pink. 'We'll see you at Easter!' she shouted, and the grinning boy waved his furry hat through the window. Then the girl wound the window up again, and they watched the raven with beaming faces. Wanting to make them happy, the raven soared in graceful waves up and down. The bird did not want the girl to forget that she could fly.

Another car raced along the cold road. It accelerated quickly, perhaps recklessly, creeping up behind the family's red car, as though intent on hunting it. The raven descended to fly level with the cars, a sense of danger ruffling her happiness.

The pursuing car was occupied by one man alone, with dark hair and a brightly coloured blue-and-red cloth around his long neck. His car began to overtake the red one with a loud purr. Before his car had quite passed, the lone man turned to the girl and boy through the windows and drew a finger across his neck. The raven did not know that the girl and boy had seen the paisley cravat and the rather handsome face before. But she knew something was wrong; the smiles dropped from their faces as they took in the driver – and the black nail on that threatening finger.

The stranger in the car surged ahead and swerved, so that the red car screeched and veered perilously towards the edge of the road before coming to a stop. There was no stopping the pursuing car now, however. It raced away, victorious.

The raven flapped on to the bonnet of the red car and peered inside. The family were wide-eyed, but unhurt. The father opened the car door and stepped out, staring at the vehicle disappearing down the road.

'Who does he think he is?' the mother seethed.

The girl and the boy stared at each other, dread mirrored in their faces. 'Nobody.'

ACKNOWLEDGEMENTS

We have imagined sharing Hedy and Spencer's story in different ways over the years. To have it come to life on page is a dream come true, but we didn't get here alone.

At the outset, the dream might have been an unrealized one if not for; Doug Ngai, the original Doug the Rug, who matchmade us as a writing team and whose belief in us never wavers; Rob Hyde, who gave us early advice when we first began writing *Hoarder Hill* for the screen; Kevin Burke, who loved the characters so much he wanted to get to know them in book form; Harry Holland, whose talent and amazing vision brought our idea to life in our teaser trailer; Mitch

Rose, who was instrumental in us being represented by CAA, and whom we owe a really fancy TV dinner.

To the cheer squad that supported our vision for page and screen, read early drafts, and listened to our ideas – we heart you:

The Holland family, especially Paddy Holland who has always been our Spencer, Genya Sugowdz, Stuart Madgwick, Jenny Wong, Christie Carr, Kelly and Carol Dann, Kristen Cherrie, Lia Brandligt, Marinka and Amanda Hudonogov Foster, Kendra Wester, Dede Grutz, Kat Rallis, Dijanna Mulhearn, JulieAnne Rhodes, on whose guest bed the idea was 'conceived', Naomi Watts for your continued support, Heidi Gomes, whose friendship and help we were so lucky to have inherited, Katherine Tomlinson, Julieanne and Dave Williams, Jamie Olds and magicians Eric Jones and Charlie Caper, Emmy Marriott, Ben Perkins, Dan Baldwin for brainstorming the painted world with us, Debbie Ujcic, Bjorn Puckler, and Lexi and Nick De Toth.

Mahalo to our amazing literary agents, Oliver and Paula Latsch of LatschLit, for once upon a time asking if there was a Chapter 2, and for their continued support and guidance thereafter.

Our thanks to Barry Cunningham for loving Doug and Stan as much as we do, believing we could be the real deal and inviting us to join the incredible Chicken House stable – or perhaps coop! – of authors.

We're indebted to Rachel Leyshon, editor extraordinaire, who always saw the forest in spite of the many, many trees, and helped us distil the story in these pages with such intelligence, thoughtfulness and tact.

Thank you to Rachel Hickman, Elinor Bagenal, Laura Myers, Jazz Bartlett Love, Sarah Wilson and the whole Chicken House team for getting behind our book and being all round lovely humans.

The hauntingly delightful cover artwork made our hearts skip a beat – thank you Maxine Lee-Mackie.

For enabling our nefarious plans for world/multimedia domination, our gratitude goes out to:

Catrin Abert and Carsten Polzin at Piper Verlag; Olivia Blaustein, our dynamic agent, and Jamie Stockton at CAA; Debbie Liebling, Zainab Azizi and Sam Raimi at Ghost House and Nne Ebong at wiip.

From Kelly:

My love and gratitude goes out especially to my parents Juliana and Michael Ngai, who gave me time to write with their boundless support in day-to-day life; to Brent Armfield for his constant encouragement, humour and loving the unexpected bits; and to Rufus and Xavier for so proudly telling everyone from teachers to strangers at the park that their mama is going to be an author.

From Mikki:

My love and thanks also go out to family! Firstly to my father Uldis who passed on his passion for storytelling, and my mother Ilze for her humour, sense of fun and unfailing support in whatever dreams I chose to chase (that day . . .), Martins, Amanda, Sharon, Adrian, Aleks, Thorley, Josie, Annika, Ryan and a special shout out to 'baby' brother Gint for suggesting that it would be 'kind of funny if you had a talking bear rug and stag head in your story'.

My husband, Colin Lish for his endless, non-wavering support, encouragement, love and keeping me focused when yet another 'shiny object' would enter my orbit!

THE LAST CHANCE HOTEL by NICKI THORNTON

Seth is the oppressed kitchen boy at the remote Last Chance Hotel, owned by the nasty Bunn family. His only friend is his black cat, Nightshade. But when a strange gathering of magicians arrives for dinner, kindly Dr Thallomius is poisoned by Seth's special dessert. A locked-room murder investigation ensues – and Seth is the main suspect.

The funny thing is, he's innocent . . . can he solve the mystery and clear his name, especially when magic's afoot?

'This mystery is a worthy prizewinner . . .
a jolly, atmospheric mystery.'
THE TIMES

'Hercule Poirot meets Harry Potter in this
mind-bending, magical, murder mystery.'
MISS CLEVELAND IS READING

Paperback, ISBN 978-1-911077-67-1, £6.99 • ebook, 978-1-911490-41-8, £6.99

THE SECRET KEEPERS by TRENTON LEE STEWART

A magical watch. A string of secrets. A race against time.
When Reuben discovers an old pocket watch, he soon realizes it has a secret power: fifteen minutes of invisibility. At first he is thrilled with his new treasure, but as one secret leads to another, he finds himself on a dangerous adventure full of curious characters, treacherous traps and breathtaking escapes. Can Reuben outwit the sly villain called The Smoke and his devious defenders the Directions and save his city from a terrible fate?

'There are some genuinely haunting and ingenious moments as the three young heroes combat the villain in his mouldy mansion.'
THE NEW YORK TIMES

'. . . the tension never flags and the hold-your-breath moments come thick and fast.'
CAROUSEL

Paperback, ISBN 978-1-911077-28-2, £6.99 • ebook, ISBN 978-1-911077-29-9, £6.99